Keep It In The Family

By

June A Sharp

Copyright © 2024 June A Sharp

ISBN: 978-1-917293-57-0

All rights reserved, including the right to reproduce this book, or portions thereof in any form. No part of this text may be reproduced, transmitted, downloaded, decompiled, reverse engineered, or stored, in any form or introduced into any information storage and retrieval system, in any form or by any means, whether electronic or mechanical without the express written permission of the author.

This is a work of fiction. Names and characters are the product of the author's imagination and any resemblance to actual persons, living or dead, is entirely coincidental.

The views expressed in this work are solely those of the author and do not necessarily reflect the views of the publisher, and the publisher hereby disclaims any responsibility for them.

www.publishnation.co.uk

CHAPTER 1

Alexandra picked up her skirts and trod very sedately down the wide staircase of Grangely Hall. She had neglected to hold the banister rail, due to her unusually long skirt, and she tripped, just managing to save herself before crashing down the full flight. She looked around in panic, then moved unusually slowly down the centre until, finally reaching the bottom step, she took a huge deep breath.

This was her twelfth birthday and she had been invited by her uncle and aunt to join the adults for their evening meal in the dining room, along with her cousins Marianne and Marshal. Twelve was the age when the children at Grangely usually ceased having nursery tea and the others had already passed that magic number, Marianne only six months previously, a fact she had not stopped telling her since breakfast time, combined with many anecdotes of faux pas Alexandra would undoubtedly make at her first dinner. She hoped and prayed she would not. Thank goodness she had not been seen on the stairs by her uncaring cousin.

As she stood in the spacious hall, her skirts still in her hand, she wondered if indeed she was quite old enough to join in grown-up conversations and eat as well. It had been so comfortable upstairs with nanny, eating various concoctions of vegetables and minced up meat but now it was time to find out what French cuisine really meant, even though cook had tried to inform her in advance, to the point of letting her dip a teaspoon into the dishes she made. Where were the others? She could hardly walk into dinner alone – or was this part of the initiation ceremony?

"What do we have here?" shouted her fourteen-year-old boy-cousin as he rounded the corner from the drawing room, sounding so much like his father, now his voice had broken, that Alexandra looked round eagerly and dropped her skirts to the floor. When she saw it was only Marshal, she smoothed down her gown and placed a hand tentatively on the side of her hair, to ensure it was still firmly secured.

"Well, is it a vision of loveliness, in its fine blue gown or just my little cousin dressed up like a lady?"

"Please don't tease me, Marshal. I feel so nervous about this already."

"Nervous? Nervous, just because you are allowed to join the adults for an evening meal. Nonsense. You must have acted out this day since you were pushing your dolls in their perambulator. All girls love to dress up. I know that for a fact."

"Playing with dolls is not quite the same as the real thing. Oh, here comes Marianne. Don't tell her I'm afraid."

"Your secret is quite safe with me, little cos. Hello Marianne, you see we have the company of our grown-up cousin this evening." It was strange that Marshal only bothered to tease *her*; he was so quiet and almost sullen with the rest of the family.

"Good evening, Alexandra," Marianne said. "I see you are wearing one of my old gowns. Such a pity your hair curls the way it does; little pieces are escaping all around your head."

She had been practising to put up her hair for weeks and she felt she had eventually made it look grown-up, with the help of Mary their maid, but Alexandra could never tame her thick, brown hair. She wished it were straight like Marianne's. Mentioning the fact that she had been made to wear the same gown that Marianne had worn to her first dinner was not exactly kind and she knew it was only because her cousin had outgrown it.

"Come along then, dears," said the older girl, as if she were collecting two little ones from the garden, even though she was little older than Alexandra and a year younger than her brother and all three made their way towards the dining room door. Marianne swept in front of her cousin and her size was very obvious. She was increasing in width as well as height and she was as tall as Marshal nowadays. With her hair up on top of her head, she looked even taller and poked her chin out in front of her as if proud of the fact, whereas Alexandra tried to hide her presence from the others, regardless of the fact that she was petite and becoming increasingly attractive.

Just as they were about to enter the large dining room, the

adults crossed the hallway and Ernestine Turner forged on through the doorway in front of them. She was handsome rather than beautiful, although *she* thought she was ravishing, always preening and trying on new gowns. Her body was slim, which meant she could wear all the fashionable padded skirts without lacing too tight and worrying that she looked too large. Her hair was straight and dark, like Marianne's and she also held her head up in the air, as though sniffing for an unpleasant scent and her nose appeared slightly wrinkled, as if she had found one. They were so alike. William Turner appeared and held the door for his wife and smiled back at the children, as they stood aside and waited for a signal that they could follow. William looked down at his little niece, the last one to come out of the schoolroom at mealtimes.

"You look delightful this evening, my dear. Allow me to escort you to the table," and he took her hand gently and threaded it through his arm.

When he reached the seat beside Marshal which had been allocated to Alexandra, he drew back her dining chair and waited until she had arranged her full skirt on the needlepoint cushion.

"Don't expect this treatment every mealtime, will you?" hissed her cousin, as he took his own seat. "Usually, Father's head is so full of business he can hardly be bothered to speak to us."

"Ssh, Marshal!" his mother admonished.

"Don't forget to use your cutlery properly, Alexandra," said Marianne in the loud pseudo-adult voice she had decided to adopt this evening. "Just work your way from the outside in and ensure you place the ones you have used tidily in the centre of your plate. Just try to remember what nanny said about the little soldiers."

As if she would have forgotten the basic rules about eating when nanny had insisted they behave properly from the day they came out of high chairs and sat around the nursery table. Marianne was behaving as if she were five years older, not less than one year.

"We will say grace," said William, bowing his head and rushing through a thank-you speech to his Maker.

The servants moved speedily in and out of the open door, until the table was full of delicious food, from a pork joint to be carved by the master to many steaming tureens of vegetables, sauce boats and dishes of apple sauce. Then they disappeared.

That first dinner of her life was one of the best Alexandra was to taste. Their cook was exceptional. Conversation was bland, deliberately so from father, to enable the young girl to involve herself in several subjects. If she only realised she was being tested on her social skills by Mrs Turner she would have been much more nervous than she had been at first. However, she was totally unaware of any ulterior motive and behaved exactly as she would have done in the nursery, answering when she was asked a direct question and commenting when she felt knowledgeable. William Turner was proud of his protégée.

After their family meal, the Turners removed to the drawing room, where an invisible line was drawn through the generations and life went on as it had before, plus one.

Father spoke first. "There, my dear Ernestine, I told you she would acquit herself well."

"Hmmph. I feel we may regret this move, even now," said his wife.

"But your fine training will out, my dear. You see if it doesn't."

"Blood has always been thicker than water, William. She is not of our blood, always remember that."

"Almost my blood, dearest. She is the daughter of my dead sister, Sarah, so there must be some of our parents' blood in her."

"Not mine, William, not mine."

"Please, Ernestine, don't hold it against her that her mama died giving birth to her. The little mite had no-one but us to care for her. I had to take her away to save her from poverty, when it was obvious that her own father would never return to fulfil his obligations and now we have a fine young woman who will be a friend to our own dear daughter. I know you can never feel this way about her but, please, try for my sake and for the sake of the Turner family."

"If your ancestors knew that you were taking in waifs and strays, they would turn in their graves. Think how they lived here in the 17th century? I'm sure the house was filled with elegance and not a whiff of scandal would have drifted through Grangely Hall in those days."

"Never be so sure, Ernestine."

"Well, I am allowed to imagine, I presume."

"Yes, yes, my dear but bear it in mind that my niece, Alexandra, stays here at Grangely Hall, as long as there is breath in my body."

Ernestine hrrmphed several times more and then picked up her embroidery, to signal the end of their conversation, so William hunted around for his copy of The Times and sank into the deep cushions of his chair by the fire. It had always been this way. Ernestine would argue and put forward her own strong opinions but she had to admit to defeat when he quietly stated what was going to happen. He would never allow her to over-rule him.

Alexandra looked over at the adults and caught the eye of her aunt. She had always been told by her uncle to call them mama and papa but she wished she did not have to call her aunt anything at all. Uncle William was different and she really did think of him as papa. Her aunt kept staring at Alexandra, as if she were one of the servants who had been told to leave the room; her eyes did not move and her mouth was set in a straight, severe line. It was tempting to stare her out, as the three of them did to each other in their schoolroom game but she knew this would incur more displeasure and she might possibly be forbidden to take meals with the rest of the family until she could become more sensible.

And her aunt knew she would eventually look away. It was obvious that the woman did not want her down for meals as if she were one of their own. Alexandra did not know that she reminded her of her own past, of a time she desperately wanted to forget.

CHAPTER 2

It was just over ten years since ironstone had been extracted in the Eston Hills for the first time. Iron was important for so many industries, not just shipping and railways, and the north of Yorkshire grew in size and became smothered in grime. Small iron plants sprang up in housing areas and the resultant homeless were rehoused in cottages where there had previously been green fields. Furnaces were built along the river front of the Tees, until they could be seen belching out fumes from many, previously quiet countryside towns. It was a time of industrial revolution.

William Turner's friends had invested in the new iron age and took every opportunity to encourage him to join them. Each time they sat at his table, the same conversation emerged.

"Will, I honestly feel you are the man to involve yourself. Don't you realise, my friend, that 32% of UK pig iron is provided by our own works and that Middlesbrough itself is supplying most of the World's railway lines. We can roll the rails here, whereas Canada and Australia have neither the means nor the expertise for doing this most basic of operations." Anthony Beecham had been a local doctor but, as soon as he retired from practice had decided to invest in iron, or as his friend often said, 'put your money where your mouth is, Tony'.

The friend in question, Walter, had spent the early part of the evening discussing digestive ailments with Ernestine but now he joined in with the men,

"He knows what he's talking about, William. These far-flung countries couldn't build up their networks of railways without us. Now the Tees has been narrowed and deepened, it means big ocean-going ships can get closer to our product. We're sitting on a gold mine."

William never could resist telling a joke. "I think you mean sitting on an iron mine. Even I know that some of the ironstone was extracted from mines under the sea and now it's been proven to exist under 200 square miles of North East Yorkshire. I know you mean well, Walter, and you Tony, but I'm not sufficiently confident that this is where I want to invest. I'll watch the situation carefully and maybe in time ... Now, pass the port and let's get back to the ladies. Have another cigar, they're very good. Old Bertie Briggs brought me a box back from South America last week. Talking about them narrowing the Tees, did you know they're planning to fill in the salt marshes just south of here with all that slag they throw out from the blast furnaces. I know it sounds like a good idea to claim back some land from the sea but what about all the birds and animals who live there in droves?"

"Here he goes again, boys," said Walter. "I think you'll come back as a bird when you quit this mortal coil. At least make sure it's one of the little buggers on your own estate; you never even get a gun out for pheasants. Anyway, they'll find somewhere else to strut around if the salt marshes go. It stands to reason; they can fly, can't they?"

William let it go. They had all had plenty of good claret and the port had gone round the table three, or was it four, times. Perhaps they should move. Ernestine would be wondering where all the men were and she would certainly make her displeasure felt.

In the drawing room, the ladies had exhausted tales of maids and interior decoration; in fact it was amazingly quiet when the men wandered in.

But Ernestine was determined to break the unnerving silence. "Do you know, William, Eleanor has just told me how noisy it is in Ormesby, now the iron works are in full swing. She even said that her sister can hear the thrumming from the, what did you say they were called Eleanor, blowing engines, yes, blowing engines. She can hear them three miles away. I sincerely hope we won't hear them here."

Her husband walked over to the fireplace and stood with one leg crossed in front of the other, elbow resting on the mantel, as he enjoyed the heat. "I very much doubt it, my love. We're completely surrounded by woodland. Trees seem to soak up the sound from most things."

"Well, if we do, I hope you will complain and do it in high places. We own the largest house in the area and if we can't enjoy peace and quiet on our own estate, well, it doesn't bear thinking about. Please replace the firescreen, would you? I can feel heat from the coals on my face."

William complied, wondering why Ernestine sat so near to the fire, when she was obviously worried about its effect on her complexion.

"No my dear, it doesn't bear thinking about," said the doctor's wife and smiled sympathetically at William.

"Let's change the subject, shall we. All we've talked about in the dining room, over our port, has been the iron industry and I feel ready for something else," William said, moving over to Tony's quiet, little wife, sitting by the brand new, crimson velvet curtains.

"Why don't you play for us, Dorothy? You know how much I enjoy the piano and especially when you play – you know all my favourite pieces."

Dorothy hunched up her shoulders and blushed bright red; at the same time starting to get up.

"Would that be alright with you, Anthony?" She always felt she had to ask permission from her ebullient husband and he merely nodded, staring into the middle distance.

Straightening herself, Dorothy walked confidently enough across to the beautiful piece of mahogany furniture which sat in the corner of two multi-paned windows. Of course the curtains were drawn across at this time of night and the gas mantle shone its light down onto the music stand. She needed no music and, sitting bolt upright as she had been instructed as a girl, began the haunting strains of Handel's Largo. Sadly, only William really listened, the other men being still absorbed in business matters and the women gossiping about women's matters.

Upstairs, in the night nursery where she was sewing with Marianne, Alexandra stopped doing her patchwork and also listened to the faint sound coming upstairs, through the floorboards.

"What a beautiful piece. I believe it's Handel, isn't it?"

"I've really no idea, Alexandra. All those music lessons mama made me suffer were less than useless to me; I can't remember a single concerto, nor a single note, come to think of it. I am so glad she let me stop banging on the piano last year and I'm sure Miss Trotter is glad as well."

"She never mentions you since you gave up, Marianne. At least I still enjoy my lessons."

"Little Miss Goodygoody. You enjoy all the boring things in life. I expect you're going to tell me you enjoy making patchwork cushions as well."

"I do, I really do. I feel I'm doing something useful for a change. Some of the estate workers would have nothing to keep them comfortable, if it weren't for our patchwork."

"Well, I think it's boring, boring, boring and I've had quite enough for one evening. I think I'll get back to my book. At least Jane Austen writes about young men and romantic encounters."

Oh, not that subject again. All Marianne thought about was men and how she could attract them – at the ripe old age of thirteen.

"We will both have to stop soon, I suppose. The light from these candles is barely enough to see by, let alone work by and Mary is sure to come up soon, to make sure we have finished sewing."

"Yes, it's about time papa installed gas lighting upstairs."

"But you know why he's loathe to do that. They say that gas takes away all the air and people who have installed it always wake with headaches." Alexandra had been listening in to the men's conversations again.

"What a clever little girl. I think I'll go and sit on the stairs, to pick up some gossip of my own. Are you coming, Miss Shankland, or do you find that far too badly behaved?"

"I think I will get ready for bed, Marianne. I feel rather sleepy." It had been a tiring day.

"As you will, my dear, as you will", her cousin said, in the exact words of her mother, as she went out. Alexandra knew that Mary would soon appear and send her cousin back to the bedroom; it was much easier to second-guess the maid and be ready before she arrived.

CHAPTER 3

Time moved on inexorably for Ernestine, the only thing making life worth living in Yorkshire being the increasing beauty of her own tall daughter. She had friends, whom she saw regularly and she would sometimes take Marianne with her on her visits. She left Alexandra behind, giving one excuse after the other, which the girl did not believe. She knew her aunt would never introduce her to high society, just as she knew she would never make the kind of marriage that Marianne would make – not with her questionable background.

When William had informed his wife that his sister's orphan child would be coming to Grangely to live, she had taken to her bed for weeks. Marianne was still a babe in arms. She had not completely recovered from the birth and he had to spring it upon her that the little bastard would be coming to stay. Oh, that word. She could hardly bring herself to think it. Ernestine was convinced William's sister had never married the child's father, even though he had said she had. But nobody had been invited to their wedding; that said it all. Oh, why did Sarah have to die in childbirth? William had always gone on about how strong his family was – and yet she, a woman with such a fragile constitution, had given birth to two children without a moment's illness. Admittedly, Marshal's birth had given her some problems but they were more of the mental kind – enough of that. Back to the Turners: Sarah had run off with the Shankland boy, completely against the wishes of her parents but that was what she was like and Alexandra had obviously taken after her, with her impudent nature.

000

The three young people were now invited to take dinner regularly with the Turners and their good friends on Saturday evenings. William tended to instigate fashions, rather than follow them and this was one of his innovations, bringing them to the table as young as twelve years old. He felt very strongly that children in a family would never learn correct social skills if they were not exposed to such occasions and he knew his good friends enjoyed the children's lively company as much as he did.

ooo

When Marshal was eighteen, he involved himself in all their activities, including cigars and port. Marianne liked to think she was a woman but she had some time to go before the others around the table would accept her into the select coterie of adults. Alexandra still felt young and remained extremely quiet. Because of her mainly silent presence, she soaked up facts like a sponge and, what's more, retained them. A girl of her tender age was hardly expected to enjoy conversations about the iron industry, nor was she endowed with the flirtatious nature of Marianne, so she was still treated as a child by the Turners' friends.

One Saturday, Alexandra came down to the drawing room, to hear a new voice. She stood for a moment outside the door, listening to the low, somewhat drawling tones of a younger man and wondered who it could be. Almost immediately, the excited voice of Marianne joined in, saying,

"Of course I've been to London, Ralph. Mama takes me often to shop for gowns; I almost know Oxford Street and Regent Street as well as I know Middlesbrough."

Oh dear, she was showing off again, how embarrassing. Alexandra pushed open the door and tried to sidle into the room before anyone noticed her. Marshal stood at the fireplace, looking like a bookend with his father. They were so alike: both the same height, just under six feet tall; both with fair hair and brown eyes; the likeness was made more so because Marshal insisted on mimicking William in every miniscule way.

"Hello, my dear. You must be the last one down," papa said. "Walford hasn't been in to tell us to go through yet, so you've time for a pre-prandial sherry. Come along, come along," he said. He was so kind to her, involving her in everything. She was rather partial to a thimbleful of sherry, particularly the sweet one, and that's all she was ever offered. She took the tiny, patterned, crystal glass held out to her and sipped it with relish.

"Now, let me introduce you to my son, Ralph," said Walter Lawrence. As he spoke, he put his warm hand around her waist and propelled her forward. At least it was meant to be her waist but the fingers of his hand had slipped up slightly and had reached her left breast by the time they approached the young couple near the piano. She found this very embarrassing now she was fully developed and was infuriated that an older man should do such a thing.

"Ralph, cease your constant conversing with Miss Turner and let me introduce her young cousin. Alexandra, this is my son Ralph. I suppose I should call you Miss Shankland, now you're grown up."

This was so humiliating. He did not have to treat her like a child in front of this nice-looking young man, although he found her old enough to grope her body. Silence was the best policy, so she held out her hand and smiled into the bluest eyes she had ever seen. He was a fine-boned, very stylish young man, who seemed to pose rather than stand and yet he was extremely masculine. She felt her face changing colour and knew that her normally peachy skin had become the colour of a beetroot. As she looked down to camouflage her inadequacy, Ralph said,

"Good evening, Miss Shankland. This is a great pleasure. Marianne didn't tell me she had such a beautiful cousin."

At this comment, Marianne also blushed but Alexandra knew it was from anger and not any form of self-consciousness, so to try to correct matters, she said,

"Good evening, Ralph. Now, would you excuse me? I have a question to put to your mother about a piece of music and I must ask her now, while we are close to the piano."

She could almost feel her cousin's breath escaping and see her bosom lower inside her apricot gown. No doubt she would suffer for Ralph's compliment later.

Not long after her short but productive enquiry to Dorothy Lawrence, regarding a certain passage in a new piece of Mozart Alexandra had started, the dinner gong sounded and they all went next door to the dining room. As usual, she took up her position near one end of the long table which was spread with a pristine, white linen cloth and laid with the good silver plate cutlery left to papa by his mother. In front of mama towered the large soup tureen and Alexandra knew from cook that it contained rabbit potage, made from those shot by a friend of papa's who had the shooting rights of the whole estate. Papa himself hated shooting anything living. And she hated watching cook taking off their skins, to leave a slimy creatures looking as she imagined new-born babies to look. Papa presided over the fish course but it was hard to see exactly what it was from the far end of the table. Later, no doubt there would be a meat joint, probably beef as it was papa's favourite and, hopefully she would have room for some pears in wine sauce which cook had allowed her to taste from a spoon in the kitchen. She wondered how long this childish habit would be allowed to continue, for she knew Marianne never set foot downstairs.

Everyone was seated and she noticed with some pleasure that Ralph was on her left, although on Marianne's right so there was little chance of conversation. The room started to buzz with polite comment and she strained her ears to listen to the interesting remarks between father and the other men at the table.

"That mine under Eston Nab's doing alright now, William, and it's been on the go since the early fifties. I keep expecting to hear it's dried up," the loud voice of Mr Lawrence shouted across the table to her father.

"I think it'll be good for a few more years, Walter," papa replied, more quietly. "It's to be hoped so, for the sake of all those workers who came from Wales and across from Ireland. Their families have a poor time of it though, in all those little back-to-back houses down in Grangetown. I believe they have to share earth closets as well. Such a pity."

"Not at the table, my dear," said Ernestine, as if she were talking to a child.

Papa merely ignored her and Mr Lawrence went on,

"Aye well, you can't expect anything better, when an industry expands at the rate the iron has. Our population's grown from under ten thousand to nearly forty in twenty years, don't you know."

Dr Beecham came in at this point, with the medical man's

point of view,

"The population won't stick at that number if they continue to treat their workers the way they do though. Those poor fellows go to work in only cloth caps to protect their heads, and there's so much dust and smoke they're all going to die of lung disease – not to mention the heat - and they're only able to tuck in sweat rags to protect their faces. It's a sin, it certainly is."

Her father thought this was quite enough for the ladies and changed the subject to that of his interest in paintings, which he shared with the doctor's wife, so the young people were encouraged to display some of their recently acquired knowledge. On this more pleasant note, the table became quite animated and Ralph turned to her and asked,

"Which do you prefer, Miss Shankland, oil paintings or watercolour drawings?"

Alexandra hesitated before she began to answer and this was enough time for Marianne to ignore the doctor on her left and dive into their conversation.

"I really prefer oil paintings, Ralph, because they seem so permanent compared with something executed on mere paper. What do you say to that?"

"I still wonder which Miss Shankland prefers," he remarked, pointedly turning to Alexandra. Oh dear, this was so difficult. Did he realise how little her opinions were valued by her cousin? To try to remove his gaze from her blushing countenance, she said the first thing that came into her head,

"Please call me Alexandra. I like watercolours myself because they are so pale and gentle. Oil paintings are wonderful for large portraits but the medium of water-based washes must surely lend itself to landscapes." Seeing the slanted eyes of Marianne in the background, she felt she must make amends and continued, "But I'm sure my cousin has more experience of the works of the Old Masters and her views are more to be heeded than mine."

Ralph had already seen the rivalry he had caused and felt he must ignore this pretty little girl if relations were to remain friendly around the dinner table. Women were so complicated in their mental make-up.

Alexandra bent over her food making it quite obvious that

she did not want to converse anymore, so her face was saved once again by her own swift thinking. Apart from the odd comment from her seniors about growing-up and becoming a young woman (all the foolishness she hated about attending dinners) she was left alone to her own devices and managed to collect several more facts about the exciting rise of the iron industry. Sometimes, as she lay in bed after one of these educational mealtimes, she started wondering why it was always men who talked about the real stuff of life and women who dwelt upon insubstantial trivia for much of their time on Earth. She would not divulge her inner thoughts to another soul but she could never stop her mind from speculating.

As the dinners were established occurrences and Ralph became a regular guest, soon, to Alexandra's surprise, he requested Mr Turner's permission to escort his elder daughter to one or two soirees given by mutual friends and it was accepted by all who knew them that the liaison was becoming permanent. It was not what Ernestine wanted for her daughter but, as Ralph's mother was prepared to chaperone the two, she obviously approved. Then Ralph went off to London.

CHAPTER 4

"Please Mama, allow me to go to visit Aunt Maude. You said she wants a companion for cousin Barbara. Just imagine how many fine balls and parties we will attend together and I might even meet some eligible young men if I keep company with my cousin, who is just about to do the season." Marianne was trying not to whine, as she mentioned the content of her mother's letter yet again. Mama might never know that Ralph had gone off to London recently and, hopefully, she could find ways of escaping her aunt's eagle eye on occasion.

"Oh Marianne, my dear, it is such a tempting offer but how could I possibly manage here without you. You are my only daughter, my pride and joy."

"You still have Alexandra, Mama. She is like a daughter to you." The pseudo daughter sat in the corner, listening to all this pleading.

"Not quite, my love. Alexandra was a doorstep baby, you know that. I need my own flesh and blood around me in my advancing years." How cruel she was, knowing Alexandra could hear their conversation.

"Tch, tch, Mama, you will not arrive at your advancing years for a long time yet." Marianne knew how to flatter her mother and sensed that appealing to her vanity would be the key to success. Nobody ever knew how old their mothers really were but, using a little intelligence in the way of addition and subtraction, she had worked out that hers was about fifty-four or five. "All my friends are amazed at your youthful appearance and quite surprised when I tell them you are my mother and not an elder sister. Just think how wonderful it could be for me to do the season with Barbara – after we are both presented, of course."

Ernestine smiled and looked down. Her daughter was so sweet. Perhaps a year in London would be the making of her. What harm could it do, particularly if she were in the care of her sister Maude and also it would help to remove her from Dorothy Lawrence's boy.

"I think I have had a change of heart, my darling. You must have the opportunity to be belle of the ball in the capital city. Our local soirees and parties are all very well but to say you have departed for London will make this family important in the eyes of our acquaintances, so I will inform your father this evening." So Marianne had won the battle.

"Oh Mama, dear Mama, I am quite overwhelmed. Oh Alexandra you must be so jealo... but surely you are so thrilled for me." She was not going to allow her mother to see her real self for a moment, not until she was on her way to London. She moved about the room, swinging her dress from side to side in her excitement, until her mother said,

"Cease your constant prattling and kindly stop causing such a draught in the drawing room. I expect you to break an ornament at any moment. I must swear you to secrecy about this, at least until I have told your father. It would be the end if he found out from a maid or somesuch."

They separated, each wearing a furtive smile – the mother because she imagined the comments of her afternoon society and the daughter because she had overcome her mother's prejudices, in a way which had not been detected.

000

The next time Marianne saw Ralph was that Saturday evening. She knew this was the last dinner he would attend at the Turner house and had decided to surprise him with her momentous news. Her father had been told and had agreed the project. Remaining detached was part of her plan and she even allowed him to converse with her young cousin over the entrees, simply because she knew he would be moving on to greater things. The entire Lawrence family were returning to London, where his mother had inherited her parents' town house; in fact the only reason for their lengthy stay in Yorkshire had been his father's desire to continue breeding horses, as his father did before him, but Mrs Lawrence came from a titled family and was an only child, so Walter had been extremely pleased when both her parents quit this mortal coil, as he put it, at more or less the same time. They were now exceedingly rich.

Alexandra did not know that Ralph felt he must talk seriously to her before she went out of his life. He found her intelligent and serious, understanding sarcasm and jokes which were meant for people many years older. She never giggled, she just nodded sagely and smiled in a mature fashion, unlike Marianne who was only a year younger than himself, although she seemed more like a twelve-year-old on occasion.

"I believe you know I am leaving for London on Monday, Alexandra," he said.

"I do hope to come back to Yorkshire on occasion, when my father inspects his investments in the iron trade, so I hope I will continue to be welcome here when I do."

"I expect you will be just as welcome as you have always been," she said, demurely. She would miss his presence at their table.

He looked down at his hands and glanced in her direction, his mouth turning up at the corners, and said,

"Welcomed by you, Miss Shankland?"

Alexandra had no experience of this kind of behaviour. Could this be what Marianne called flirting? Her cousin was leaning across the table, talking to Mrs Beecham, who looked as if she wore a horse and cart on her head because she sat directly under one of her father's paintings, and this made her smile. This was a good way to disguise the real reason for her happiness because, in the last few minutes, she felt as if her heart had become detached from her body and was moving around in her chest. She must say something in reply.

"Of course, Ralph, as you will be by the whole family."

"But by you in particular, I wondered?"

She cast caution aside and said, "Yes, by me in particular." If this was to be her first experience of flirtatious behaviour, then she would enjoy it. Marianne had been taken to many evening engagements, where she had been introduced to young men, so she had been able to practise the art of flirting but she had always been kept at home because aunt said she was young for her age.

"I am so very pleased," he said, just before her father indicated that the ladies should remove and she continued to smile at him as she left her chair.

When the ladies took up comfortable positions in the drawing room and she found herself side-by-side with Marianne, she had a feeling of guilt as if she had taken something belonging to her cousin, like a doll or a toy bear instead of just a flattering comment from her beau. Her face began to colour and she was glad when the girl started to speak rapidly about her own plans for the later part of the evening.

"I want it to be a complete surprise, when I tell him. Mama has already informed papa that I will be going to stay with Aunt Maude and tomorrow I will be measured by the dressmaker for some new gowns in the London style. But my coming out dress will be fashioned by a London dressmaker with the longest train ever.... Of course nobody will know that I intend to continue to keep company with Ralph. I don't suppose the parents have even linked the two events, so don't breathe a word about Ralph to anybody in this house – ever – or you will be in very big trouble. Do you hear me, Alexandra?"

She was still remembering her final words with Ralph and only came back to her senses when Marianne nudged her in the ribs. "Ow! What do you think you're doing?"

"I've just finished telling you to remain silent about Ralph Lawrence at all times and you obviously didn't hear a word I said."

"I will remain silent," she said quietly, wondering how he would take the news that her garrulous cousin was following him up to London.

She did not have long to wait because the men came through and took up their seats at various points around the room. She wondered how they ever found subjects to discuss, as they had been meeting here for months and the men saw each other during the week as well. Admittedly, ladies always had some gossip regarding staff or mutual acquaintances but this time of the evening, when their husbands felt honour-bound to enter into some general conversation interesting to both sexes, must be a most trying time. Usually a safe subject such as music or art was discussed and never a friend's name was mentioned, unless to express a compliment or to comment on some kind of move either into or out of the area. The discussion on one particular sofa was, however, altogether different.

"Hello again, Ralph," said Marianne in her sugar-sweet voice.

"Hello, Marianne."

"I wish to inform you of a change in my own circumstances, to coincide with your removal up to London this week."

"Oh yes. What might that be?"

"I, too, am travelling to London, to stay with my Aunt Maude and her daughter, although not as soon as you – probably next month."

Ralph's expression did not alter. He was a master of concealment, which made Alexandra suspect an element of masquerade in his character. This calm exterior could only have come from much practice.

When he spoke, it was in a dispassionate and totally unemotional way,

"How pleasant... for you. Perhaps we will meet at some mutual acquaintance's home."

"I do hope so," she said, somewhat breathlessly.

"One never knows," he smiled and started to get up.

"Where are you going, Ralph?" Marianne questioned.

"I have business with your father. Please excuse me," he said and giving Alexandra a quick smile, walked across the room, his fine bottle- green coat swinging as he went.

"Well, what do you think of that?" said Marianne, when he was out of earshot.

"Typical of a man, I would say," said Alexandra, trying to sound worldly.

"I expect he wanted to appear nonchalant because you were beside him," her cousin whispered. "I'm sure there will be more contact between us before he leaves. Perhaps you should take yourself off to another seat and give us some private space."

Not wanting to discuss Ralph or Marianne's forthcoming expedition, she went off to talk to Mrs Lawrence and Alexandra noticed that, when the party broke up, there was no further contact between the two young people.

000

Marshal hardly ever spoke to his sister and seemed to spend

most of his time following his father around like a hunting dog. He hung on William's words and repeated them verbatim to anybody who would listen but as most of it was about the iron industry, not many people in the family cared to join in. Unfortunately, his father treated him in the same way as he treated his two Labrador Retrievers and he was never seen in conversation with his son, despite his extremely kind attitude to the boy. Boy was not exactly the right description for Marshal because he was approaching his nineteenth birthday. There was no potential marriage partner on his narrow horizon, nor were there many male friends and Alexandra had begun to worry about this introspective life-style. How could such a fine-looking young man, find himself on the shelf? He had attended many events and met several girls of marriageable age but he never seemed to have the confidence to continue an alliance. In his childhood he had travelled to the Quaker school daily, because his abortive attempt at boarding school was a disaster and he had begged to be allowed home. He showed no signs of wanting to further himself, taking pleasure only in the vicarious pride of his father's achievements. Marianne had told Alexandra in a rare confidential moment that he had told her he wished his papa would truly notice him and wanted his mama to love him as much as she obviously loved his sister. He was very handsome, resembled his father in many ways, but spoilt his looks by stooping and allowing his face to settle into frowns on many occasions.

One Spring morning, as Alexandra left the house to go for a walk in the woods, Marshal came down the wide staircase behind her. She could hear his slow footsteps, so knew it was not papa, who rushed everywhere. She turned and smiled.

"I was going for a walk, Marshal. Would you like to accompany me?"

"I don't suppose you want my company; you probably want to commune with nature."

"We can do that together, cousin. Why not come along?"

"If you're sure?"

"Come along," she said, taking hold of his hand and leading him outside.

The trees were losing their leaves and the ones remaining

were beautiful shades of red, rust and ochre. The grass below them was a bright carpet of colour and the path leading into the woods appeared like a runner laid for Royalty, directing them into the darkness.

"I simply must scuff in those leaves. Come on, let's run down the slope and under the copper beech." Alexandra wanted to bring some element of fun into the sad-looking face beside her. She was so glad she had decided to lace herself gently most days and not to appear like Marianne, as if she were a fragile vase, not to be touched.

"You used to do this as a small child, cos. You must grow up sometime, you know." Marshal's head had risen and his brown eyes looked almost yellow as they caught the sun. There was an expression of excitement, like that he used to exhibit in his childhood, and she could feel his hand clutching hers tightly as they started to run across the lawn.

"Parts of me will never grow up!" she shouted as they careered forward into the crunchy layer of leaves.

Marshal took away his hand and started to kick around frantically, raising the leaves all about them and totally ignoring her. It was as if he had forgotten her presence completely. Then he reached down and took a huge armful of the golden harvest, throwing it high in the air and waving his head around in a shower of dusty leaves. Just as suddenly as he had started, he stopped and, brushing leaves from his curls, looked anxiously back at the house.

"I hope my father didn't see all that," he said, picking the odd piece of leaf from his jacket pocket and his flannel sleeves.

"I don't suppose he would worry in the slightest. After all, we're still children to him and children do such things."

"No. You've got it all wrong Alexandra. I'm a man now and I must behave like one. I can't let father think I'm superficial. I think I'd better be going. Thanks for ... thanks for... oh, I don't know what to thank you for. I'll see you at dinner. Goodbye."

He walked off in his usual studied fashion, staring at the ground and still brushing leaves from his clothing, whilst Alexandra turned to go in the opposite direction, away from the house and into the dark comfort of the woods, not looking back even once. Her mind kept reverting to the sight of Marshal flinging leaves around himself as hard as he could, in the area where a croquet lawn had been set-up during the summer. If only his young friends could have seen him. If only those bright, young girls, invited especially for him, could have seen him. But they would all have probably joined in with Marshal and ignored her as usual.

CHAPTER 5

As Marshal entered the white double doors at the front of the large stone house, beneath the portico, he bent to remove some final pieces of flaky, autumnal leaf from his new checked wool trousers. He bumped his backside on one of the round pillars and glanced around to see if anyone had noticed him behaving like a childish fool. Using the iron boot-scraper on his now damp ankle boots, he tried to look casual, as if he had just returned from a relaxed walk around the policies. His unusual (that is for NorthYorkshire) interest in fashion had been noted already by father and, now he was more mature, he was considering whether to change his mode of dress to something more suitable for a country gentleman. Walford, the butler/footman/valet, stood in the hall and greeted him. If there had been a male equivalent to a maid-of-all-work, he would be it because he had known Marshal's father since he was a boy and knew so much about the estate that he more or less organised everything. Walford would have seen him leaping over the grass with his cousin, so there was no point in pretending.

"Hello Walford. Alexandra and I decided to relive our childhood and scuff in the newly fallen leaves. Very childish but I have to humour her sometimes."

"I saw you, Mr Marshal. It looked like good fun to me. I'm sorry my days for scuffing are over."

"No great loss, I assure you. Have you seen my father recently?"

"Nowhere in the house, sir. Perhaps you could try the stables."

"No, I won't bother just now. I think a change of boots is in order."

"Just as you like, sir."

The old man had been friend and confidant to Marshal throughout his childhood and teens but now the boy was older, Walford stuck by the rules and called him Sir. Mr Turner would have something to say if he didn't and according to the downstairs family, rules were there to be kept. His sister, Aileen, was the cook and between them they ran Grangely Hall efficiently. Any gossip between the general maids and the scullery maid was passed on to Cook and any news from the stable lads and gardeners came straight to Walford, as well as nuggets picked up from the family – hence they knew it all, from how many letters the mistress wrote to where the carriage went every day.

Their most important secret of all – and one neither of them would ever divulge to another living soul – was that of the demise of Alexandra's mother. Cook knew the downstairs family of the man who got her into trouble and was more instrumental than anyone realised in having the baby taken away by William. Cook's own mother was about to take the infant home with her, after young Sarah died because she was about to be taken to an orphanage. The older Nevilles believed she was the daughter of one of their footmen. But Cook knew better.

Aileen Walford had asked her brother to organise an appointment for her to see the master and, once he had been told realistically what was about to happen to his sister's child, he had taken steps to adopt the baby himself. It was a very sad affair, with young Sarah eventually marrying the footman, after many arguments with her own parents and then dying in childbirth shortly after. She had cut herself off completely from the rest of the Turner family when she left home but she and William had remained good friends nevertheless. Ernestine had never liked Sarah and knew nothing of her husband's clandestine meetings with the girl, so his arrival one afternoon with a babe-in-arms was the biggest shock she had ever had.

How she had cried when that child was brought into her genteel home to be cared for alongside her noble children. William seemed to think it was the acceptable thing to do – to take somebody else's rejected child into his home. She knew he had a soft heart and that was how she had always managed to get her own way, whether consciously or unwittingly on his part. However, to instruct her to employ another wet nurse and decide that the nursemaid would look after two children instead of only Marianne, was totally unacceptable – to any mother. She had tried to make him understand how it hurt her to have a baby in the house to which she had not given birth. She had fumed and fainted, she had begged and pleaded, suggested alternatives, but to no avail. His heart was hardened against her.

Cook knew that William had used many bribes to ensure his niece was cared for by his own staff with his own children but there was never any love forthcoming from his pretentious wife. The whole situation was brushed under the carpet and all she ever told her acquaintances was that Alexandra's mother had died and William had taken the child out of the goodness of his heart; which was indeed the truth.

ooo

Marshal changed into clean clothes, then went downstairs to find his father. He had no interest in horses or those who looked after them, so he gave William some time before making an indoor search for him. He had no specific reason for wanting to see him but felt there was something missing from life if he spent too much time away from papa.

The drawing room was empty, although a fire leapt up the large chimney and all looked exceedingly comfortable, as if only just vacated. No doubt his mother had taken tea recently, as the maid came to collect her tray.

Next door was a smaller room, used as study and library mainly by his father but sometimes by himself. He hesitated at the closed door and had an involuntary impulse to knock. This was ridiculous at his age. Why was he so deferential to all adults, when he was one himself? He had told Alexandra it was time she grew up and the same applied to himself so he turned the handle and walked straight into another warm, airless room. There was a desk over at the window, with a bentwood chair behind it with rolled arms and tall back; it was occupied. As he faced out to the garden, his father's clothing pressed out from gaps in the wood, like a puffy eiderdown and Marshal saw that he was deep into one of his large volumes, his reading spectacles noticeable from the back by their curled wire ends.

As he heard the door close, William turned slightly to see who was intruding on his privacy. He had fair hair in the same side parting as Marshal, with a greying moustache. A large cigar hung from the side of his generous mouth and he looked over the top of his glasses at his son.

"Hello there, young man. To what do I owe this pleasure."

"Nothing in particular Papa." He must stop calling him that childish name. "Nothing at all Father. I merely wondered where you were and, as the rest of the house is full of women, thought I would search you out."

"Then sit down by the fire and get warm. The days are becoming a little chill, don't you think?" All conversation between the two was formal. Marshal could not remember an occasion when his father had asked him anything personal.

He did not think they were but said, "Yes, I'm sure you're right, Father," not wanting to put forward a different opinion.

"Well, take down a book and let's have a quiet read together – just the men of the family, eh?"

Marshal was delighted. This was more than he had hoped for. Ever since he had realised at a young age that his mother had no affection for him, he had transferred his devotion to his father. There was a deep need inside him for love and tenderness but he was unlikely to experience this from papa; he was too much of a masculine man.. So, Marshal was prepared to sit at his feet and clutch at the crumbs he let slip. Had he only known that William wished he had a stronger, more independent son, someone who would grow up to be a bit of a rake, taking risks as he had done in his youth, not this bibliophile who dogged his every footstep. Still, he felt Marshal was young and there was no need to make the boy suffer for his personality, which made him behave very much like himself at his present age, not like a wild boy should.

Marshal went across to the room-high shelves on the right of the door and took down a large tome of Shakespeare's works. He knew many pieces by heart but felt it would do no harm to reread the bard. It was so pleasant to be with his father, alone and so comfortable. There was no talk, as Marshal had anticipated, because William had the capacity for losing himself in a book for hours on end. In fact, reading was his main occupation. He knew everything there was to know about current affairs, due to his perusal of The Times every morning, and Yorkshire must have been etched onto his mind, as he read book after book after book about the geography and industry of the county. What he did not know, he looked up immediately and was a mine of information to his friends as a result. When Marshal was a young boy, he had only to ask a question and he would be brought into this room and told to find out from the books on the shelves, not being allowed to leave until he had the answer.

William was engrossed but he allowed himself a moment to reflect on the age and aptitude of his son. It was amazing that this boy resembled him so closely; Darwin had written at length on the question of adaptability of animals to their surroundings in the Origin of Species and even touched on the subject regarding human beings in the Descent of Man, so it should not be so surprising. He had taught this boy all he knew. Sadly, that was where it ended because Marshal was so lacking in confidence that he doubted this would ever be a man who could earn a fortune by character alone. Unfortunately, he would have to; there would be little left of his own money to hand on when he died. That was the true test of a man and Marshal would have to develop the instinct of survival for himself. It was disappointing when the young did not rise to a challenge, as he had when little older than his son.

He loved his children and that included his adopted daughter but children were women's work - even when they ceased to be dependent - until they left home. His big worry in life was Marianne. She was skittish and showed no desire to be a helpmeet to anybody. What sensible man would want a doll to dress up and exhibit to his friends? It would not be so bad if she could relax into orderly housekeeping once the parties and dancing were over but she seemed incapable of thinking seriously. Alexandra was the one for thinking; she seemed to be lost in thought most of the time and found her sister outrageous and trifling; she was more like him than the other two children. He must try to marry off Marianne to someone level-headed. What about that son of Walter's. He was a nice-looking young chap who would appeal to the show-off side of his daughter and he had a few brains as well. An accountant, I think he said he was. This might be worth pursuing. Now, where did I stop reading?

CHAPTER 6

Marianne spent the next two weeks in a paroxysm of excitement. Ernestine had dispensed with the services of a daily dressmaker, because she had tired of the woman from the village who spent more time chatting to the household staff than plying her needle. Anyway, it was good to be able to take on the services of any good woman mentioned by her friends, without having to explain about Aggie first - but the daughter of the family was peeved.

"How can I possibly exist in London without enough gowns to see me through the winter, Mama? I'm sure cousin Barbara will have a wardrobe full to overflowing."

Ernestine's first thought was to say borrow hers then but she realised how much Marianne wanted to appear fashionably elegant on her first trip to the metropolis. "I dare say we could call on Mrs Lawrence's dressmaker, now she's gone away. I'm sure she said they were going to London last week."

"That sounds absolutely perfect Mama and I could do some of the sewing myself – plain sewing of course."

"You're such a good girl, Marianne. Such a very good girl. Yes, I have a note of the name of Dorothy's dressmaker and I will send a note to her this very day. You will have several new gowns to take with you and everyone will see how up-to-the-minute we are in Yorkshire, even if she charges your father a large amount."

"Thank you, dear Mama, I am so pleased."

Even if she had to sew some of the simple pieces herself, she was determined to take a reasonable collection of gowns with her. The last time mama had employed a dressmaker, Marianne had sewn the whole of the skirt for her in the afternoons and, once the intricate bodice was attached, her gown had looked splendid. Perhaps Alexandra could be cajoled into helping. When they had stitched samplers together in the schoolroom, she had been a quick and accurate needlewoman and surely she had plenty of time on her hands these days, despite the never-ending patchwork.

There was no time like the present, so she left her mother and went upstairs to her room. The maid was coming along the corridor from the staff staircase, carrying a tottering pile of ironing and almost crashed into her.

"Please, watch where you're going Mary. You almost knocked me down with that unwieldy pile of clothing. I would have thought two, or even three, trips would have been better than wobbling about with such a mountain."

"Sorry, Miss, it's just that it's such a long walk from the basement and to do it three times, well …."

"I don't care about such trivialities. Don't do it again, I said, or my mother will have to be told."

"Yes Miss." The poor girl staggered along the corridor and stopped outside Marianne's bedroom.

"Oh, you were coming to my room, were you. I sincerely hope that nothing of mine has been dropped on the way. If I see the slightest crease, you will do it again."

"Yes Miss."

As the girl waited for the door to be opened so she could slip in, Alexandra appeared in the doorway.

"Oh dear, what a lot of ironing you have today, Mary. Let me help you place it on the bed."

"Not on my bed, Mary," said Marianne, gesticulating across the room.

"We can sort it and put it away together, Mary."

"Speak for yourself. I will not be used to this casual service when I go to London, so come back later and put it away for me, Mary."

The young maid was in general service, meaning she had a bit of everything to do in the busy household. For the past two weeks she had been rushed off her feet by Miss Marianne, fetching and carrying, up and down three flights of stairs and no sooner had she reached the kitchen than the bell rang again for something else. If it hadn't been for her ma and pa being so unwell and needing the money, she would have run away from home before now.

After she left, Alexandra said,

"I think you were rather hard on Mary, Marianne. There's no reason why she should behave like your personal lady's maid. It's bad enough that she has to see to mama's toilette, without adding to her workload."

"Oh, have you become a spokeswoman for the working classes these days. You must know that they expect this of us whenever they go into service. Being too kind only reflects on the family and the whole village would know we were amenable to such behaviour within hours."

"I'm sorry, cousin, but I happen to think they deserve some appreciation. They do so much for us and most of them work for a pittance."

"They get their board and lodging, don't they? Oh, don't bother me with insignificant details, as I just came up to ask if you would do some sewing for me, that is when the dressmaker arrives and makes up some toile models for my new gowns."

"I don't know…"

"Oh, come now. You must be dying of boredom most days. All you ever seem to do is go for walks and read. Do it for me, dear cousin. I so need your help."

"Oh, alright. I suppose I have some afternoons to spare and I've almost finished making my own winter gowns."

"Thank you, my dear," she said and walked out of the room, leaving her pile of ironing for the maid to put away.

Alexandra set to, placing Marianne's things in her drawers. She would make a point of going down to the kitchens and telling Mary that all was finished. In a few days' time, her cousin would be away and there would be so much less work for the young maid-of-all-work.

000

William was very pleased that Marianne seemed to like his friend, Walter's son. The two men had spent a fruitful evening at their club in Middlesbrough and when he suggested the young people should get together, Ralph's father had been delighted and a letter had been sent to him immediately, asking the boy to return for the weekend with a view to making a proposal of marriage before Marianne left for London.

Ralph was in two minds about his father's proposition but knew there was a need for William's intellectual expertise in a planned business venture and his reputation as squire in his village would make him a superior father-in-law. One female was very much like another and as he had decided to move back to Yorkshire with his accountancy firm and definitely wanted to become more involved in the iron industry, albeit as an investor, he saw no reason not to comply. So, several days before Marianne left for her aunt's town house, Ralph appeared on the doorstep with his father. Walford ushered them into the morning room, where Ernestine and William had been sitting together for once, expecting their good friend to call..

"Hello William. Good morning, my dear Ernestine. Please forgive us for turning up so early but I know there is a sense of urgency, as the lady in question goes up to London shortly."

"All is forgiven, Walter. After all, it was at my suggestion you both came today. I trust you had a comfortable journey, Ralph?"

"Yes sir. The railway is most accommodating, apart from having to change from one platform to another at York."

"Railways are our future, my boy. You bear that in mind," said his father, accepting a cigar from his host and ignoring the moue made by Ernestine.

"Let me ring for the maid, so she can tell Marianne you are here." William got up and pulled the cord, at the same time inviting both men to partake of a glass of sherry while they waited.

Some minutes later, Marianne arrived, having been briefed on the Lawrences' errand and having been ready and waiting for some time upstairs. This was not what she had expected, when she had tried to convince Alexandra that Ralph would come to see her before she left for London. The whole idea of going down, or rather up as she had been told to say, to London was to enjoy the social life, with or without him. She loved the handsome young man desperately but that was no reason for her to miss the season. Oh, what should she do?

She entered the room, wearing an enormous smile, then, thinking better of it, closed her eyes and fought back her excitement, choosing instead to rearrange her face into an expression of strained curiosity.

"I expect you're wondering why we're here so early in the day, my dear," said Walter in his normal glib fashion. "I think Ralph wishes to ask you something, don't you Ralph?"

"Yes I do, father, but I would appreciate a little privacy in which to say what I have come to say. Could we retire to another room for a while, Marianne."

Everyone looked slightly disappointed and also surprised but then the two fathers glanced at each other in appreciation of the boy's sensitivity and the two young people left the room together.

Marianne could think of nowhere better than the dining room because no-one ever entered it before meals and Ralph pulled the door closed as they entered.

"This is probably the most important day of my life, Marianne, so perhaps you would like to be seated, while I say my piece."

"Thank you, Ralph, I would," she said, knowing exactly what was coming and wanting it to be a proposal she could remember for the rest of her days, even if she was unsure of her answer.

He came close to her chair and went down on one knee in front of her delightfully frothy new gown, worn for the daytime deliberately today, although it had been made as an evening dress for London.

"Marianne, would you do me the honour of accepting my proposal of marriage?" he said, gently and quietly. This was the moment when she could really live the answer she had rehearsed so many times, ever since her mother had told her the wonderful news. She held out her hand to be kissed and looked into the deep blue eyes of the man of her dreams, then said,

"No, Ralph. I'm very sorry but I will have to refuse your kind offer of marriage."

He looked aghast and rose from his ridiculously subservient position.

"But, why? I thought we were becoming close. You behaved as if you would say yes. In fact, every time I came to this house, you hovered around me like a bluebottle."

"I don't think I wish to be known as a dirty little fly, Ralph. Wait until you hear my reason for refusing you, before you go off like a firework."

Ralph looked down at her with a pained expression. She was not as attractive as he had at first thought. In actual fact she was rather masculine in looks. Very much like her mother. Isn't that what they always said to you. If you like the look of a girl, take a look at her mother to find out how she is going to turn out. Not that Ernestine Turner was ugly; she was just a long, tall lady.

"Ralph, are you paying attention to me. You have just proposed to me and I have said no."

"I'm very aware of that, Marianne. Now I will have to go back in there and explain that I am a rejected man."

"Not if you listen to me first."

"Go ahead then. I don't suppose I can become any lower than I have."

"Ralph, I refused you for one reason and one reason only. If I am to become the sort of wife that men, that you, would wish to have, I must go to London and come out properly. I have been invited to go to my aunt's home and do the season with my cousin and all I want to do is to accomplish this before I make any firm promises. Now, do you understand?"

"I think so. Of course, you do realise that I will be in London, not exactly doing the season but spending my time in the homes of debutantes as well."

"I do realise that, Ralph and I think we will have a wonderful time together, regardless of the fact that my London aunt will be looking for a prosperous match for my cousin and myself. Now do you understand. All you have to do is become that prosperous match towards the end of my time in London and we will be back where we have just started."

"You are a scheming woman, Marianne Turner and, if I might say so, very much like me. So what do we tell them, out there in the other room?"

"The truth of course. We say that I have decided to go to my aunt's house first and will reconsider your offer when I return."

They returned to the waiting party and tactfully explained the reasons why Marianne had refused Ralph's offer of marriage. Walter looked more annoyed than downcast, Ernestine was pleased but tried not to show it and William was definitely puzzled. This wayward daughter had chosen a season of frivolity, spent with people she did not know, over a lifetime of luxury with a man she obviously cared about. The mind of a woman was beyond the understanding of a mere man.

CHAPTER 7

"Do you mean to tell me, Marianne's turned him down and she's going off to London to Aunt Maud? The fellow must be unhinged. How do you suppose she'll fill her time with our socialite cousin; at dances and supper parties, that's how?" Marshal almost shouted.

Alexandra had heard raised voices coming from the morning room, just as she had been about to enter, so she had hovered in the doorway and heard some significant sentences. Father was discussing the situation with Marshal, who was anything but calm.

"I believe Ralph and his parents are in London just now, Marshal. I expect they will both attend the same functions anyway," he said, trying to accept the situation, but failing miserably.

Marshal merely bit his lip and looked back at the book he was reading on the subject of sewerage in their area. Alexandra had entered the room and glanced down at the huge tome. How could he find such a topic of interest?

Alexandra reverted to the subject under consideration. "However, I felt you both should know that no-one chose to inform me of this momentous situation and I presume you were kept out of the secret also, Marshal?"

"I wouldn't expect them to tell me. I don't even like the man. If he were to be my brother-in-law, they would never see me at their table – not that I would expect to be invited. The man's a charlatan and a show-off; he likes nothing better than to dress in London styles of clothing and wave himself around the North of England for all to see and admire - of course." A small note of jealousy about Ralph's superior clothing had crept in.

"Now, now, Marshal, I thought he was rather pleasant. Although Marianne would never allow me to hold a sensible conversation with him. Even now, I don't suppose she will even let him recognise me in a crowd."

"So, you like him do you? I expect he used his mock

gallantry and trifling ways to win you over. I am a much shrewder judge of character than you, little cos."

Alexandra felt their conversation was at an end, if Marshal wanted to exhibit his obvious jealousy for a man who was much more knowledgeable and more worldly than himself, so she went off to think her own private thoughts.

When Marianne was ready to travel, her dressing trunks had to be seen to be believed. Walford had to solicit the help of two gardening boys and a stable lad, just to lift them onto the carriage and the driver was exhorted to find help before removing them and depositing them on the train. How several gowns and the other garments of one girl took up quite so much room was a mystery to Alexandra. She must have persuaded her mother to invest in lots of extra clothing. She departed amidst great excitement on her part and immense sadness on that of her mother. Alexandra attempted to console Ernestine by placing a hand on her shoulder, as she waved her lace handkerchief at the receding picture of her daughter's transport going off down the drive and was rebuffed by a swift hand moving hers away.

"Don't touch me, young lady. Can't you see I am exceedingly distressed?"

"I'm sorry, Mama. I really am. I quite understand."

"No. You don't understand at all – and don't call me Mama. My one and only daughter has left me and don't think you can ever take her place in my affections."

This was dreadful. She had always called her adoptive mother mama, under duress, and now she was being rejected completely. What could she call her? aunt? Mrs Turner? She would try not to call her anything at all, at least until the woman had come to terms with her great loss. As for taking anyone's place in the affections of this person, that was impossible; she had no affections in which to take a place.

When William Turner came home, his wife had retired to her bed and refused to come down for dinner. At least the gathering around the dining room table was cheerful tonight and conversation was not peppered with Marianne's whining comments about which gown had taken too long to make and which frock was from the wrong fabric. Even Marshal involved himself in several discussions about the significant growth in population around the ore fields.

"I believe the population has grown tremendously in our area, father. In fact a combination of increased births and immigration figures puts the birth rate much higher than the death rate and there are many more males than females."

"I don't know how you come by these facts, my boy, but you are indeed correct, according to my professional sources."

Marshal looked suitably rewarded for his research and glowed both inwardly and outwardly, his face beaming like the Cheshire Cat.

"Sadly, due to this speedy increase, much habitation is unfit for iron workers and their families. According to our Dr Beecham, there is a danger of disease spreading through these unhygienic communities, particularly when large families reside together in small houses. Overcrowding has been seen to be one of the reasons for epidemics of cholera which are far too prevalent in this area. Oh dear, here we go again, talking about unwholesome topics at the dinner table. If your mother were here, she would stop this immediately." His father was much more knowledgeable than he was but he was also more sensitive.

Marshal's pleasant glow receded and his gaze descended once more onto his plate. His moment of glory was over and now, no doubt, they would commence talking about Marianne and her travels. However, William was not to be denied the opportunity to take over the conversation and directed his next comment to Alexandra,

"My dear, what do you intend to do now your sister has left home?"

If only he knew. Sister, oh dear.

"I have no real plans, Papa but I have become interested in reading about famous cooks, such as Mrs Beeton   I find this fascinating and absorbing. So much so that I would like your permission to spend some time in the kitchens with Cook, to bring my reading to a practical conclusion."

"Well, well, well, my young lady wishes to turn into a cook. Whatever next? I suppose you will require a set of aprons and some wooden spoons as a gift?"

"Oh, Papa, you are so funny. You know it is merely a hobby for me, like embroidery and tapestry-making."

"Only not quite so clean," put in Marshal, between bites.

"May I have your permission, please."

"I don't know what your mama will say. Perhaps we should ask her."

"No! No! I mean, no, there is no need to bother ma... her for such a triviality. I will forget all about it and take up some other more suitable occupation."

"Now, Alexandra, that is so unlike you. I know that once you've made up your mind to do something, be it ever so small, you will do it. Therefore, I feel it would do me no good to refuse you, so give you my permission – with or without the corroboration of mama."

Thank goodness. Now she could quote dear papa when she went downstairs and nobody, not even Cook, could deny her access to the kitchen.

000

The following day, Alexandra made her way down to the basement kitchen and sought out Mrs Walford. Although she was not the wife of Walford but his sister, tradition decreed that she should be Mrs something-or-other and she had decided on her maiden name. It hardly mattered what she was called because her name was Cook and everyone, from the master down to the scullery maid called her Cook.

Alexandra held her in some respect, so took a deep breath before saying,

"Excuse me Cook but I wondered if I could have a word with you."

The rounded woman was stirring a huge pot of soup on the iron stove and glanced up, expecting to see one of her minions begging leave to quit the kitchen, but instead saw her favourite young lady standing by her side. Her face creased into one of its rare smiles, as she knocked the wooden spoon on the side of her large copper saucepan and put it down on the wooden surface.

After wiping her chubby hands on her pinny, she placed them on her hips and looked at the lovely young girl. She seemed unsure of herself and surely this was a new experience for her. Cook thought she would put her out of her misery and said,

"I suppose it's about coming down 'ere to cook once in a while, after reading all them fancy receipts in them books you're allus reading."

"How did you know that, Cook?"

"Oh, I have spies all over this house – but the spy in question is the master on this occasion. He trotted down to tell me he'd given you permission to join me in this wonderful palace of fun down 'ere. Why do you want to go soiling your pretty little hands and your fine dresses by cooking, Miss Alexandra? I can get all that stuff done for you, can't I?"

"I know you can, Cook but you're the best person in the world to teach anyone about cooking. That's why I want to come down and try my hand at it, for myself. You've no idea how exciting it all sounds when it's written down by Mrs Beeton.

"Well, if you must, you must and who am I to gainsay the master. When he makes up his mind to do something, there's absolutely no stopping him. So when do you intend to start? You'll need to get dressed up in something a bit more workmanlike than the things you're wearing now."

"I thought…" but Cook would not let her answer.

"Now, what if I get you a dress from my store. I allus ask for them back when one of me girls leaves me, so I've plenty of sizes to choose from. I'll provide you with a kitchen frock and you make sure it's kept nice and clean by wearing a pinny every time you come down 'ere."

"Of course, Cook. I thought I might make a start tomorrow. Would that be convenient?"

"As convenient as any other day, if you ask me. Right! Tomorrow it is. Report for duty at nine o'clock in the morning. Better bring one of them fancy books with you."

CHAPTER 8

Alexandra took down Mrs Beeton's Book of Household Management from her bookcase. How amazing that someone in her twenties could consider starting such a knowledgeable manual; what a wonderful thing it must have been to apply herself for four years to perfecting it. Oh, how she wished she could address such a project during her lifetime. There was so much of interest in the world and here she was being trained to be nothing but a lady, who would someday marry and have perfect little children, dressed up in sailor suits and frothy dresses. Was there nothing a woman could do? If she remained a spinster, it would probably be better than marriage; at least she would have time to investigate life itself – unless she was bound to an old relative.

It was 7.30 in the morning and she had washed and dressed already; excited that she was to do something entirely different today and not wanting to be late for Cook's inspection. She hoped she would be allowed to get on with some simple cooking herself and would not have Cook or one of the kitchen girls constantly looking over her shoulder. She had never in her life cooked a bean and was longing to know what it felt like. Surely anyone who could read could follow a receipt.

Marshal had always said that. Cookery was the same as science; once you knew how to follow an instruction manual, the experiment would attend to itself. Of course his Bunsen Burner, or source of heat, could be adjusted to suit the raw materials and some shaking or stirring could take place by the operative but the end of the experiment depended on the correct temperature achieved. Alexandra knew nothing about scientific experiments but she was sure Marshal was quite right in his comparison.

Now, she must read for the umpteenth time what apparatus would be required to make a simple batch of scones, or maybe a cake. Out came the receipts. She had omitted to tell anyone what she finally intended to do with her culinary efforts because this might elicit cynicism or even laughter. She had seen how poor some of the people in the village were and watched as they tried to obtain cheap food, or even yesterday's bread, from the local shops. In the past, people from the big house had always felt it their bounden duty to help their villagers survive and she saw no reason why it should not happen today. The poor of the community must be cared for and who better to do it than the ladies of the Hall. Of course she knew that Ernestine had no interest in anyone without a title of some kind, so her part in the charity work must be taken on by someone who cared; why not herself?

Once the time was right, she took herself downstairs – not by the front staircase but by the staff stairs, as befitted her new station. They were stone and cold and she looked way up to the only source of light, a large skylight separated into a cone of individual panes. Up the stairs were the attics and what used to be maids' rooms, now unused because most members of staff were local and came each day. Cook and Walford had rooms near the kitchens. No-one ever went up those stairs, she was sure, and the one time the three children had investigated the large, empty rooms, they had felt quite shivery from ghostly feelings they inspired. All was musty and still, until their small feet had stirred up a great deal of dust; windows had been uncleaned for many years and it was only by rubbing a clean patch in the filth that they had been able to see lawns, flower beds and trees below them; so far below. They had run back to the wooden staircase, feeling spiders' webs across their faces and squealing with fear.

As she made her way down to the kitchens, holding on to the narrow banister tightly to avoid falling, she saw a square of rails which marked an entrance to the cellars. Perhaps there were dungeons down there with the bones of dead ancestors or their prisoners. Rats would have picked the flesh off any corpses left lying there years ago. But she must stop her over-fertile imagination; it was where they kept the wine and ale of course.

Entering the warm kitchen, in her striped dress which reminded her of pillow ticking, she saw the scullery maid and a kitchen lass look around and cover their mouths with their hands. To the true workers, her appearance in such garb was very funny. They must think she was going to a fancy dress party and no doubt they would expect her to prance about like a lady at a ball. They were so wrong.

"Oh, hello Alexandra," said Cook, deliberately loudly, then continued so the others could hear every word she said, "We will dispense with the 'Miss' whilst you're in my domain. All you are is another girl down 'ere. If it doesn't suit, get yourself back where you belong."

Alexandra got over her surprise, then realised in her perceptive way that dear old Cook was merely trying to make her fit in with the maids and there could be no giggling and gossiping if she were treated just like the others.

"I understand, Cook," she said in reply, looking down modestly. She was acting the part; nobody realised but her, and maybe Cook herself. She glanced around and saw Walford sitting in Cook's rocking chair by the range. His expression remained serious but Alexandra caught the twinkle in his eye and only just stopped herself from laughing.

Cook went on, "I'm glad of that. Now, have you brought some receipts with you, that I can get you started with. First, go out to the scullery and wash them hands. I won't 'ave dirty paws in my kitchen."

Although she felt her hands were perfectly clean compared with those of the kitchen girls, she did as she was told for appearance's sake and when she returned the others had started work. Her acceptance had been effortless.

She showed Cook the two pages she had chosen and she decided that scones would be a good way to start. She was told where to obtain her ingredients and given the shortest of explanations then left to her own devices while Cook got on with preparing lunch. Her reason for curtailing the process was summed up in one sentence,

"You know your letters and can read it yourself, my girl."

Never in her young life had Alexandra felt so nervous. She could feel the blood rising to her cheeks as the heat of the kitchen closed about her and this did nothing for her confidence, as she pointed a finger along the lines of print and weighed out her ingredients on the large set of scales. There were beautifully polished brass weights from half an ounce up to several pounds And the scales themselves, although made from painted metal, had a brass pan which made her blink as it shone in her eyes. So many duties fell to the kitchen minions, which were unknown to those upstairs, and polishing equipment must be one of them.

Eventually, after pouring milk from a jug dipped in a churn and stirring it into her mixture, she was able to stand back and admire the large piece of dough in front of her. She had no idea what to do next and looked around for some inspiration. Up marched Cook.

"Right, lass. You've got your dough and here's a cup."

Alexandra thought she must have forgotten one of the ingredients but no.

"You can see it's a broken piece of china but it's just perfect for making the scones". She pronounced it with a flat 'o', not like Ernestine who always said scones to rhyme with thrones. "Roll your pastry out a bit. No! not too thin, girl. Pick it up and squeeze it up together again. Now, have another go and this time treat it like something fragile – like a little baby bird you've rescued from the ground. The less you 'andle it, the lighter the scones. That's better. Now you've got the hang of it, make me a round dozen, grease this baking sheet and I'll show you where to put 'em in't oven."

She felt truly excited. She was well on the way to making her first batch of scones. Doing exactly what Cook had said, she cut out twelve perfect rounds and placed them on the old, black baking sheet. It looked as if it had baked-on grime from a thousand scones but Cook, being cleanliness itself, had not mentioned it, so it must be alright. She left the remaining cut-off dough on the slab and carried her precious cargo across to Cook who was already at the stove.

"Now, lass, very, very carefully put your tray of goodies into the oven. It's alright to do it without a tea cloth round your 'ands when you puts 'em in but remember, you never take anything out of the 'ot oven without suitable protection – and I mean protection, not just one layer of cloth but two or three. I'll show you how to wrap up your hands when they're ready to come out. Take a look at the clock on the wall and give 'em ten minutes to start with. That oven's very 'ot, so that should do it but if they're not brown on top, given 'em a bit longer. Got that?"

"Yes, Cook, I'm sure I have."

"You better 'ave, or I'll know the reason why. Oh! By the way, what 'appened to the rest of the dough, after you'd cut out the rounds?"

"It's still on the slab."

"Still on the slab - Cook!"

"Cook."

"Well go and roll it out and make a few more. We can't 'ave waste in my kitchen and when you get to the last bit, make a little 'un for me to try."

Oh, this was so difficult, keeping Cook happy. Would she ever get it right? She went back to the dough and cut three more scones, then formed the last bit into a round thing with her fingers. There was another baking tray by her side, as if by magic, and she could see Cook over by the range watching her every move.

At the end of her first session, which lasted until lunchtime, Cook took a bite out of her tiny scone and she felt her heart move to a position somewhere near the back of her throat. The round face, wearing a spotlessly clean mob cap, ground her jaws backwards and forwards, then she swallowed dramatically and wiped her mouth with her index finger.

"Not bad for a beginner, not bad at all," she said, wiping her finger back and forth on her capacious apron "but next time, see if there's an egg hanging around and paint a spot of beaten egg on the top before you bake 'em. It'll give 'em a more professional look."

She had turned to walk away, leaving Alexandra feeling like a child who lifts his spoon to feed himself for the first time; pleased by his success, yet looking forward to the next mouthful. Cook's head turned on her invisible neck and gave her a quick, maternal smile, before marching off to the scullery.

Alexandra was elated. She had mastered a new skill, with only minimal instruction from her mentor. Now she could make scones until they were piled high – but that was probably the most ridiculous thought she had ever had. Everyone knew how scones went stale a couple of days after they were made; Ernestine had even sent first day scones back to the kitchen, saying they were hard; in a fit of picque, 'to make them sit up and pay attention down in the kitchen' she had said. So, maybe scones were not something she should churn out in their hundreds. She would try something new tomorrow but, in the meantime, she must scurry off upstairs, using the route she used previously, to be in the dining room in time for lunch.

The maid looked totally disinterested as she brought various items to table. Not a smile at Alexandra, although she had worked with her all morning, so it was obvious that she had been given her orders before coming upstairs. Lunch was uneventful, with Ernestine picking at her sparrow's portion and Marshal reverting to his usual silent self. William did not mention her new hobby and she saw no reason to discuss her morning with the others.

She had two more sessions with Cook in the kitchen and had started to feel like one of the maids; at any rate all the girls accepted her as one of them. Her new occupation filled her hands at lesson time and filled her head for the rest of the time, so much so that she had not been outside for her usual exercise.

One afternoon, missing the clean air outdoors, she walked in the autumnal woods alone. It was a fine, sundrenched day and the trees looked even more beautiful in their crisp, multicoloured gowns, with sunbeams finding their way through the fine branches onto the flattened paths. Taking a different direction from her usual route, she came upon an open field of parkland and decided to walk along the edge until she arrived at the main drive. A little way along the fence was a tall oak tree and casting her gaze down to the base of the trunk she saw a small stone. It looked for all the world like a gravestone, only much smaller, and she squinted into the sun to read the words carved out of it. Loyal Major – 1820. It must be the grave of an animal belonging to the Turner family. A little further along, there was a sycamore with another stone bearing the words, Devoted Prince – 1822. By now, Alexandra had become curious and had to know whether there were more trees planted to commemorate the death of other Grangely Hall pets. Just before she crossed the field to walk up the stony path to the house, was a Scots Pine. Underneath, was a much larger stone, with the message, Faithful and true – Captain – 1800. Probably a horse. She wondered if there were more scattered around the parkland but, by now, her boots were wet from the grass and it was approaching afternoon tea time of four o'clock, so she slipped her small, silver pocket watch away and skipped across the remaining damp field and, from there, up the drive to Grangely.

She returned for tea with her head full of thoughts but was unable to sit quietly and think them through because Ernestine had received a missive from Marianne.

"My beloved daughter has already been on a drive in Windsor Park and has attended a musical soiree with her aunt and cousin. She wore her mid-brown suit and the beige hat with a peacock's feather, on the drive, and her pale blue ensemble for the evening event. Aunt Maude was overcome by her elegance and said so, in front of Lady Marsham ..."

"Good, my dear. I am so glad she has settled into London life so quickly. Can I pass you something to eat. Which will you have, the cucumber sandwiches or the scones?"

"Oh William, how can you speak of food at a time like this? But I will have a scone, if you please." She reached out her slim hand and removed one of Alexandra's scones from the plate. Taking a bite, she muttered, "At least they're light today. My words to Cook must have done some good."

Alexandra's smile widened and William caught her expression. He knew now what the girl had been making today, so he raised an eyebrow in her direction and nodded imperceptibly. Success was sweet.

Seeing that her aunt was engrossed in rereading her letter, she turned to her uncle.

"Papa" she said, "I went for a stroll in the woods this morning and turned to the left, which took me around open parkland on the way to the main gates".

"You certainly take long walks these days, my dear. Most young ladies are content to sway elegantly around the drawing room, gossiping to friends."

Alexandra laughed at the picture conjured up for her, then continued, "I saw some small gravestones underneath trees and wondered what they denote."

"Ah, the animal graveyard. Well, not a graveyard in the true meaning of the word; more a rural resting place for some fine animals belonging to the Hall."

"I saw two which appeared to be for dogs and one larger stone."

"The large one is the stone which started this tradition. It was a fine, bay gelding belonging to my father. He carried him to hounds on many occasions, then spent his last years accompanying young horses and, no doubt, instilling some sense into their thick skulls. That horse died before I was born but I remember all the stories my papa told me of his affectionate and responsible nature. After that, any animal that died was buried with its own headstone. The two dogs, Major and Prince were my childhood companions and there are several more dotted around the estate. Always look at the foot of a tree as you take your long walks and you will be surprised to find many of my friends there."

"Oh, Papa, what a lovely idea. Now they will never be forgotten."

"They would never have been forgotten anyway, my dear, but a headstone will encourage future generations to think twice about cutting down those trees, don't you think?"

"I do hope so," was all Alexandra could say, as her eyes filled with tears. To think that her uncle was so sensitive about such things was a revelation to her and yet she had always known that beneath his gruff exterior was a more than kind heart.

CHAPTER 9

A few days later, Alexandra was called down to the morning room, where William sat in his usual seat by the window, talking animatedly to someone out of her line of vision. As she entered the room, three men rose from their seats and papa greeted her.

"Ah, here you are my dear. I have a visitor who would like to take a turn in the gardens before we dash him off to the Club for lunch. I'm convinced you're the right person to entertain Ralph, on behalf of the family. So, off you go and please don't be long; I've already called for the carriage."

What a surprise, to see Ralph with his father and to be asked to escort him around the gardens. Surely that was not a correct thing to do, without a chaperone, but this was Yorkshire and papa's rules about such things were more relaxed. It was just as well that Ernestine was not present. They filed out and, once in the hall with the morning room door closed, she turned to see Ralph smiling down at her in a way which could only be described as affectionate.

"Hello, Alexandra. How good to see you."

"Hello, Ralph. What brings you back to Yorkshire?"

"My firm of accountants has decided I can do more good in the centre of industry, so I find myself reinstated back here. I shall make regular trips to London, to liaise with my head office – and to see Marianne of course."

"You are very lucky, Ralph, to be able to rush up and down the country on a whim."

"Not my whim, Alexandra. The whim of my employers and, of course, the whim of my father, who organises everything."

"I still think you're very lucky."

"Some may call it luck, I call it connections."

"And what does my cousin feel about this. No sooner are you removed to the city than you are moved back to the smoke of industry."

"If you want to see smoke, you should go to London. People walk around with pieces of soot on their faces, like the

48

patches of Regency times and may not hang out their washing for fear of its turning grey in an hour. Nobody, who's anybody travels with a window open in their carriage and rooms are totally bereft of air for the same reason. I had to come back to Yorkshire to breathe again."

"That I would hate. Fresh air is a tonic to me."

"Well, my dear, don't get too used to it because the iron industry could well remove the 'fresh' from your description, if it continues to expand the way it is doing."

"What a dreadful thought."

In the space of one conversation, they had donned outdoor clothing and walked through the rose garden at the front of the house. The smell of roses in autumn was aromatic and somewhat heady, as all blooms were at the height of maturity and almost ready to fall to the well-tilled soil. Ralph stood quite still and cast his eyes around the many bushes; when he found the object of his search, he rushed forward and snapped off the head of a beautiful red velvet flower. He trimmed away a vicious-looking thorn and several leaves, then handed it to Alexandra, with a flourish.

"For Mademoiselle, the most beautiful rose in the garden."

She was delighted and smiled her appreciation; then hesitated. This was all totally wrong. His words were ambiguous but she chose to imagine she was the 'most beautiful rose'. This fine man belonged to Marianne and she had been about to accept a red rose from his hand. A red rose, which meant I love you. No-one could accept a red rose from anyone but their sweetheart. Surely, he knew this, so she made light of it.

"How utterly dramatic, Ralph Lawrence, but surely you know I am not my cousin. Fetch it indoors and I will press it for you to give to her when you return to London."

He looked disappointed. No, he looked angry. He started to throw the rose back into the flower bed and Alexandra said,

"No! no! Give it to me. I mean what I say. You can give your beloved one of the last roses of summer from her own garden, when you return to the land of smoke and grime, to remind her of the beauty of Yorkshire. I expect it will encourage her to come home…to you."

He held out his hand and passed over the crimson flower with its two dark green leaves and Alexandra felt the rough underside of them as she took hold of the round stem. If only this could have been given to her for all the right reasons, she would have taken it and raised it to her lips, then treasured it forever.

They heard papa calling from the front of the house and the carriage was waiting on the drive. Ralph ushered her forward before rearranging his features into a pleasant smile then he turned and said,

"Thank you for your time, Alexandra. I will see you ere long."

"Come along, lad, we must be moving on now," said his father and William touched her gently on the shoulder before joining the others. If only he were her true father. She had known no other but the thought of some man, somewhere in Europe, who knew he had a daughter and cared nothing about her, troubled her so much. How she would love to know what had happened to her mother; had she indeed married for love?

Later in the day, when William returned home, Alexandra greeted him in the front hall and he was reminded of her question about the animal graveyard when he hung up his coat and knocked a once-used collar and lead still left hanging on the hallstand. Dogs were such good companions and perhaps he should consider getting another to take on his regular walks when he inspected the policies.

000

On her next foray into Cook's domain, Alexandra decided to make cakes; not the fancy, sweet little cakes enjoyed by Ernestine and her friends, more substantial items which could be eaten by children lacking the basic nutrients of life. She had found a receipt in one of her books by Mrs Beeton, for Dripping Cake and she intended to ask Cook to save any excess fat from the regular joints of meat cooked for the family. There were other ingredients which would make the cakes more palatable and nourishing, such as a small amount of sugar and a handful of dried fruit. Full of charitable ideas, she skipped into the kitchen, wearing a clean apron as instructed and waving her book around for all to see, her finger keeping the place where Dripping Cake could be found.

Everyone seemed to be busily at work when she entered and one of the girls glanced up at her, frowning as she did so. She looked around and noticed that all was silent in the normally cheery, domestic hub of the house.

"Now, let's see what you have decided to play with today, Miss Alexandra," called Cook grumpily, as she thumped down on a huge wedge of bread dough. She grabbed at the sides of it, as if strangling an enemy and whammed it down on to the vast kitchen table in a flurry of flour. Stopping to run her fist under her nose to remove a flour-induced tickle, she bashed it apart once more and began the whole series of moves again. Alexandra stopped dancing forward immediately, realising something was wrong, and looked down at the floor in penitent fashion.

"I…I…er…thought some tray-bakes…er Cook."

"You did, did you and who, in this family of gentility do you think is going to eat tray-bakes?" She whacked and walloped her dough in time to her words, never once looking up and Alexandra realised she had said the wrong thing. How could she explain to Cook, when she was in such a fierce mood, that she was not making anything for the family. This was obviously not a day for her presence in the kitchen. She moved a little closer to the fuming cook and said quietly,

"I can see you have more to do than teach me baking today, Cook. I'll come back another day…"

"You're right about that anyway, young madam. Your fine mama has given me a day's notice to prepare a veritable feast for them ladies what come for lunch once a month – and it's not even the right week for it, what's more – changed their minds they 'ave – would rather come tomorrow, they would and she doesn't want any old thing this time, she wants somep'n special she says – and me not seeing the butcher 'til Friday noon." She went on and on without stopping her banging and crashing about and Alexandra could see that the rest of the staff had also had the rough side of her tongue long before she came downstairs. It was time for a rapid removal, back where Cook thought she belonged.

Walking peevishly up the stone staircase, she looked up to the skylight
once more. She had little to do today and the thought of joining her aunt in the drawing room, to sit in silence with her patchwork, was more than she could bear. The thought of the ladies coming for lunch tomorrow cheered her up slightly, as they usually brought their daughters for Alexandra to entertain. However, today a climb to the top of the house would fill in her morning.

The old door creaked on its hinges as she entered the first room of the old staff quarters. Her childhood fears remained and she looked quickly around her. Nothing. The small window was once more covered in grime but today the sun shone on the glass, showing her the full extent of the filth which had accumulated over so many years. How long was it since maids slept here? Perhaps in her uncle's childhood. There were so many questions she would love to ask him, if only she could talk to him alone without her aunt's interference.

There was a small, black fireplace in the room, with a grating on the hearth and the last occupant had covered the place which normally held coals with a piece of newspaper. This would answer her question, so moving slowly through the dust motes, Alexandra bent down to pick up the paper, when there was a loud rattle and she flung herself backwards in sheer fright. Her stripey kitchen dress landed in the dust and there was a cloud surrounding her, as she fought to regain her feet.

As she scraped on the floor and pushed with her hands, she saw the newspaper move in the grate and out flopped a soot-covered starling. It was weak and could only hop a little way across the wooden floor, looking around itself in fear. Poor thing, it must have fallen down the chimney and been unable to get out of the fireplace. Forgetting her own agitation, she bent down and gently placed her two hands around the small, warm body. It felt so feeble; she could almost feel its skeleton beneath the covering of feathers. How long had it lain there, in its paper shroud. How long would it have remained, its life trickling away day by day, had she not taken it into her head to come up here. Some actions were meant to be and her day, from the moment she awoke, could well have been planned for her, just so she could save this bird from its sorry fate.

There was no point in trying to open the window. Without a free hand it would be impossible and if this tiny mite should fall again, it could well be the end for it. Instead, she retraced her footsteps, feeling glad she had left Mrs Beeton in the kitchen when she made her rapid escape. At the foot of the stairs, where corridors went into the main house, she managed, by deftly manoeuvring her index finger, to open the door and then it was easy.

Slowly to the front door; sitting on the top step, the precious bird on her lap, she waited. Little by little, the starling started to move; first its head almost completely rotated on its scrawny neck, then one wing was flexed followed by its partner. Eventually, after one or two flaps in situ, the life force returned and Alexandra's starling flew from her skirt to the nearest tree in the garden. She watched, as it started to preen itself, no doubt removing the alien soot from its feathered body, then it left.

There was no need to worry about its finding food, for the Grangely birds did extremely well from kitchen scraps and it was to be hoped it knew where to find them. Her job was done.

As she got up unsteadily from the stone step and looked down at her dreadfully creased and filthy kitchen garb, Marshal appeared around the corner and approached the entrance. Amazingly, Walford was nowhere to be seen.

"Alexandra, is it really you?! What on Earth have you been doing? You look as if you've just completed sweeping the chimneys!"

"It's such a long, dreary story, Marshal but I would appreciate it if you say nothing about this to the parents. I must get away upstairs and remove this awful clothing."

A carriage could be heard coming up the drive and, before Alexandra could move, it was upon them – at least it had stopped outside the building. Ernestine's strident voice was heard, moaning about her cold feet and Walford appeared behind them, rushing to help his mistress to enter. All he said, when he saw the grimy apology for a kitchen maid standing before him was,

"Oh, my God!" Then he more or less bundled her bodily

into the nearest door, which happened to be the library – and closed it behind her. From her safe haven, Alexandra could hear the voices of her aunt and Marshal and surmised that the lady of the house was being divested of her outdoor clothing. There were footsteps going past the door, then silence. She breathed a sigh of relief and stood back from the door, where she had been listening to the commotion in the hall then smoothing down her dress and filthy apron, she prepared to peek out.

"I don't think that's a very good idea," a voice said from the window and, when she looked round, there was her uncle, his spectacles down on his nose, sitting in his usual position, a book in his hand.

"Oh, Papa, you frightened me."

"Oh, Alexandra, you frightened me," he said, smiling.

"What can I do now? You've seen me, Marshal's seen me, Walford's seen me…"

"Has your mama seen you?"

"No, my aunt has not seen me."

William wondered why the girl had suddenly started to call his wife her aunt but chose to ignore it, due to the more important task in hand – that of getting her upstairs to her room. The story of how she came to look like an urchin could wait until another time.

"Come along, my dear, come along. I will escort you, with my fingers pinching my nose, to your bedroom. I'm sure you have a good excuse for playing fancy dress in the middle of the day" and he took her by the elbow and led her up the main staircase to the first landing. Patting her bottom, as if she were a child of five, he pushed her towards her own door and departed.

After dinner, Alexandra told Marshal the full story of her adventure and begged him to tell papa secretly. She knew there was no possibility of either of them giving her away to Ernestine, so the episode was at an end, apart from the washing of a filthy dress and an extremely soiled apron – but she had now gained the trust of the maids and the garments were sneaked into the washing without anyone being any the wiser.

000

It was three days before Alexandra dared to approach Cook regarding her baking project, mainly because her kitchen clothes were unwearable but also because she had been treated so badly by one of the people she admired most. When she did pluck up courage to enter the kitchen, she was very surprised to be greeted warmly by all and sundry. The story of her starling rescue and her subsequent adventure had been relayed from Walford, to Cook, to anyone who cared to listen downstairs and she was now a heroine.

She explained to Cook about her plan to feed the hungry of the village and it was greeted with great enthusiasm.

"I have to say, I would often have liked to take bits home for me own family in the village but I've been warned on pain of dismissal never to remove so much as an old crumb – by the missus o' course."

"That's dreadful, Cook, particularly when you make everything yourself. What harm could it do to hand our leftovers on to the needy. They must be very hungry, particularly in the cold weather?"

"Aye, your heart's in the right place, lass, but that mama o'yours, she's a different kettle o'fish."

Alexandra fought against the desire to snigger at her aunt being called a kettle of fish and asked,

"I didn't know you had family in the village, Cook. Who is it and where do they live."

"Just me cousin, her hubby and the bairns now. I had an old auntie who looked after them all but she's gone to meet her Maker now, so there's only Doreen left. She lives down the lane, just opposite the gates you know."

"That sounds like a good place for me to start then. Do you think your Doreen would mind if I took some food for the little ones?"

"I'm sure she wouldn't. Her man had a bad accident in the iron works last year and still can't walk, so she's only got what she earns from taking in washing to keep them and those two scallywags. You tell her you know me, if you go that is."

"Oh, I shall go Cook. There's no doubt about that and I'll ask her if she knows anybody else who would like some bits and pieces to help out."

"You're a little saint, Miss, you really are. Now, let's get on with your baking, if you want to start doing your bit. By the way, I know the master says you can come down here and knock up a few receipts in your spare time but what about the mistress?"

Confident in the knowledge that papa knew what she was doing, Alexandra became sure of herself and said,

"I think the least said about that the better, Cook."

She's growing up, that lass, thought Cook, and a fine woman she's going to be an' all.

CHAPTER 10

In London, Marianne waited for Ralph to come to collect her and her cousin, to take them to a soiree in Grosvenor Square. It was being held by Lady Betty Medway for her daughter, who was being groomed to come out at the same time as Barbara and Marianne. They sat in their finery in Aunt Maud's drawing room, keeping an eye on the door so they could compose their features suitably when the butler announced Ralph. It did not do to be seen laughing or even smiling in the presence of a presentable young man and to Marianne this man was the most presentable she had ever seen. She had been introduced to many gay blades in the past months but none of them compared with the handsome looks and elegant bearing of her Mr Lawrence. Of course their chaperone would have to attend with them. Aunt Maude had dragged one of her own aunts out of the shadows for the irksome job of watching the two girls and it was so easy to pull the wool over her eyes when required.

There was no sound, either of a carriage or a knock on the door and Marianne began to fidget.

"There's no need to worry, dear cousin," said Barbara. "If Mr Lawrence does not appear in time for us to leave, we will go in father's carriage with great aunt anyway. He will then see how independent we girls can be."

Oh dear, don't say that; he must come. Barbara knows so many of the aristocracy now that I will be left sitting alone – or worse with great aunt – until the end of the evening.

"I'm so glad we decided to wear our matching gowns this evening, Marianne. Of course yours is slightly lighter than mine but we still look like sisters, don't you think?"

This girl was driving Marianne wild with her desire to have a sister, even to the point of asking a dressmaker to copy some of her gowns, right down to the ruched trim and looped fringing. It was so annoying because Aunt Maude's London dressmaker used more lavish materials and all this copying did was draw attention to the inferior quality of Marianne's own fabrics. She must ask mama to allow her to use the same woman for some winter outfits. Velvet trim was all the rage at present and the new high waist would be extremely flattering. However, she had discovered that Peter Robinson, the large store in London, sold un-made dresses which were merely a made-up skirt and the trimmings to make a bodice, so this was a possibility. Of course the bodice would need professional fitting if it were to be skin-tight as today's vogue dictated. After gossiping to some other girls of her own standing, she had been told that a velvet ready-made could be bought now for as little as £2.19.6d, a serge for about £4 and many winter dresses sold for seven guineas, whereas a dressmaker could charge anything up to £38. All these avenues were worth investigating, if she were to stay ahead of Barbara in the fashion stakes.

Luckily, her straight hair had grown sufficiently for it to be coiled higher on her head, whereas Barbara had the same curly mane as Alexandra and could not twist it around without pieces escaping. She was wearing so many velvet bows this evening that she looked like a gift box in flight, particularly with that demeaning, oh so tiny feathered hat.

Too much sitting was bad for the back of her gown and the crinoline would poke out so. She stood up, a signal for Barbara to do the same and at that moment the door was opened by the family butler. This must be Ralph, it must be.

It was Aunt Maude, followed obediently by great auntie.

"You must go without Mr Lawrence. I fear he has been detained, perhaps by other carriages on the way; there is so much traffic in London. Should he appear, I will send him on to Lady Betty's. Here is your great aunt and the carriage awaits. I will expect you at the usual time, dear girls. Please give my regards to your hostess." She patted and poked her daughter as she left the room and smiled casually at Marianne, thinking, she is such a sullen young thing. It would be a good day for all when she went away to the back of beyond where she belonged, but that would be some time yet and she had promised the girl's mother, her sister, to take care of her and bring her out.

000

Little did they know in London that Ralph had started out

that very day for the 'back of beyond' and the following afternoon was making his way to Grangely Hall, in the company of his father of course, to pay a call on Miss Alexandra Shankland.

This was the first time Alexandra had decided to visit Cook's relatives across the road from the big house and she had planned to walk, bearing her basket full of food gifts for the Seymour family. Half way down the winding drive, she saw the Lawrence gig coming towards her and stood back so it could pass unimpeded, thinking it was one of Mr Lawrence's regular calls on papa. As it came abreast, she heard the driver shout 'Whoah boy!' and she was staring into the smiling face of Ralph, heaving on the reins for all he was worth.

"Good afternoon, Alexandra. My father was coming to see Mr Turner, so I offered to drive him in the gig, the day being so fine for December. Can we offer you a ride back to the house?"

"No thank you, I am heading in the opposite direction," she said demurely, wishing she had left her charity visiting until the following day.

"In that case, I'm sure father won't mind taking over the reins and I'll accompany you on your walk."

This was difficult. How could she explain to Ralph, of all people, that she was going to visit some poor people down the lane. Yet to change her mind at the eleventh hour would be so unkind. What if Cook had mentioned her proposed call to her relatives? She must try to put him off.

"I'm sorry, Ralph, but I am on an errand of mercy today and I fear you would be totally bored by it. When I return, I presume you will still be here – I will see you then."

"Oh no indeed! I intend to come with you now. How could I not, when you have a heavy basket and no servant with you? I will be your protector."

He was not to be put off, so she let it be.

Ralph dismounted from the trap and his father took over the reins, after wishing her good-day and smirking at the young couple in his usual, annoying fashion. Thank goodness he made no comment about her cousin – but what would he say to papa? Ralph was hardly a suitable companion for a long walk." The two walked off down the stony path, listening to the gritty clip-clopping of the Lawrence horse and soon approached the main gate. On the left was the lodge house and dear old Mr Stubbs dashed forward to open the large, heavy gate again, although they could easily have passed one at a time through the small pedestrian entrance.

"It's a fine day for a walk, Miss," he said, as he tipped his cap and nodded briefly to Ralph. She replied in the affirmative and they continued on, past the stone half-moon of the entrance to Grangely and across the dirt road to a copse on the other side. As they walked briskly along, Ralph carrying the basket and supporting her arm through his, Alexandra felt as if he were hers and they were off to see mutual friends. It was a pleasant feeling and she smiled up at him as the sweet thought overcame her.

"Why do I have the honour of one of your rare smiles, Miss Shankland?" He waited for a reply.

"I thought how lucky I was to have company on such a fine day."

"Your companion is the lucky one. How fortuitous to meet you when we did."

"You do realise where I am going, do you not? I have spent some time cooking nutritious items in our kitchen, which I intend to give to the poor of the village and this is my first visit. I fully understand if you would rather not come any further."

"How foolish. I must come with you now, to see how the poor live if nothing else but you do have some strange pastimes, Alexandra."

She knew now that this was a big mistake. Ralph saw this as some kind of entertainment and would be sure to say the wrong thing to the Seymours. How could she put him off?

"I hope you will not be affronted if I say I want to do the whole thing myself and you must wait for me outside their home. If I walk in in the company of a fashionable young man, the lady of the house will be sure to think I am playing some upper class game, using them as something to ridicule." She stopped and took a deep breath.

He grinned and said, "But is that not what you are doing?" However, he saw the furious expression on her face and said, "As you wish, Alexandra. I will obey your rules," and gently replaced her arm in his.

They reached the old cottage at the foot of the lane and noticed that it was sited on the edge of a field, where the grass was yellow and there were no grazing animals beyond the fence now it was winter. They opened a small, unpainted wooden gate.

"No, don't come in Ralph. I want them to see I am alone. I should not be too long." There was a stile in the fence a little farther along and he pointed to it, as the place he would wait for her, hoping she would not keep him waiting, out here in the cold.

Her first knock went unanswered, so she tapped a little harder and this time the squeaky door was opened by a boy of about ten years old.

"Yeah, whatja want?" he said.

"Is your mother home? I come from Grangely Hall. Our Cook said it would be alright to call."

"Mam!" he yelled over his shoulder. "There's one o' the big nobs from over't road at the door."

A slim, dark-haired woman of about thirty appeared behind him and, grabbing him by the ear-lobe, pulled him out of the way, causing the boy to squawk like one of Walford's chickens.

"Sorry, mum, he doesn't know no better. I keep trying to get him to use his manners but it just falls on deaf ears. All his pals talk like that, so I haven't a hope in hell. Oh, sorry mum, I didn't mean to cuss."

"It's alright, I understand. I told the boy your cousin, our Cook, said I could come up with some bits to eat for the children – and you of course. She said you would appreciate a little extra. Is it alright? I mean, you don't think I'm pushing in and trying to be like one of the big nobs from over the road, do you?"

The woman, creased up her eyes and started to laugh. She pulled her apron up to her face and pushed part of it in her mouth to try to stop herself but she couldn't. Alexandra found it totally contagious and joined in, until they both finished by heaving in large gulps of air and wiping their eyes.

"Oh, mum, I haven't laughed like that fer years. You're a right tonic, you are."

"I didn't mean to say anything funny, I just copied what your boy said."

"Ah know but he was bein' cheeky and talking slang. I never expected you to do the same. Oh well, now we've had a good giggle together, why don't you come in and show me what you've brought."

This was more like it. She ushered Alexandra into the small room and at first it was so dark she could hardly see but eventually her eyes got used to the dimness and she noticed a tiny fire on the opposite wall. Even in her thickest outdoor coat, she felt cold in this room. There was a black range surrounding it and a mantelpiece full of knick-knacks and pieces of paper held down by a single brass candlestick. At the side of a tiny fire, his feet splayed out on a multi-coloured rag rug, sat a man holding a newspaper on his knees. When they eventually entered the room after all the laughing and gasping, he looked up from his reading. It was so unusual to hear his Annie laughing that he thought he must have died and gone to Heaven. What the hell was going on?

"Look what I've found on t' doorstep, our Ted. It's the young mistress from over't road and she's got a basket full of stuff for us."

"I don't want no charity," he said gruffly, looking down at his knees.

"It's not charity, Mr Seymour," Alexandra said quietly. "Cook always has plenty of ingredients in her kitchen and I wanted to learn to bake, so she said I could bring my efforts down the lane, so your children can tell me what they taste like."

"That's a hell of a tall story, if ever I heard one. You've just come round with your basket, like the lady of the manor, because you know I'm good for nowt and can't look after me family proper."

"Now Ted, I'm sure that's not what it's all about at all. This nice young lady is trying to do somebody a good turn and here are you givin' 'er a hard time. Where's your manners? You're as bad as our Jeff."

"I'm sorry, love. I'm not meself these days, since I 'ad that accident down the mine. I'll be alright when it 'eals and I can get back to work."

"I'm sorry to hear about your bad luck, Mr Seymour. Can't you walk at all?"

"Aye, I can wobble around a bit but I'm no good to the bloody manager of an iron mine unless I can use meself prop'ly and get out of the way quick, should anything untoward 'appen, yer see?"

"Yes, I quite understand. Well, I hope it won't be too long before you're back on your feet again and back to work."

"That'll be great, won't it? Back to that bloody hell hole, they call a mine. Oh, 'ere I go again, cussin' and swearin' when there's a lady present. Please accept me apologies."

Alexandra had a bit more of a chat with Mrs Seymour, who told her to call her Annie, then she put out the baking and a few pieces of bruised fruit she had taken from the pile meant for the pigs. There was some of yesterday's bread and butter and a jar of jam from Cook and Annie seemed quite overwhelmed by it. During their talk, as she emptied her basket, young Jeff had appeared at the back door, followed by a little girl of about seven or eight. He was obviously displaying her to his companion as a strange beast, like an animal in the zoo. She raised a gloved hand and waved to the children as she left and, telling Annie she would see her in a few days' time, she gently closed the door behind her.

Ralph was sitting on the stile, smoking a cigar and looking blue with cold, when she reappeared. It was just as well he also was wearing a substantial coat to keep him warm while he drove the gig. He pulled down his soft, felt hat and replaced his gloves.

"Righto! Come along Florence Nightingale. She was the lady with the lamp; I expect you want to become known as the lady with the basket."

"Please Ralph, don't poke fun at a very brave woman. She did a great deal more for mankind than I could ever hope to do. For one thing, she went to war with our soldiers in the Crimea, never knowing whether she would return. As it is, I believe she has been confined to her bed for nigh on twenty years and she still works, writing books on training for nurses and the improvement of conditions for patients in field hospitals."

"Phew, I didn't expect a full lecture on famous women of our time. Perhaps you should follow it up with a talk on Queen Victoria."

This was dreadful. She had left Ralph sitting in the cold for too long and now he was overcome with sarcasm to make himself feel better.

"I'm sorry, I really am. You know you shouldn't have come with me."

"I wouldn't say that, exactly…"

"I would, Ralph. I am the kind of person who likes to carry out a project alone. Other people only confuse me."

"You are a woman, Alexandra, and they very rarely even say the word project, let alone involve themselves in one. Why not accept that such things are done by the male of the species?"

"Never. I would die of boredom if I had to occupy myself with sewing and dressing-up from morning 'til night. God gave me a brain and I intend to use it."

"Going into dirty hovels is not what I would call using your brain, my dear. There must be much cleaner and more satisfying ways of occupying yourself."

They had almost reached the hall and Alexandra felt this conversation was exhausted and she had no intention of walking into the house arguing, even if it was about a subject nearest to her heart. Walford came forward and took Ralph's hat, pointing elegantly up towards the drawing room, where tea would be served. Alexandra wanted to change her shoes and remove her oldest loose coat before her aunt saw her, so she left Ralph to the butler and skipped away to the staircase.

When she came into the room, suitably tidied for tea, everyone was discussing yet another outbreak of cholera among the working population – not the best subject for the drawing room, prior to afternoon tea – but it seemed to fascinate every one of them – Marshal, Ernestine, Ralph, Walter Lawrence and papa.

"It was made very clear by Mr Ranger, when he did his town-by-town inspections for the General Board of Health, that the cause of much disease is the state of the sewers. Sort the water hygiene out and medical improvements follow," said Walter.

Marshal, who had made this one of his pet subjects, intervened at this point – which Alexandra felt was very brave, most people in the room being older and wiser.

"Many problems are caused by poor drainage conditions around the Tees estuary. There is often reflux at high tide, leading to…"

"Never mind what it leads to, my boy. I think this conversation has gone a little too far into the realms of specialization," said papa, after watching his wife's nose visibly curling.

Tea was served.

CHAPTER 11

After a whole week when Marianne could hardly bear to talk to anyone, let alone be an entertaining companion to her cousin, due to her clinging vine behaviour, it was made very clear to her by Aunt Maude that her person would not be required in London if this continued. The whole situation blew up when Barbara had insisted on sitting beside Marianne and paraphrasing her every sentence in a conversation with several slightly more interesting young people.

In fact, Marianne had decided that she could accept the absence of Ralph, as long as she had the company of another young man, Gerald, who had been invited to call specifically for Barbara. But Aunt Maude was not amused at this turn of events and felt her sister's child superfluous to requirements.

"I have written to your mama, Marianne and her reply arrived this morning. She requires you to return home as soon as possible, for reasons of her own." This was not strictly true, as she had complained to her sister that the behaviour of her niece was not what she had expected from a companion to her daughter.

"Oh, I will be so sad to leave, Aunt Maude. I was just starting to find friends of my own," Marianne said.

Knowing to whom she referred, Aunt Maude glanced across at her own ineffective daughter and smiled. This would mean she had more of a chance to capture a beau, without the interfering presence of Marianne. "I am sure you have many such companions back in Yorkshire, many of whom are longing for your return."

Marianne hoped that Ralph had said this to her mother and Aunt Maude had read it in her letter. Regardless of all the well-dressed and beautifully mannered young men in London society, she still felt a twinge of longing to see Ralph whenever she took time to think about him. Perhaps Yorkshire was the best place to be, and mama surely had good reasons for sending for her. It was a pity she would not come out with the other girls but her love for Ralph was more important than her light feelings for Gerald, now she had time to consider it.

Her travel arrangements were made and, after a long and tedious journey by rail in the company of an elderly couple who were friends of the family, Marianne eventually arrived at Darlington station, where she was collected by the Turner carriage.

The first time she saw her mother, she was prepared to find her lying in bed ill, due to the urgency of her return home. But no, Ernestine was in the drawing room as usual.

"Dear Mama, I am so glad to see you looking well. I was convinced you were at death's door when Aunt Maude sent me home, after receiving your letter. Why was I required at all?"

"I have had second thoughts about your continued absence, my dear and have missed you so terribly," Ernestine lied. "I also feel that Ralph Lawrence is the husband for you – particularly as your father is so keen on the union. You must come home and settle down. I insist." There was no point in telling her all the details written in Maude's letter. Obviously Marianne was far more appealing to young men and she had become jealous for her own, plain daughter.

000

Ralph once more accompanied his father to Grangely Hall. Neither of them had any idea that Marianne had returned, perhaps due to an oversight by William but more probably because he usually chose not to inform his business colleague of his personal affairs.

As they alighted and made to enter the Hall, Ralph caught sight of Alexandra leaving one of the doors from the kitchen quarters. She was bearing her basket once again.

"Would you excuse me on this occasion, Father. I see Miss Shankland with a heavy basket and feel I must lend her some assistance."

"Do you realise what you are doing, my boy," blustered Walter. "This girl is young and single and you have accompanied her on one walk, unchaperoned, already. I must insist that you have no more to do with her and take yourself off to be with your own friends.. This behaviour could be the ruin of me, doncha know!"

Ralph looked straight at his furious father and said, very quietly, "I really don't see what it has to do with you, Father. If I wish to act in a gentlemanly fashion to the cousin of the family, then I will do it."

"No, you will not. You forget I have known you since birth, my boy, and I know the way your mind operates. If you continue to see Miss Shankland, then you are up to no good! Have you forgotten that you are promised to Marianne Turner, just as soon as she returns from doing the season."

By now the conversation had become too loud for politeness and Ralph was aware that Walford had appeared to open the door for them. He looked at the father and son quizzically, then started to retreat slowly so they could enter the house. At the precise moment when Walter issued his final sentence of, "Come inside with me to talk business, as previously planned and leave that girl alone," Marianne appeared at the first landing and heard him. She hesitated, as if about to return to the upper corridor, then picked up her skirts and continued down. On reaching the foot of the stairs, she held out her hand to Ralph and, behaving as if nothing had happened, greeted him warmly,

"What a lovely surprise, Ralph. I had no idea you were coming today. I expect Papa told you I had returned from London."

Nothing in human relationships ever phased Ralph Lawrence and he took her hand, raising it to his lips and said,

"No, Marianne, I had no idea you were home. I often accompany my father on his business calls – in my professional capacity, you understand – and today is one of those times. I must add that I am delighted to see you visiting home, happy and well I trust."

She chose to forget the previous comment made by Walter as they entered, thinking it nothing to do with her and probably some men's talk for which she had no interest whatsoever. Whoever the girl was, she would have no place in the life of Ralph Lawrence after they were married. She would make sure of that. However, she did mention her unwitting eavesdropping to Alexandra on her return from her charity call.

"Can you believe that Ralph is still involving himself with

women of easy virtue at this late stage before our wedding. I have decided to tell papa I intend to marry, now I have been called home from London. I know a man should always have some experience of these things but it seems his father is not of the same opinion. 'Leave that girl alone', he said and I sincerely hope that Ralph is a good son and does what his papa says."

"I had no idea these things were spoken of in polite society. Are you quite sure that is what his father meant?" Alexandra said, her heart jumping around in her breast as she said the words.

"What else could he mean, you silly creature. It is not as if my Ralph will be seeing another person of our class, now is it?"

"No, I suppose not." Of course she was not seen to be of their class anyway.

"You suppose correctly. Ralph will marry me when I decide."

The conversation was closed, as far as Marianne was concerned. She found it so easy to change her mind – and about something as important as marriage. She had not explained why she had come home from London half way through her grooming to be presented. Oh, she was such a fly-by-night. Alexandra wondered if she had a sensitive bone in her body and as for her powers of perception, they were non-existent. Suppose Ralph were seeing someone else – apart from her, that is - she must find out and she must end whatever fragile relationship existed between them. Playing with fire had never been one of her favourite occupations.

The opportunity arose as the two men were leaving that same day. They did not stay for luncheon and Marianne had gone up to titivate herself. As they started to leave, Alexandra was returning from her walk and papa was in close conversation with Walter. This meant that Ralph had wandered outside and was waiting impatiently at the front of the house, tapping his black leather boot on the dusty ground and grinding one foot backwards and forwards to see a cloud of dust fly up in front of him. He looked like an overgrown child and Alexandra had to smile as she watched his antics.

"Whatever will your mother say about this?" she called out

as she approached him, smiling gently.

Ralph also laughed when he realised who it was and he took her arm and led her around the end of the house.

"I am so glad to see you. I had intended to accompany you on your walk today but father put a stop to it. He feels it is not quite correct for me to be escorting a beautiful young girl in the absence of a chaperone."

"And he is correct in that assumption."

"What? You mean to say you agree with his outmoded ideas regarding who I should and should not see?"

"Yes, I do and particularly as you have returned to Yorkshire without mentioning anything about it to my cousin, who is absent no more and believes you two will now become betrothed. What do you think she feels about your views?"

"Very little, according to her behaviour since my return here. She seems not to care one way or the other."

"I think you are wrong."

"And I think, no – I know - I am right."

"What kind of a marriage will you have, if you have no thoughts for her feelings and she none for you?"

"The kind of marriage that was planned for us by our parents, I expect. You must know it is just a marriage of convenience, organised by our fathers to bring them closer together in the iron industry. Feelings have nothing at all to do with it. In fact, if we are talking about feelings, you have more of them in one little finger than Marianne could hold in that basket, down by your feet." This was treading on dangerous ground.

"I think we should stop there, Ralph. I do not wish to be the reason for a problem between my cousin and yourself."

As if by magic, Ralph's father came down the steps at that very moment and started looking around for his absent son. They could hear William saying,

"I don't suppose he's far away, Walter. Probably just looking around the garden, although there's little to see at present, apart from a few late roses."

"I'd better go," Ralph whispered and smiled conspiratorially at Alexandra.

She turned and, picking up her basket, walked off silently to the kitchen block. She still had not told Ralph to keep away from her, although, when she had first seen him that was the only thought in her head. Once again she had been distracted, hearing that he appeared not to care for Marianne in the slightest.

Ralph joined his father and William, climbed aboard their gig, collected the reins from a stable boy and trotted off down the drive so by the time they had reached the first bend, Marianne had arrived in the kitchen.

Regardless of the maids and Cook herself, she took hold of the sleeve of her cousin's coat and pulled her unceremoniously through the door into the hall.

"What, do you think you are doing?!" she hissed. "I was watching from my bedroom window and saw you talking for quite some time with my intended husband and the conversation was not based on polite conversation. I saw both your faces and they were screwed up into expressions of …of… torment…argument…distress. Why?! I must know what has been going on behind my back! What were you saying to him?"

This was dreadful. It was so wrong. She was so wrong, if she thought for a moment that Ralph had been encouraged in her absence. How to explain such a situation.

"Marianne, let me try to find the words to tell you what we were discussing…"

"I think that is a very good idea."

"Ralph has been meeting me on the way to my charitable visits in the village and I was unable to dissuade him from accompanying me on two occasions. I asked him not to come, but you know Ralph…"

"I don't think I do know Ralph. It sounds as if you know him much better than I do."

"No. I have no interest in him, apart from the fact that he is your friend." This was a lie and she had only just realised it. She had a great deal of interest in Ralph.

"Well, I have suddenly lost all my interest in him and think I should have stayed in London, where a certain gentleman had more than a passing fancy for me. As far as I am concerned, Ralph and I mean nothing to each other."

"Oh no, Marianne, not because of me. I swear I did nothing to encourage him, nothing at all."

"No, nothing apart from wandering around the grounds every time he appears and apart from smiling and laughing into his face. I mean it, Alexandra, I will never marry Ralph Lawrence." She swirled around and started to mount the stairs. Then, thinking better of it, she came back down and marched off to the morning room, where she knew her mother awaited a call to luncheon.

Alexandra watched her disappearing behind the closing door with a feeling of dread, almost fear, because she knew what her aunt would do if she thought she had played any part in this fiasco. She could do nothing to change what had taken place, so she turned towards the stairs and sought solace in her own room.

She heard the gong for luncheon but ignored it. How could she appear in front of a furious woman and a frantic girl? She would rather starve. As for papa, he obviously would be told everything and, no doubt he would believe his daughter and his wife above his niece. This was the worst time of her young life, just when things had started to make sense and she had come to terms with being part of a rich family in a poor neighbourhood, just when life had commenced being worth living because she was going to help others, rather than sit up on a pedestal looking down at the deprived population of the iron towns. There must be a way to keep her position at Grangely and for Marianne to go ahead and marry the man of her dreams. She would lie and deny any interest in Ralph at all. She must give up any friendship they had ever had; she must.

All afternoon she anticipated the arrival of her aunt or Marianne – or both – but nobody came upstairs. The house felt as if it were empty, apart from a rattling in the drawing room, which she knew was the housemaid making up the fire afresh for the evening. Even after this, there was no movement on the stairs of people going up to change for dinner; nothing. She started to feel nervous. What was happening?

Rising from her chaise longue, she went to the window and looked out on the now wintry-looking scene. Apart from a few stray birds heading for their roosting places, there was nothing outside either. The gardener would not be working at this hour anyway but it would have been pleasant to see papa coming back from his club, or one of his business friends departing.

She pulled herself into some semblance of tidiness. She was not prone to playing with her hair or changing too often during the day, so it was easy to look normal and she decided to go downstairs, if only to dispel the feeling that everyone had left. On the way down, she met Marshal coming up.

"If I were you, I would about-turn and avoid the fracas downstairs, Alexandra. There is nothing but anguish and distress – and in the morning room of all places."

"Why, what has happened, Marshal?"

"It seems that Marianne presented mama with the news that she no longer wishes to marry Ralph and mama collapsed to the floor, just before luncheon. The silly girl flew off to find papa and gave him the anxiety of lifting my mother to her chaise, instead of waiting until the fainting fit had passed. Lunch was taken in rounds and my dear parent was fed from a spoon. Now, both of them are sitting beside her, pandering to her every wish and I have escaped to continue my studies."

"Oh what a dreadful thing to happen. Has the doctor been summoned?"

"Of course not, dear cos. But there is absolutely nothing wrong with mama. She heard something from Marianne which displeased her and sent her into a bout of swooning. The thing is, I cannot understand it. I heard that she was the one who wanted Marianne to do the season in London and the last thing in her mind was the marriage of her beloved to Ralph Lawrence."

"So, what did she hear? Do you know?" Alexandra was afraid she had been the cause of her aunt's illness.

"The spoilt child has decided she will go back to London, to stay with some new friends and finish all that hoo-haa regarding meeting the Queen."

"Why?"

"No particular reason. I personally think she has met someone she prefers, when she was off on her maidenly jaunt to London."

"So there is no specific cause and nobody else is involved,

apart from this figment of your imagination?"

"No. I have just told you so. Why this sudden interest in the affairs of Marianne, when I know you care nothing for her."

"That's a very cruel thing to say, Marshal. I have never said I care nothing for my cousin, not to you, not to anyone."

"You hardly need to put it into words, my dear. You appear to care more for her suitor than for herself."

"And what do you mean by that?"

"Don't think I haven't seen you in his company the last few weeks."

"That was nothing to do with me. I asked him to go away and he refused."

"Perhaps it had something to do with Marianne's decision."

"Why should it? You haven't said anything to her, have you?"

"What do you take me for, the village gossip. I have more important things on my mind than the potential marriage plans of my sister. Now, if you will excuse me, a book awaits upstairs."

"No doubt on the fascinating subject of sewage," Alexandra muttered to his disappearing back, thinking he was out of earshot. She was wrong because Marshal whipped round and said,

"Don't make fun of me. There will come a time when the study of such subjects will be more important than you realise." His mouth had compressed into a fierce straight line and she knew she had truly upset him. But she was dreadfully worried.

000

Ernestine lay on the chaise longue in the window of the drawing room, accepting sips of tea from her husband or her daughter and groaning quietly on occasion. It was good to have her two favourite people so close. William looked suitably upset and Marianne bore the guilt of one who had created a dreadful accident. How could she try to steal Barbara's young men and have to be sent home by Maude? Not only that, but she had, in the past, stated quite categorically that she would indeed marry that foolish boy, Ralph. What she saw in him was beyond her but she knew her husband wanted it to happen.

When the decision had been made before the girl went off to Maude's, William had become quite animated and said what a good decision she had made. Later that evening, he had explained to her how much depended on her acceptance and explained that the boy's father, Walter, was planning to make William privy to much secret information which would ensure that his investments did extremely well. In other words, Marianne was a pawn in the game which had to be won for the sake of the continuation of Grangely Hall. So, when her girl entered into conversation at tea time and declared she would never marry Ralph Lawrence if he were the last man on Earth, she had felt her consciousness just slipping away. She would most likely feel like this for days and all due to the naughty girl's changing her mind like that.

CHAPTER 12

The Saturday evening dinners continued and Ralph Lawrence accompanied his parents to Grangely, and the Beechams also attended on a regular basis. A second proposal of marriage had been accepted, due to Ernestine's determination and many threats of illness brought on by her daughter's thoughtlessness. Marianne returned to London, to stay with her new friend – a girl she had met whilst with Aunt Maude - and she had left to continue to be groomed by the new family. She and Ralph would marry when she returned. Sadly, Ralph was sick with desire for Alexandra, who now treated him badly in an attempt to reassure her aunt but he was convinced that it was only a matter of time before she succumbed to his manly charms.

Talk was of the country-wide, some said international, depression and its affect on the iron industry in Yorkshire. Engineers had worked out how to convert low quality ironstone into exceedingly high quality rolled products and a by-product of pig iron could now be converted also, using de-carburisation and puddling hearths. It had become large scale industry and yet, with the depression, any subsequent growth was slow and unimpressive. There had been talk of a process pioneered by Bolckow, Vaughan & Company Limited, which instigated the conversion of pig iron into a new product named steel and many local investors had become quite excited by this at the time. However, when the slump occurred in 1874, it was not seen as a viable gamble and William was glad he had not succumbed to the persuasion tactics of his friends. Both Anthony Beecham and Walter Lawrence had lost money but intended to hold on to their investments in the hope that events would change.

"I understand how you feel about the lack of confidence in local companies at the present time, William, but believe me it will all come right eventually. There is no possibility of such a massive development falling foul of a mere cyclical slump. It has to bounce back," said Walter.

"I sincerely hope so," nodded Anthony. "Every penny of my savings have gone into the new industry. If it fails, I shall have to live off my wife!" and he laughed. Only Alexandra noticed that there was no laughter in his eyes; just a cold, fearful expression. Marshal had remained silent throughout this exchange but he felt this was the time to make his presence felt.

"May I make a proposition, gentlemen," he said, looking extremely confident, Alexandra thought. "Surely this is the time to think about investing in something as important as the new steel industry in our area. As Mr Lawrence and Dr Beecham have mentioned, they, and no doubt many others, expect the industry to revive as soon as the employment potential is corrected – by government or whoever. Personally, I would choose this time to invest, when shares have reached a rock-bottom price and are almost guaranteed to rise in a two or maybe three year period."

"My God, Marshal, all your book learning is certainly paying off. I hardly recognise my own son – and, yes, you may be right – but, sadly I have no money I wish to squander on a gamble which might not pay off."

Marshal seemed visibly to shrink, as the other men laughed amongst themselves and then turned to other topics of conversation. Alexandra felt sorry for him because she knew his ideas were good. From the conversations she had heard over the years, it was obvious that such a large-scale operation as the invention of steel could not wither away and die; rather, it would spring into life as soon as conditions were right in the country as a whole.

When the meal ended and fanciful female discussions came to an end in the drawing room, the men reappeared from their port and cigars and Ralph made his way towards Alexandra. He felt this cousin was much more attractive than the other and she was available, whereas Marianne was not. He had spent some time discussing relationships before she went off to London and had been told in no mean terms that he was definitely betrothed. Seemingly the dragon of a mother would not hear of a break-up, despite the fact that her daughter had desperately wanted to remove Ralph from her circle; so who was he to argue. The marriage would take place, no doubt his father would persuade William Turner to join their syndicate and life would go on as before – with Marianne swanning around in London and he spending his time as profitably as he could – in every way possible. So here was his chance to revitalise his friendship with the independent Alexandra. What a catch she would be – even with her too-particular ways. Come to think of it, she had never mentioned any social events involving herself. All she wanted to do were her so-called good works. What a waste. No doubt the frightening Mrs Turner would find a goofy, chinless suitor for her niece in time.

He moved towards her. "Good evening again, Miss Shankland. May I sit with you for a while?"

"Please do," she said in an almost friendly manner. This augered well.

"How are your charitable works progressing. You note that I have taken your advice and avoided any close contact with you during the day."

"So sensible, Ralph. My trips into the village are much appreciated by the poorer people and more so since the big depression. I know I can only visit so many houses in the vicinity but every small amount of food must help, particularly in families where they have children."

"And what does your mama feel about such rash squandering of her provisions?"

"Shhh! You know I have never mentioned my kitchen training, nor my house visits to her, as she would put a stop to it immediately." She wished he wouldn't call her mama because she wasn't. She continued in a whisper, "Please remain quiet."

"I don't know if I wish to. In fact, I too object to your magnanimous behaviour. You put yourself in so much danger when you wander around the village streets alone. Who knows what might happen."

Alexandra wished he would go away. This was one conversation she never wanted to hold with anyone, let alone this man. "Please change the subject, Ralph, or I will have to leave the room. I do not want to discuss this topic."

"Oh, I fear I have annoyed the oh-too-good Miss Shankland," he said in a voice too loud for private discussion and William got up from his chair and came across.

"What do I hear? I trust this is merely banter. How have you annoyed my girl?"

"I told her that I object to her wandering around the poor houses of the village, bearing provisions. I feel it is a dangerous exercise for a young lady alone."

"What's this? What is he saying, Alexandra. Do I hear right? Are you visiting the houses of the iron workers?"

"Yes, papa, I am and I don't think it is anyone's business but mine. What I choose to do in my own time is my own business." She was so annoyed, she wanted to leave and now the whole room was listening.

"I forbid you to continue with this ridiculous farce. Do you hear me?" Then, knowing he had drawn attention to them and not wanting to involve anyone else in this foolish charade, he bent down and whispered in her ear,

"Please go to your room. We will continue this discussion tomorrow."

Feeling like a child, Alexandra rose and left the room, all eyes upon her. This is not how it should be. Now her aunt knew what she was doing and all because of Ralph. How could she possibly have thought he enjoyed her company. He had gone out of his way to denigrate her in the eyes of their friends and she could never keep company with him again. Her sadness overtook her on the stairs and she climbed the final half-dozen in a mist of tears.

In her room, she gave way to her anguish and sobbed into her pillow until there were no more tears in her heart. She had even had foolish thoughts of loving that irrational man. How could she have entertained such ideas, about such a selfish individual, who had no thoughts for anyone except himself?

000

It was not until after his own morning walk around the estate that William Turner decided to have a firm talk with his wayward ward. He had spent his time alone tossing over her actions in his sympathetic mind and, despite changing his views several times, had finally decided that her charitable visits must stop. Partly it hinged on his wife's knowledge of the affair and the dressing-down he had suffered after dinner last night, and also he had become aware of the danger hinted-at by Ralph Lawrence. All the villagers knew of her gentrified upbringing and it would only take a gang of like-minded youths to turn Alexandra's compassionate calls into a game for them. He would hate to think of such a caring girl finding herself upside-down in a ditch surrounded by vicious hooligans. It certainly did not bear thinking about. So, he sent up a message that he wished to see her in his study.

Little did he know that his niece had been preparing herself for such a summons since she had skulked away from the drawing room the previous evening. All her intellectual energy had gone into the problem during the night when she should have been sleeping and she had come to the bitter conclusion that everybody was right about her forays into the villagers' homes. She knew that she alone could not make a sizeable difference to their situation by delivering such a small amount of sustenance to such a small number of people. She had been living in cloud-cuckoo-land and truly believing that she could make a difference to their plight; in her generosity she was merely being childish.

When she went down to the library, or study as it was now called, she wore an expression of acceptance, coupled with a smile of understanding, which pleased her uncle considerably. Without being told, he knew she had accepted his decision and really felt any further lecturing on his part was totally unnecessary. However, he went through the motions of parenthood.

"Ah, Alexandra, I expect you know why we have to have this little talk alone."

"Yes, Papa, I do," she said, calmly. She was so different from his own daughter.

"I must insist you stop your foolish jaunts into the village, bearing pastries and what-have-you."

"Jaunts they are not. Pastries and what-I-have is correct. I hope you will not think me impudent if I ask one proviso."

"Ask away, young lady, ask away." Now, he was smiling his comprehending smile.

"Have I your permission to continue to cook? I so enjoy preparing food and watching a solid, edible confection appear out of the conglomeration of liquids and dry ingredients which go into the bowl."

"Will Cook still have you, if your results are left lying around the kitchen, instead of being toted around in baskets to the needy?"

"That is part of the question, dear Papa." He could not resist such fond remarks and she was aware of this.

"Tell me all, Alexandra. I can only say no."

"I hope not, because it is something your ancestors probably took for granted. I wish to reinstate the policy of giving away our left-over food the morning after dinner parties and such. Too much good and edible sustenance goes into the pig swill – far more than they need and our villagers are still poor and needy. It is only due to my aunt that the habit ceased…"

"Why have you stopped calling her mama?"

"I…I…was unaware I had…"

"Come along, my dear. I have known you too long for such dishonesty. I have noticed, so I'm sure others have."

"Alright, Papa. It was due to an argument we had when Marianne left. I will not say more than that but as a result I cannot say the word mama without thinking about what was said."

"Oh dear," was all he said and the subject was never raised again.

As for the handing out of excess food, including Alexandra's studiously made samples, they were collected by Annie Seymour's husband, as soon as he could drive a cart once more. This led to a permanent job on the estate for him, working with animals, for a man who had trained at his father's knee to be a stable hand and then decided to go off into industry as a rebellion, when the new employment became lucrative. Alexandra's attempt at charitable works was taken over by someone much more able to communicate with his peers and more capable of knowing which families needed help at which times.

CHAPTER 13

There was no other way for Ralph to see Alexandra, apart from the monthly dinners when she made a point of avoiding even eye contact, than for him to call on some pretext or other. He had worked out when William would be elsewhere on the estate and when Ernestine took her afternoon rest and arrived on a borrowed horse, supposedly to consult the girl on a private matter regarding her cousin, Marianne.

Marshal saw him in the gravel turning-circle below and watched from an upstairs window as he handed over his reins to one of the boys. Even his riding clothes were of the latest fashion – more suitable for Rotten Row than a Yorkshire village – and very dashing.

Walford came to the door, after hearing the bell clanging as he drank a second cup of Cook's valuable tea in the kitchen. His legs were getting stiff and it took several steps before he could adopt his usual, straight position.

"Good afternoon, Mr Lawrence. I'm afraid the master is out and about today."

"I know, Walford. It was Miss Alexandra... Miss Shankland I came to see. Could you inform her of my presence, if you please."

What a puppy. He treated everybody like an underling. He even tried to lord it over Mr Marshal, who was worth three of him, when it came to intellect. However, he was paid to be a butler and a butler he would be. It was a long way up to Little Miss's room but he staggered along the corridor and knocked on her door.

Alexandra was doing some more patchwork. If she could not run around with food parcels, she would go back to doing her sewing for the estate workers. How annoying, somebody wanted her, just when she had planned a quiet afternoon. She placed her stitching on the seat behind her and opened the door.

"Hello Walford. Does someone wish to see me?"

"Yes Miss. It's Mr Ralph Lawrence at the door. He wonders if you'll come down."

She definitely did not want to see Ralph but how could she explain that to Walford.

"Alright, Walford. Could you ask him to wait in the drawing room. I'll be down shortly." This was a surprise. She and Ralph had not spoken since his outburst about her charity visits. Such a pity. He was an attractive man and they had been so friendly in the past. What could he want with her? She glanced in the looking glass and then went a little closer and pinched her cheeks, twirling her side ringlets into shape and smoothing down the small plaits at her ears. She would have to do.

Down in the drawing room, Ralph had taken a seat at one side of the fireplace and was leaning back so his head rested on the back of the sofa, one leg lifted and crossed over the other knee. As she entered the room, he stood up and moved towards her, his hand outstretched. Alexandra had no idea what to do. Was their unfriendliness at an end? Who had decided this? There was really no need to continue their feud, as the situation which caused it was at an end, so she held out her own hand and he took it in his. He was sensitive enough not to kiss it and merely squeezed it gently, before bowing in front of her.

"To what do I owe this pleasure," she said, in the words of a character in her latest Regency novel. The ice between them was broken and Ralph started to laugh; it was more of a low rumble, which rose and escaped from his nose and mouth like a horse's whicker.

"I wish to take a present to Marianne for her birthday when I go up to London next week and, as I was unable to remember which are her favourite gemstones, felt I should ask someone who knows her well, before I go to the jeweller. Who better than her sister, or should I say cousin?"

"I don't know if I can be of much help to you, Ralph." Even saying his name made her insides feel strange and she had thought these feelings gone forever.

"I'm sure you can. I will tell you what I had in mind and you can say yea or nay."

"So be it." Will things ever change? Why is she always sought out to choose gifts for another woman?

"I thought of a ruby pendant. What do you say?"

"That is a nay, I am afraid. She would not wear a stone which denotes July, when her birthday is in the month of March."

"Now I know why I came to you. I had no idea that different months meant different stones, so tell me please, what is the stone for March?"

"It is the aquamarine. Perhaps you could find a pendant with such a stone."

"Find it, find it? I intend to have a stone set into the gold pendant which I have had designed specifically for my future wife. My jeweller waits with baited breath until I return with the information he requires. I will tell him aquamarine and he will be a happy man. No doubt he could have given me more advice, had I known about precious stones denoting months of the year. Thank you again, Alexandra."

"I am pleased to be of assistance. Now I must go. I have many things to do. Goodbye, Ralph."

"Oh, surely not. Please stay and talk awhile, Alexandra. It has been so long since we were together."

"You know that is the wrong thing to say. Please stop now. I will ring for Walford."

"No, no, not yet. I must know that we are still friends. After my ill-timed and ill-chosen remarks some time ago after dinner, I have not been able to get you out of my mind."

"Ralph. You are betrothed to my cousin. Does that mean nothing to you?"

"It means as much to me as it means to her. Alexandra, you know this is a farce, a marriage of convenience, so why do you continually refuse to listen when I say I have feelings for you. If you wish, I will refuse to take Marianne's hand but you know what happened the last time we wanted to part. Your aunt suffered an illness and Marianne said we must marry to ensure her health. What can I do about that?"

"Please, Ralph, don't say such things." Her heart beat so she could feel each stroke and she knew in that minute she had not forgotten his intense attraction to her. He came closer and took her hand again, looking into her eyes as he did so. His face was so close, too close and she was unable to move away because of the pressure on the veins of her hand. He was pulling her towards him and she knew she should struggle or call out for assistance but did she want to? Their faces touched and she could feel his breath and the warmth of his skin transferring itself to her cheek, just before his lips sought hers and they fused, like egg yolks into warm milk. She could smell the scent of his hair cream and feel the light stubble of his chin, as he gently ground his mouth over hers. She had never expected this sensation, which was not one of the lips or even the whole face; the rest of her body tingled and blood rushed along feverish nerve endings to many parts of her anatomy and the feelings were so exciting and pleasant that she had no power to stop him – or to stop herself.

When they drew apart, held together only by their eyes, Alexandra wanted it to happen again and only the noise of a footfall on the gravel outside the window brought her to her senses.

It was papa, returning from his inspections.

"Please, Ralph," she started to plead but before she could finish her sentence he said,

"It's alright, my dear, I will go now and explain my presence to Mr Turner as he comes in. That way I can walk past him and avoid further questioning but, believe me, I will not forget today and I hope you will not. Goodbye, sweet Alexandra."

He was gone. She stood in the middle of the room, beside the centre table and had to put out her hand to steady herself. The blood was rushing to her face and she hoped papa would not come into the room, not yet. These were the kind of moments written about by Jane Austen and she longed to know the end of the story. She could hear voices in the hall, then the door closed noisily and she heard papa giving Walford an order, in a completely relaxed and pleasant tone, so she knew there had been no altercation between him and Ralph.

It was almost afternoon tea time and her aunt had not appeared. It was just as well, otherwise she could well have found herself leaving with Ralph, accompanied by a trunk and a flurry of clothing. What a fool she was. This must never happen again. She pulled herself together and walked towards the half-open door but, before she could pull back the brass knob and exit elegantly as planned, there was a loud bump followed by a crash and she heard Walford calling,

"Are you alright, sir! Are you alright!"

She rushed into the hall, to see her uncle collapsed under a criss-cross of flower stems and blooms; he had fallen onto the hall console, knocking over a vase containing flowers in water. The crystal vase was in pieces over his chest, the water had soaked his shirt and waistcoat and the table leaned at a precarious angle from the wall. Falling to her knees at his side, she gently lifted his head onto her lap and stroked his wet cheek. Walford had, by then, replaced the table onto its legs and was staring down, with an expression of sheer horror, at the prostrate body before him. As they maintained their tableau, a maid appeared through the staff door with a tray. On seeing the spectacle, she halted, stared, then turned and ran back to the kitchen, yelling,

"Cook, Cook, the master's on the floor!"

That is all they heard, as they patted William's hand and gazed down at his closed eyes, willing him to return to consciousness. In a minute or two, out came Cook in full baking dishabille and rushed forward to where Alexandra was kneeling. A damp cloth was produced and she joined them on the floor. After a few minutes of mopping and more affectionate stroking, the beloved brown eyes opened and moved from side to side as he assessed his position.

"Ohhh! Ohh! What happened to me?" he mumbled.

It was Alexandra who took control and she said, "It's alright Papa. You fainted clean away and knocked the hall flowers on top of you. It's alright now, though. Cook and Walford have brought you round and I'll call for assistance to help you to move. She turned the knob of the nearest door. It would be so much easier to move the disorientated master onto a chair in the warm morning room, rather than trying to heave him upstairs to the drawing room or a bedroom.

Still issuing orders like the mistress of the house, Alexandra asked for tea and told Walford and Cook to return to their work, after calling a couple of the outside staff to lift her uncle. The brother and sister looked at each other conspiratorially, enjoying the sight of their Little Miss taking over the reins and organising the household. This is how they had expected her to grow up.

When the doctor had been and the wheels of his gig could be heard taking him off down the drive, Alexandra and Marshal remained standing at the front door, looking down at their feet and then at each other. They had asked for an honest appraisal of the health of papa and Dr Benbow had given it to them, although he said he had not been quite so straightforward with his patient – mainly due to his optimistic outlook on life.

He had an incurable heart problem.

"Should we tell him, do you think?" Marshal was the first to break the silence.

"I don't know. He's always been honest with us, about everything, but this is such a dreadful truth to impart to anybody. Perhaps we should keep it to ourselves for a while; let's wait and see if he asks."

"I trust your judgment when it comes to matters of health. A woman is much more sensitive regarding such things. Anyway, perhaps the doctor is wrong. Stranger things have happened. He may make a complete recovery and, in that case, it would be wrong to depress him with a negative prognosis."

"I thought you were logical and scientific in your approach to life, Marshal. Did Dr Benbow seem to be telling us a fairy story? He told us how weak papa's heart was and was convinced himself that another such attack would be the end of our dear father."

"I suppose not. Let's get back to the morning room before papa thinks there is something wrong. Oh, I know there is but it will do no harm to dissimilate, as you suggest."

They went back to the invalid and affected a mock cheerfulness and, unbeknown to them, so did he for he knew without being told that his body was quitting the world of the living. It would have taken more than a lying doctor to assure him that he was going to be well again. His self-knowledge was paramount. The two adult children did not fuss around him, as Marianne would have, nor did they behave in a sad and selfish way, as Ernestine would have. They both accepted they had a job to do and that was to make papa's life as happy and unburdened as possible, as long as they had him.

Another serious conversation took place later between them

and that involved pledging that neither of them would tell either their sister or Ernestine about William's collapse and its resulting prognosis. Alexandra also committed herself secretly to keeping her knowledge to herself as far as Ralph was concerned because she doubted his capacity for keeping a confidence - which saddened her.

CHAPTER 14

Ralph and Alexandra met in the woods, when they could. It was cold and dark among the trees but, wrapped up in furs and leather, they were afforded an amount of privacy they could find nowhere else.

Their closeness was limited to kissing and holding each other – to the point of opening both their coats and clutching the other's body within the confines of possibility. They could not have lain down on the hard, wet ground, even though they desperately wanted to, but this was nature offering them contraception of her own making. How Alexandra longed for more, when she felt his strong, muscular arms about her and heard the beating of his heart reverberating on her own chest.

Ralph was not so frustrated, apart from wanting to add her virginity to the wonderful embraces and loving they shared together. He had ways of taking care of his basal needs, whenever the urges became too strong. When he disappeared down to London, which he did on a regular basis, she fumed and wept alone in her room, knowing he was seeing her cousin but never knowing about the other degenerate women he met in backstreet rooms.

It was so tempting for Alexandra to tell him she would not keep company with him ever again unless he gave up Marianne but the thought of losing what little she had for the sake of his arranged marriage kept her sane and she returned to her hobbies, desperately waiting to receive a note from the man she thought of as her lover.

Now that her cooking expertise was as good as she required and she had worked her way through most of her receipt books, her time in the kitchen was in danger of becoming commonplace – even boring, when she reflected upon it. She was in need of a new project and nobody could decide what it would be except herself. Her aunt was absent more often than present at family meals, so she and Marshal found sitting around the dining room table rather enjoyable. Papa was prepared to discuss most subjects with his young companions and she was made aware of how knowledgeable Marshal had become about the iron and now steel industries. He was aware of, and often visited, the Royal Exchange, which had been built in Middlesbrough as a centre for financial dealing and even tried to encourage papa to revive his interest in investing, knowing full well that he would not live to see the fruits of his labours. This was his way of pretending there was nothing wrong with father's health. He described the sheer black sea cliff at Cattersty, near the village of Skinningrove where a large iron works had produced masses of metal and plenty of unnecessary side products, which were used to form a false barrier against the sea, and went on at length about the steam, smoke and general industrial effluent along the coast from Stockton to the gares, which had increased in quantity throughout the 1800s.

Papa enjoyed being able to discuss such technical topics in full detail and showed a certain amount of pride in his son's knowledge and intellectual ability. Alexandra was pleased for both of them and sat quietly thinking about Ralph whenever the conversation at dinner turned to local industrial expertise.

000

After one of his trips down south, Ralph and Alexandra met in the west woods. Their method of contact had become one of the village boys whom she had befriended on one of her final visits to Skipper's Lane. When she had mentioned to Ralph that the youngster kept coming up to the Hall, talking to gardeners and asking for odd jobs around the place, he had taken a great deal of interest in the young tyke. One day, after a call between the fathers, he had seen little Bert and beckoned him over while he waited for Walter.

"I've seen you around the estate very frequently, young man," he said imperiously and he could see adoration in the boy's eyes.

"Yes sir," he mumbled, looking down at the gravel path.

"I suppose you're looking for odd jobs, at your age."

"Yes sir," he said, this time looking up under the peak of his cap.

"How would you like to be my messenger on occasion?"

"Yes, sir. I would really luv that."

"I would have to know my messenger was prepared to keep things to himself, no matter how tempting it was to spread the word around."

"Y'u c'n trust me, sir. I w'uldn't breev a word, not even to me dog."

"Well, I would need proof of that. You see there's an old saying – don't shoot the messenger – but I would just miss out the don't bit."

"Ooh, sir, I don't like the sound o' that"

"Well you wouldn't have to worry about it, if I could trust you. You come and see me outside the village inn tomorrow morning, not too early and I'll put you to the test – alright?"

"Yes sir!" he said and Ralph waved him away, before his father saw him talking to the lowest of the low.

The following day, he had written a pointless message to Alexandra about Marianne and it had been delivered secretly as required and this went on for some weeks, before young Bert was trusted with a real message containing an assignation and that is how they acquired their go-between. The boy was unable to read so their venue was safe.

After Alexandra had found out about papa, she was quiet and sometimes unapproachable but she knew she must protect her air of fun where Ralph was concerned because he had told her that the main reason for Marianne's unsuitability for him was her dour attitude to life. So, whenever Ralph appeared, her dismal thoughts flew over the treetops and it was good for her as well as for their association. However, this time she had something else on her mind and she simply must share it because it affected Ralph also.

Two days before, she had come into the drawing room at afternoon tea time to find her aunt surrounded by cushions in her usual place by the fire. Of course the screen was in front of her to protect her far too pallid complexion but she was holding a conversation with her husband, so things were looking good.

"Good afternoon Aunt," Alexandra said, forcing a smile onto her face and attempting to look pleased to see the usually absent woman.

"Good afternoon Alexandra. You must come and join us for

some tea." What had happened to cause this improvement?

"In fact you must come and hear my news. I have just been telling your uncle that Marianne arrives within the week, to pay an extended visit – or should I say to come home. Her hosts have an Italian holiday and wish to take along their daughter, so our girl is returning home for the duration. What do you say to that, niece?"

"What a lovely surprise. You must be so pleased – and you also, Papa. It is months since we have seen our sister."

"I do wish you would stop using those childish names for this family. We all know who we are, except you. William, please tell her to stop."

"I will not, Ernestine. Alexandra has been our daughter since she entered this family circle as a baby. I do not expect her to suddenly become a niece at this late stage – unless she wants to of course."

Alexandra did not know what to say. She would always call William papa but she had stopped herself from saying mama to her aunt; not that she ever noticed what she was called. Now she was being told not to call him papa. Instead of involving herself in such a pointless argument, she decided to try to change the subject.

"Have we any idea when Marianne will arrive? I would like to arrange some flowers, or at least some greenery at this time of year, in her room, to welcome her home."

It worked because William said, "What a delightful idea, dear girl. I think you thought Thursday, did you not, Ernestine?"

"Yes, it will surely be Thursday. I must also find some knick-knacks to welcome my only daughter back to the fold."

Alexandra had let it rest there and left the room as soon as politely possible. At least she knew when her rival for Ralph's time would be appearing and she could tell him to forget their own meetings until Marianne returned to London. There was a chance that he already knew, due to his regular trips to the metropolis – she would have to find out.

So she walked purposely towards their meeting place, wearing an expression of sadness. How had she let herself become involved in such a problematic situation? Because she had fallen in love was the honest answer; fallen in love with the only man her cousin wanted, the only man papa wanted his daughter to marry.

Ralph was leaning by the oak tree which looked like a tall, angular skeleton waiting to whisk them away to Hades. He put out his hands and drew her towards him as soon as he saw her.

"I cannot believe what I am seeing. My usually cheerful and beautiful companion is in the depths of misery. What can have caused such a change?" he said, as he held her at arm's length and looked at her closely.

"Marianne has happened," she said, forcefully.

"You mean she's here, now?" Ralph asked, starting, and looking very worried indeed.

It only took such a foolish mistake to make her smile. "No, silly one, not now. She comes home on Thursday, my aunt said and she has made a complete recovery on the strength of it. I can't believe that someone who has been languishing in her room for weeks should suddenly feel like rushing around the house, laying out a red carpet for the return of her selfish daughter. Oh, I shouldn't have said that. You must think I am a shrew, talking about your future wife in such a way."

"If you cast your mind back, it was I who said she was selfish. I can hardly blame you for repeating what I have told you."

He was so kind and forgiving. She must forget about the misery ahead and enjoy their last time together for some weeks. Looking into his eyes, she moved forward and felt his welcoming arms come around her body. They kissed and Ralph drew her in towards the wide tree trunk. He changed places and pressed her back against the ridged base of the oak and, before she realised what was happening, she felt his hand sliding up and under her several petticoats. She wore a simple, walking gown of green, with a pleated hemline and she could already see the pleats around her hips, as Ralph fumbled to find his way in amongst the complicated undergarments.

This was not what she expected today of all days. They had always been so circumspect, knowing that there was an invisible line in their relationship beyond which they could never pass. Not having a mother, she had no-one to explain to her the vagaries of the masculine mind; how could she understand that a woman could hold herself in control, whereas a man was unable to think beyond the sexual act when a woman behaved as if she would be available.

"Stop this at once!" she yelled. "I will not be treated like a farmer's lass in my own woodland." Is this how she felt – that it was her own?

"Don't be so prissy, Alexandra my love. We are unlikely to see each other for some time and I must have a sweet memory to keep in my heart until we meet again."

It was so tempting to give him something of herself before they parted. Her body cried out for him but her sensible mind fought with it. When all this sadness was over, when Marianne went away again, she would have to have him for her own. She loved this man.

"I cannot and will not behave like a strumpet. Please think what we are doing, Ralph. Here we are in the middle of a wood, pressed up against a tree like two rough farmhands, when we should be sitting in the house, drinking sherry with our small fingers crooked and talking about the next art exhibition in Middlesbrough. I must go. No doubt I will see you in the company of my cousin, at lunch or tea or dinner, whatever. Goodbye, Ralph."

She ducked below his arms and pressed past him, stopping only to pull down her skirts and pat her hair into place under her hairnet, as she ran from the wood, past the animal graves and onto the firm surface of the drive. She was afraid but excited by her own emotions. The sooner they had something more permanent arranged the better.

CHAPTER 15

Marshal sat in the study with his father. He was unable to discuss illness or recovery or anything to do with the human body without Alexandra's sensible approach to such things, so he had said nothing about papa's situation to him since hearing the doctor's verdict. It was unlikely that another man wished to converse about ailments to another man, was it? They were both reading and had been for the past hour.

There was a loud noise down the chimney, making both men start, then William started to laugh aloud.

"Oh, what a shock! That must be a crow on the roof, calling to its friends in the trees over yonder. They have such a loud caw, I almost fell from my chair!"

"Me too, Father. I've quite lost my place in my book."

"In a way, I'm glad we were interrupted, Marshal. Ever since the doctor gave me the death sentence, I've been wanting to talk to you about the estate."

Oh God, he knew, but why did he have to say that, so easily, so calmly? It was obvious he knew what was happening to himself. Was nothing sacred? But he should have guessed papa would treat death as he treated everything else. It was a commonplace occurrence, which happened to everyone. Why ignore it as if it were not going to happen?

"What did you want to ask me, Father?"

"It's not a case of asking, my boy, more telling. I want you to know what's been arranged for when I go. No, don't look like that. I know, better than anybody, that my time on Earth is almost at an end but you, you my son, have many years left to enjoy.

"I want you to sell up, Marshal. You see I have little to leave, apart from a sum in the bank and, of course, the house. There will be enough to set your mother up in a house befitting her station, some to pay for Marianne's wedding and she will be alright with the Lawrence fortune; why do you think I wanted this match so badly. Alexandra should be given a house as well, although I expect she will make a good marriage some day and then she can sell her property and use it as a dowry. You must have the rest; the money in the bank, the house and contents, the horses and other animals around the estate – you're a bright boy and will handle it well.

"Right, I've said my piece and I want you to mull over what I've told you. Come back to me if there are any insurmountable problems. Thank you for listening, my boy. Now, leave me alone for a while. I want to commune with myself for a bit."

That was it. Papa had issued his decree, then returned to his book. There was to be no discussion, he wanted no sympathetic comments from him, no arguments. Marshal was glad of an excuse to leave the room because his eyes had filled with tears and he was certainly not going to haul out his handkerchief in the presence of his ill father. He rose and walked straight to the door and then realised what a traumatic experience his father had been through, so he turned with the handle in his hand and, with a superhuman effort, stopped the tears from spilling down and said,

"Thank you for telling me all this, papa. I fully understand and I want you to know that the family and the estate will be in good hands. I will do everything the way you would do it yourself."

Not expecting a reply, Marshal had almost left the library, when he heard the strong tones of his father which he had known since childhood, saying,

"I hope you will do better than I have, my boy. Don't forget, I have left you nothing, apart from this house and your native wit. Do with them what you can."

This time Marshal did leave and had to bury his face in his linen-covered hands, until he reached the comfort of his own bed, where he lay and sobbed until he could face the world again.

He missed lunch and missed afternoon tea, while he thought about what his father had said. He was hardly expecting to find out he was penniless in his twenties. It was a good thing he had no wife and family to care for, otherwise they would end up in the workhouse. Why had papa not invested carefully, to ensure his own wife had enough to keep her in the style to which she had become accustomed? It was almost as if he didn't care –

but he had always put his family above all other things. Perhaps he expected mama to take off to London and live with Aunt Maude or Marianne when she was married but it was so unlike him, to want his dependants to sponge off anyone else.

000

Marianne returned in a blaze of glory. She loved London and fashionable living, so much so that, in her inconsistent manner, she had decided to finish her alliance with Ralph, such as it was, yet again, against the wishes of her mother and father and return to her new friends permanently. That is until she had her unsettling shock.

When she first arrived, mama had been at the door to meet her and she had been guided, or rather manhandled, up to the drawing room, even though she wanted to go up to her room and change for dinner. Her mother had a breathless air about her and Marianne felt she must go along with her plans, if only to avoid a swooning or somesuch. They sat opposite at the fireside.

"Marianne, my love, my child, my Marianne, how wonderful to have you back."

"Yes, Mama, it is good to be home – but only for a short time, you understand. As soon as the Brownlies return from Italy, I have been invited to return to London. I will save all my incredible news for after dinner but I can tell you here and now that I have been the toast of the assembly rooms for some time now. Ever since you gave me my own dressmaker, my costumes have been the envy of all my friends and acquaintances…"

"Yes, yes, Marianne, my dear. I'm sure that is so but I must ask you, have you seen much of the Lawrence family recently?"

"A little but you must know that Ralph divides his time between London and Yorkshire, so I attend functions with him when he comes up to town and the rest of the time I am accompanied by other friends."

"You see him a lot, I hope. It is not quite the done thing to parade around without one's betrothed – particularly at dances and soirees." She must encourage Marianne to bring forward her marriage date; the sooner she was married the sooner life around her daughter would settle down.

Marianne thought, it must be said. "That is the point I was coming to mama and I thought it should wait until we were together tomorrow."

"No, it cannot wait until then. Tell me what you have been wanting to say."

Oh dear, she expected some good news. "I have become used to being without Ralph this year, Mama, and I would like to terminate my betrothal."

Ernestine threw her hands in the air then allowed them to drop silently into her lap. Her head fell forward also and slowly her body appeared to slide from the sofa onto the floor. Marianne screamed, in an extremely unlady-like fashion, then ran to the bell at the side of the fireplace, to summon help. When the maid appeared, she said the one word, 'Walford' and young Mary flew off to find the butler, as fast as she could run.

Once again, Ernestine was bundled up the stairs back to bed, where she stayed for the rest of the evening. Dinner was taken without the mistress and peace reigned at Grangely Hall again.

The following day, Marianne, being concerned about her mother's health, went to her boudoir and found her surrounded by people. Her father sat in a chair by her bed, holding her pale hand in his, Marshal stood at the foot of the bed gazing down and maids bustled about the room, removing a tray and placing glasses, as if there were three or four invalids there. She went to her father and asked,

"Is mama recovered? Was it anything to do with my sudden arrival? What can I do to help?"

"Yes, my dear, she is recovered. See, she opens her eyes to your voice. I do believe it was the excitement of your arrival, after waiting so long for you to come, which caused her to faint. Think no more about it, Marianne. Come and talk to your mama."

She approached the bed like someone in the jungle moving towards a tiger but her mother's face seemed serene enough. She even smiled at Marianne.

"Mama, oh dear Mama, what have I done? You were alright until we started our serious conversation and then… and then… I cannot bear to think that I upset you once more."

"Then do not, my dear love, do not. I think you must realise now that your poor mama cannot undertake serious conversations of a worrying nature and when anything is said that I find unbearable, I am afraid I just faint away, in front of your very eyes."

"I am so sorry, Mama and I will never do such a thing again."

"That is what I hoped and indeed expected you to say, my dear. I want to hear no more talk of your giving up your… Oh you know what I mean. I can hardly bear to say the words, they are so distasteful. You and Ralph will be married, as discussed, yes?"

"Yes, Mama, of course."

All visitors were told to leave by the maid in charge of Ernestine's recovery and, as she went back to her own bedroom, Marianne knew she could never leave Ralph, not if she wanted to ensure her mother's health. This was the second time her negative views on the subject had caused indisposition and it must now be well and truly closed, for good and all. There must be a way around it.

The following day, Ralph came to visit Marianne and they spent some time together in the morning room, chaperoned by Alexandra. What a part to play, that of companion to the beloved of her lover. She sat the whole time, book in hand, in the window seat, listening to their talk and thinking how trivial it was. Marianne told Ralph about parties she had attended without him and giggled girlishly when he enquired whether she had been sought out by any gentlemen. She watched as her cousin's hand covered that of her betrothed and wondered how he could bear to sit there doing this in front of her but this was the strong character of the man – he could act the part much better than she could. Never once did his eyes stray to the corner of the room, as he imagined he became once more the man of Marianne's dreams.

After he left and the girls were alone, they talked as if they were real friends and Marianne asked Alexandra whether she had met any potential suitors.

"I have decided to remain single," she said, softly and calmly, half believing her own statement.

"But you can't mean that. Spinsters are the lowest form of life. It is your duty to marry, so as not to reflect on the rest of the family. Where do you go to meet gentlemen? You cannot be attending the right gatherings, if no-one has asked for your hand."

"I do not go anywhere any more. Once I used to accompany friends to soirees and at-homes but now I care not for such engagements."

"Your words upset me, Alexandra. I do not believe that you have not infiltrated Middlesbrough society at the highest level. Surely, there are balls and social evenings where ladies such as yourself meet their beaux."

"You are speaking in the language of London, Marianne. Here, we remain with the family, in the country. Oh, there are balls and dance evenings at other large houses and I used to attend with the girls I have mentioned."

"I am sure Marshal would escort you to assemblies. Have you asked him?"

"Certainly not – apart from the fact that Marshal is not prone to attending soirees either. He associates with old school friends on occasion but we never hear where they go."

"Well, I am glad I decided to uproot and go south. I have little time to myself these days and find I am surrounded by gentlemen wherever I go. The occasions I attended when at home were dull compared with the London social scene."

"So what about Ralph – does he object?"

"As long as I am happy, Ralph is happy. He will be the perfect husband because he believes in the modern tenet of independent women, as do I."

"That sounds unbelievable. Surely, if a man loves a woman, he could not bear for her to be surrounded by other men when he is away from her?"

"Alexandra, you must know that we are marrying for the good of our families and not because of that elusive emotion, love. If I tell you something private, will you promise never to breathe a word of it to anyone?"

"Of course, haven't I always been trustworthy in the past."

"Yes, you have cos and that is why I feel I can talk to you, as I talk to my lady-friends in London." She broke off to take a breath and settle herself more comfortably in her chair. Even day dresses made in London had complicated back drapery and sitting was not something one did for long periods, due to the discomfort. It would have been better if they could have walked around the room gossiping but the room was too small for that, compared with those in the houses to which she had become accustomed. "When I came home this time, the first thought in my head had been to finish with Ralph Lawrence forever.

Alexandra felt herself take a loud gulp of air and hoped her cousin would not notice.

"Then I made the big mistake of mentioning my plan to mother. Can you imagine my horror and distress when she swooned away to the floor, just as I was going to tell her my reasons."

"What were those reasons?"

"I find myself so much in demand that I think, no I will rephrase that, I know I can make a better match – both for myself and for father's business requirements. After all, Ralph is only the son of a small-time investor in the iron industry. I am in the habit of keeping company with the sons of earls and members of the true aristocracy. However, since mama has proven to me that she cannot accept any changes in the structure of my life, I must marry Ralph and be damned." She enjoyed saying this and paused to note the shock on Alexandra's face, before continuing, "Once we are married and settled in our ways, no doubt he will continue to visit Yorkshire regularly, as well as having a London house and I will continue to keep company with my other friends – only they might become a little more than friends." She laughed into her smooth white hand, then looked up for Alexandra's reply.

It was not long in coming. "So, you intend to marry Ralph and cuckold him."

"I suppose I do, my dear. Isn't that the way with married people?"

"Not here it isn't. I would expect loyalty and honesty from anyone I married."

"But as you've told me you never intend to marry, that comment is what they call academic, is it not?"

"I find you very difficult to understand, since you took yourself off to London, Marianne. Is it so very different down there?"

"Up, my dear, up. One never says down to London. It is so vulgar."

"Then I must be vulgar in the extreme but you always knew that didn't you? I can see that nothing has changed between us. I feel I must bid you good morning. I must get some fresh air."

As she left the room, she could hear Marianne talking to herself and saying, "Fresh air, my dear, it's like poison. Give me a London drawing room any day." But if she imagined she had organised her life so well, she must think again.

CHAPTER 16

Marianne had only been back for a week, when her father collapsed in his study. She and Marshal had been sitting with him, discussing the heavy fall of rain the previous night. Alexandra sat in the window seat, as usual, listening to the conversation around her.

"I wonder if there will be more today, father," Marshal said.

"I shouldn't think so. Look up at the sky. It is far too clear for rain. However, it could happen. You know what April's like."

He got out of his chair and walked slowly across to the library shelves. They watched while he skimmed the books with his eyes and then almost pounced up to the red leather copy he had been searching for. It was high above on the top shelf and the effort of reaching up caused an audible click in his shoulder and he gave a slight groan.

"Here, let me," said Marshal, getting up quickly – but he was too late because his father seemed to crumple into a heap of clothing, as he sank down, still holding a copy of Tennyson's poems, open at The Lady of Shallot. His head dropped onto his chest and he clutched at his clothing.

Marshal was first to him and said, "Father, Papa, how can I help?"

"No help now, boy. Take care of your sisters," he whispered, closed his eyes and died. He must have known it would happen soon and, in his sensible way, mumbled his priorities, before ending it all.

Marianne started to shriek and bubble at the mouth, flinging herself onto the prone man and tugging at his arm.

"That will do, Marianne," Marshal said firmly and pulled her to her feet. He turned her round to face him and looked into her tearful eyes. "We knew he was ill. He knew this would happen soon, so it was no shock to him. He didn't want you to know, or mother. Just accept it, Marianne."

She ran off and Marshal heard her loud footsteps going up the stairs.

From that moment Marshal took charge, ordering the servants around and planning the funeral, even though he was distraught. His mentor, his hero, was dead and now he would have to step into those capacious shoes, that held so much knowledge of life in general and of business in particular. He must try to be strong for his father; he would expect it of him. The only thing he felt it was impossible to organise to his satisfaction was the reaction of his mother. When she was told what had happened, she took to her bed and refused to eat. It was as if she had died when William did and no coaxing would bring her back from her self-imposed invalidity. Dr Beecham had no experience of such behaviour and had to depend on his sensibilities and sensitivity to know how to handle such a patient.

So Ernestine Turner began her widowhood lying in a bed which had never been a conjugal couch. William Turner was laid out on a bed which had been their marital bed for a few short years only and then had become his place of solitary solace for the rest of the time they were together.

Walford went downstairs to the kitchen with a heavy heart. He had been called into the study by Marshal and told to find some strong lads to carry his father's body upstairs and it was the worst thing he had ever had to do in his life. The boy was totally in control of the sad situation, behaving like an army officer ordering his troops around. He was doing everything automatically, as if he had practised for years to get his reactions right and yet Walford knew this was the first real sadness he had ever experienced. It was only when he had said,

"Can I offer my condolences now, Mr Marshal, before anyone else comes along. I have worked for your father and his father all my days and my sadness is so deep that I am unable to voice it." Then he took out his handkerchief and blew noisily into it and turned away to the window to hide his face. Walford wished in that moment that he had kept quiet – but how could he, knowing the dead master so well?

In the kitchen, he had grabbed his sister by her apron and dragged her with him into her sitting room.

"He's gone, Aileen, just like that. The poor lad was with him at the time and so was Little Miss and that other one. Our girl stood there so quiet. I think she was trying to be invisible, trying to forget what had just happened but Marshal sent his sister off upstairs, she was so noisy. But he's gone, sure enough. Our master's dead, Aileen. Now what's going to happen?" He bent his head and surreptitiously wiped a couple of tears away but Cook saw his unhappiness and, despite feeling dreadful herself, she took him in her arms and hugged him close to her bosom.

Upstairs, Alexandra had watched as the gardener's boys lifted the prostrate body of the man she had loved as a father. Her dear papa was no more. All that remained was this disordered clutter of clothing, hanging around a floppy heap of bone and muscle. Certainly, the way the boys heaved him up the stairs was something he would have hated to see himself. One had his shoulders and the other his legs, so the middle part sagged down towards the stair treads and she imagined them dropping him at any minute. If she had not felt so drained of emotion, she would have shouted as loudly as Marianne but what did it matter, he was dead and could feel nothing. A huge part of her life had gone and Marshal was treating the whole thing like a business transaction. How could he? Yet, would she have wanted to see her cousin ranting and raving like his sister. The clear answer was no. Marshal had to be the man of the house, even at such an early stage.

They had known this would happen but girls were not as good as men at handling such crises. She wanted to run to her room and cry, yet her mind and body would not allow it. Instead, she was glued to the spot where she had been for some time – since papa had folded onto the floor – and she felt more like a statue than a human being.

After his dear father had been unceremoniously removed, Marshal turned to her.

"It's alright, cos, you can come upstairs now. It's time to give vent to your feelings. Don't hold them in. We both need to grieve for the best man in the universe."

How right he was.

000

The funeral cortege left Grangely Hall quietly. All the

sound that was heard were the horses on the gravelled drive and the noise of metal-rimmed wheels rolling away to the village church. Alexandra had hoped that her aunt would leave her bed for such an important and solemn occasion but she did not and she wished Marianne had decided not to attend either. The three of them sat in a closed carriage behind the hearse, dressed from head to foot in black, the women wearing heavy veils over their faces. The only item of colour was Marianne's white handkerchief, which was held constantly to her face, under the veil and she moaned and sniffed, groaned and mopped for the whole two and a half miles to the church.

It was a sign of William Turner's popularity that the whole road from Grangely gates to the church was lined along one side with villagers. On the other side, the trees seemed to dip their branches and sweep the ground in respect of their master and the horses pulling the carriages walked slowly, sedately along, nodding their black plumes in time to the rhythm of their slow gait. As they passed each group of people, the men removed their caps and the women looked down and curtseyed. It was enough to turn the hardest heart to jelly and Alexandra noticed Marshal's black gloved hands gripping each other so hard she expected to see flesh fly out through the leather at any moment. Marianne continued to cry and took not the slightest bit of notice of the respectful citizens outside. Even the children had turned out to say goodbye to the kindly squire of Grangely Hall and they stood, some of them without shoes, in perfect silence until the cortege passed.

The church service was longer than usual, because there was so much to say about a man who had been born and lived in the same house for so many years. The vicar was well-known to all three, as he had visited the hall regularly on various church errands, usually involving the collection of money for some good cause and he was truly upset as he took their hands at the end of the burial.

"How can I comfort you for the loss of your father?" he said quietly, as they filed out of the churchyard. "All I can say is that if anyone was assured of a place in Heaven it would be William. Try to remember his good times on earth, in the certainty that he has gone to his Maker."

Marianne blubbed her thanks, Marshal shook hands and murmured something unintelligible and Alexandra smiled neutrally, with dead eyes and pale face. There were no words that could express her thoughts on this, the most miserable day of her life.

After the funeral, Marianne could not wait to get back to London and this time Ralph went with her. Before he left, he and Alexandra met in the wood to say goodbye. The spring leaves had opened but appeared pale and colourless. Birds were flitting from branch to branch and occasionally a squirrel's grey body would snake along from one tree to another, making a silent leap into the air at the end of the leafy perch. She had covered her clothes with a waterproof coat and wore a light hat but Alexandra still shivered, regardless. It felt as if the sun had left forever because the sky had been one large sheet of grey cloud for weeks; it was also in mourning for the loss of one of the finest men on the planet. Because she had arrived at their assignation early, she stood hugging her arms about her and jumping up and down, to try to warm the soles of her feet, which were as ice in her short leather boots. The patch of earth beneath her had been trampled into a muddy morass and the beauty of the new grass was now ruined, leaving brown-coated, yellow grass where there had been fresh bayonets of green.

"Hello, my love. You arrived before me today. How can I ever apologise enough for your discomfort." He looked so handsome, his muted colours matching the woodland tones of brown and green. His coat hung loose and she saw a brown tweed suit of clothing underneath. He wore a tie with a tight knot at his throat. This must be some new fashion purchased for his trip to London. No doubt he would become even more stylish once he and Marianne were married; he would never allow himself to be overshadowed by a mere woman.

"Yes, I am cold at present due to the rain but I expect I shall dry off soon," she said, feeling the old desire spring to her assistance now he had arrived.

"Come to my arms and let me hug you like a bear until the cold leaves your beloved bones," he said, opening his coat to let her in.

Their embrace was long and warm, their kisses affectionate

rather than passionate, as she lifted her face to his and felt drops of water run down between their faces and Alexandra began to wonder whether he had accepted Marianne's ultimatum with his heart and not just in words.

"I will miss you, my love," she said, offering the first terms of endearment instead of waiting for him to persuade her into intimate conversation.

"And I will miss you but not for too long. I will return before the spring grass turns to summer pasture."

So, it would be a long time before she saw him again. Summer was months away and he intended to taste the delights of London society for that length of time. How could she survive without their regular meetings?

"I had no idea you would be away so long, Ralph."

"Unfortunately, yes, my dear. Father has business for me in London this time and I must not throw up the chance to earn an honest crust."

"But I thought you worked for the firm of Carruthers."

"I do, my precious but if other opportunities arise, I must clasp them to my chest. You, of all people, must understand that the world runs on money and not on fine promises – of which I have had far too many from my own company. The time will pass quickly until we are together again."

"We must have a serious talk when you come back. I cannot stand sharing you for much longer." She had not intended to say this but now it was out in the open. A flock of crows made a loud noise, as if to corroborate her statement and Ralph waited until they had finished flapping their wings about, cawing in concert, before saying,

"Yes, dear heart, we will talk then but come, give me another sweet kiss to speed me on my way and I will have to disappear as quickly as I arrived. I leave tomorrow at first light."

They clasped and clutched each other, their kisses seeming to heat the very raindrops as well and their breath was a fog in front of their faces, hiding the start of tears in Alexandra's eyes. When they eventually parted, their wet fingertips separating finally, the light had started to leave the sky and it was now even more murky than it had been earlier.

Alexandra trudged her way home, with a stone where her heart had been, and the first person she saw as she approached the Hall was Marshal.

"Why do you find it necessary to go walking in the wettest of weathers, young cos? I would have expected you to be in a chair by the fire, a book in your hand?"

"I must feel the air in my lungs, Marshal and watch nature coping with seasonal problems. I wonder how many birds died from lack of food and warmth during the cold spells in winter."

"Please, do not depress yourself over something we cannot alter. I believe Darwin called it the survival of the fittest, so that the birds and animals which remain to breed in the spring will be physically strong ones – and so their line continues."

"I have never really considered that point of view but, no doubt that is why human beings remained superior to other animals; they had the mental capacity to build shelters for themselves and to wrap themselves in the fur of those which died."

"You understand the principles of laws of nature and yet I have never seen you pick up a book on the subject."

"Just one more advantage of being a woman; we deal in matters of commonsense."

Once again they were laughing and Alexandra had put aside her sadness regarding Ralph, to concentrate on an academic riddle with her serious cousin. She supposed she would have to get into the habit of being the poor cousin of the family, now that the man she had always called papa had gone. She would have to put up with taunts and the outright dislike of the woman she could never call mama – her bereft aunt. The story reminded her of the wicked aunt and the ugly sisters in the tale of Cinderella but where was her Prince Charming? He had left and gone off to London, without discovering her glass slipper.

000

It was a strange house without William, without Marianne and with an aunt who closeted herself upstairs constantly. Alexandra set herself the task of winning over the woman who had completely disowned her, because she felt she owed it to papa.

Maids drifted in and out of the stuffy bedroom, offering food and drink at appropriate times of day but nobody troubled to stay with the mistress for any longer than was strictly necessary; it was a sad state of affairs.

So Alexandra made it her resolution to try to interest her aunt in the workings of the house, at least. The garden was her target, for she knew what a great part nature played in the psychological health of a person. She tapped on the door of Ernestine's room, then entered. Her aunt lay in a pristine bed, on her side, eyes wide open and blinking and Alexandra wondered what thoughts went through her head.

"Hello Aunt." she said, clearly and firmly. This was no time for hovering or dithering.

"Go away, I'm ill," she said.

"I shan't go away and your illness is of your own making," Alexandra chose to take a strong line.

"How do you know?" So, there was a conversation starting.

"You took to your bed when my uncle died and you have not appeared downstairs since that day. How do you think he would feel about that?"

"Go away, you wicked girl. I am not to be disturbed. How could you talk about my husband like that."

"Because I feel that is what's wrong. You have not spoken about him since he died. You must allow your grief to come out, Aunt, otherwise it will poison your mind."

"I will not talk about my William to you. Where is Marianne, my daughter?"

"You must know, she has gone back to London."

"Left me, like her father. Now I am all alone in the world."

"No, Aunt, you have Marshal and you have me."

Ernestine, buried her head in the sheets and Alexandra could hear her sniffing. At least she had caused some reaction and would leave matters today. She left the room quietly, promising to return the next day.

In the meantime, meals were served, fires were lit in the morning and dampened down at night and the rest of the house ran like clockwork.

When she did return, Alexandra carried a small book of poetry. It was an anthology she had been given as a child and it had seen her through many childhood illnesses, such as measles and chickenpox, so she felt it was the right one for this occasion. Her aunt lay on her other side, which meant she was turned towards the door and she watched as her niece entered once again.

"Good morning Aunt Ernestine." The words sounded strange but that is who she was.

"Oh, it's you."

"Yes, I have decided to be your visitor on a daily basis. I'm sure the company of maids is not what you desire or indeed require."

"I need no-one. Go away."

The answer was the same, "No, I shall not go away. Marshal sends his regards and he totally approves of my visiting you."

"Huh, I don't see him with you."

"You have only to ask and he will come up to see you."

"I don't wish to see him. He only reminds me."

"Of your husband, my uncle. Yes, he is very much like him, particularly in manner."

"He's nothing like him. I should know."

She chose to ignore this childish retort and continued, "Today, I thought I would read to you, Aunt, and I've brought a book of poetry you and uncle gave to me some time ago." She refused to ask her aunt if she wanted to hear the poems but just ploughed on regardless. This was no time for asking, it was time for telling. She began.

Late lies the wintry sun a-bed,
A frosty, fiery sleepy-head;
Blinks but an hour or two; and then,
A blood-red orange, sets again.

Before the stars have left the skies,
At morning in the dark I rise;
And shivering in my nakedness,
By the cold candle, bathe and dress.

Black are my steps on silver sod;
Thick blows my frosty breath abroad;

And tree and house, and hill and lake,
Are frosted like a wedding-cake."

Her aunt retorted, "Wintertime by Robert Louis Stevenson but you missed out two verses, you silly girl. Anyway, he's too childish for me. I do like the mention of wedding cake, though. It will soon be time for Marianne to be married as William wished."

Good, this was working. If Aunt was thinking about such things, she was not lost in her own thoughts. "Then I'll read something more mature."

"Not today, young lady. I wish to sleep. Perhaps tomorrow, when you come."

This was a definite breakthrough. "Would you like me to ask Marshal to come to see you, Aunt?"

"No."

That was all she said and went down into the depths of her bed again. Alexandra did not push her case. This was going well and the last thing she wanted was for her aunt to deny her entrance to her room the following day. She must be handled with kid gloves.

CHAPTER 17

As the century moved on to its final quarter, Alexandra started to take an interest in Grangely Hall. In Yorkshire, there was little sign of a resurgence in the wealth of towns along the Tees in areas such as the Ironmasters' District and the cognoscenti knew that the only industry to save them all from abject poverty was steel. Some forward-thinking pit owners had travelled as far afield as America, to study the workings of blast furnaces there but none had yet returned to spread the gospel.

There were so many families crammed into a relatively short stretch of land along the riverside, many from Ireland and Wales and some from the Fenlands to the south. The only way to accommodate them had been in back-to-back houses, with small backyards and outside privies. The removal of night-soil from so many back-lanes was a mammoth task and was often done by even more impoverished men with a distinct, yet necessary, lack of intelligence required for such work; therefore it was often not done at all.

It was little wonder that cholera crept into many supposedly clean, humble, crowded homes, spread on the fingertips of unwashed hands brought straight from the pits, where hygiene and toilet facilities were totally absent, men squatting where they could find dark places, then returning to their work.

Alexandra knew nothing of such poverty and lack of cleanliness. Marshal did but chose not to mention such dreadful unhygienic habits at home. Maids carried active bacteria in their pockets, as they left poor domiciles where hand washing was a luxury and entered the luxurious rooms of Grangely Hall and other upper middle-class homes. William Turner's decision to employ local girls, rather than take on a full staff of live-in employees had eventually worked against his family.

After weeks of cosseting and persuasion, Aunt Ernestine consented to take meals downstairs. Alexandra had been looking forward to reinstating this habit for she longed to be able to say, 'Her room can now be fully cleaned', as she would not allow a maid into her domicile, regardless of the lack of hygiene. Two housemaids were to undertake the mammoth task and they came to the person they thought of as mistress of the house for instructions,

"Remove everything from the room and wash all woodwork. I do not want to come upstairs to check on you every five minutes; you are trusted to do the job thoroughly and, if done to my satisfaction, it will earn you a bonus. Do you both understand?" She was enjoying her new position of authority but tried to do it with kindness and not with an expectation of obedience, as had her aunt.

The elder girl spoke for them both. "It will be done prop'ly Miss Alexandra, don't you worry about that. You'll be able to run yer finger round every bit of wood and not a fingerful of dust will be there. You see, according to me mam, God rest her soul, cleanliness is next to Godliness – and we all know diseases can be blown in by the wind, so I won't open any of them winders."

"Don't even consider that, Mary. Lack of air in rooms is a result of old wives' tales. Just open the casements wide and let the fresh air do its job."

"Ooh! Are you sure Miss. I would 'ate to think that chol'ra or typhoid got in to the Missus."

"I don't think that's possible. Neither of those diseases are airborne – they spread by bact... by bugs in the water. Now, just forget all about them and off you go to get on with your work."

"Yes, Miss, o'course Miss" and they trooped off to collect their pails and mops.

Marshal was delighted when she told him what she had arranged. The main reason for his not visiting his mother more often was the dreadful smell in that room. A window was never opened, for the reason the maids described and also because the wind blew soot and ashes around the room, not to mention the fact that many people, including mama, thought they could die of cold air coming into a room.

When the bedroom was completely cleaned out, it became pleasant once more. Now it had ceased to be the room of an invalid, Alexandra instigated regular 'airings', when the windows in all bedrooms would be left open for a set time each morning. This took away the smell of food from downstairs and that of bodies and chamberpots upstairs.

Alexandra was turning her domestic skills into a hobby as, without anything more intellectual on which to dwell, she saw the running of a great house as her main pastime. After one of his long forays into Middlesbrough, Marshal sought her out and found her surrounded by mountains of sheets and pillowslips, in the linen cupboard.

"Oh, hello Marshal," she grinned, from the bottom of a pile on the floor. "What brings you into my domestic domain?" She often saw him but he was nearly always heading out the door on one errand or another and she often wondered whether he had a girl tucked away somewhere.

"Once you have reared out of that heap of linen, I would like to talk with you. I'll be in my study."

He was the master of the house now and he spoke just like papa. How proud his father would have been. She carefully folded the large sheets and kept aside those to be mended; some only required a darn but several needed to be turned, outsides-in, so they could continue their useful life. It must have been years since Ernestine did this, such a regular, but no doubt to her, menial, inspection. Her job was soon accomplished and she left the dark cupboard with a pile of sheets to work on in her spare time. The only trouble with such a job was the size of the piece of material but there was space in the morning room to spread it over the central table.

Making her way down to the library, as she always called it, which had become Marshal's study, she looked around and admired the many paintings, some of them portraits. There was china on shelves and now vases of flowers placed strategically around open expanses of hallway. Some people enjoyed the care of small items, like silver or porcelain but she saw the whole house as a work of art, under her aegis. Papa would have said, 'Think big, my dear; it's good to think big'. How she missed his sensible comments.

Marshal sat at his father's desk in the window and motioned for her to take a seat. "I expect you're wondering why I wish to talk to you formally, my cos."

"Yes, I do."

"There is something I want to get off my mind and it can't wait."

It had to be something to do with a girl. He must be planning to marry and wants me to know first. How exciting.

"This will affect you, as much as it affects me, so I want you to be the first to know."

How it could affect her, she was at a loss to know – unless he wanted her to move out, to make room for his new wife. Yes, that must be it.

"Well, don't worry about me, Marshal. I am quite capable of taking care of myself."

"I am quite certain you can but wait until you hear what I have to say."

"Please go ahead, Marshal." He was hesitating a great deal. Why did he not tell me and get it over?

"You know Father was not one for investment. In fact, his friends were constantly trying to include him in their schemes but to no avail. He always said he could live quite comfortably from his inherited money – that is from grandpapa and grandmama. Well, admittedly it served him throughout his lifetime and he was able to leave an honest sum of money for me and one for Marianne. Mama has also been taken care of. I am sorry about you, Alexandra. You deserved more than anyone, but... there you are... there was no more to spare. Your allowance will continue, as it did in Father's time – I will see to that.

"Anyway, what I am trying to explain – not very well, I'm afraid – is that there is no more in the coffers to keep Grangely Hall going. We will not have enough to do repairs to the building, or in fact to pay the staff much longer. The old house will have to go."

"Oh no!" This was a nightmare. "Oh no! Not Grangely. It's not possible."

"I'm afraid it is, dear girl. The good old place will have to be sold. I told you it was something that would affect you as much as me."

She felt sick. This was almost as bad as losing papa. All her memories of him were integral with the stones of the house. Her heart was here.

"Don't you have anything to say? I expected more reaction than this from my little sister, my little cos."

"I'm sorry, Marshal, I truly am but I must ask you to excuse me. I must leave. I am too upset to talk further. Perhaps later…" and she ran from the room, not stopping to close the door, just flying upstairs past all the items she had just admired, to her bedroom.

000

Marshal knew he had done his duty. Alexandra was the only woman who worked in this house – worked for this house. Her hurt was obvious and he hoped she would soon get over her distress and disappointment. He was hurting inside as well. To think, his father had been handed this house and estate on a silver plate and had done nothing to ensure that he, his heir, could take over and continue to keep it alive. It was a sadness he would bear all his days. Why was it so?

Of course there must be things he could do, even now at this late stage, to earn enough to keep it all intact; why must he tear his childhood home apart and sell the pieces to the highest bidder? However, earning was not something that came naturally to him, the son of the squire of Grangely, and where to start? He had lost contact with papa's friends in the iron industry and anyway that form of business was dying now. There was nothing to be done.

He delayed telling his mother for as long as he could. Then, just when he felt he had the courage, a letter arrived from Marianne to say she was coming home for a visit. That would be the ideal time to pass on the bad news to both of them and if mama became difficult again and took to her bed there would be two women in the house to care for her. So, one small problem had been solved by being circumspect – or perhaps he was just being cowardly.

His mind brought back the image of Alexandra and he sat, wondering how he could find a girl like her to take care of him and guide him through life. He wanted to marry but could never meet a suitable partner. Those introduced to him by his Quaker friends, usually sisters and cousins, were far too particular about their behaviour and wanted to put on a show of goodness and kindness far beyond that desired by a red-blooded male. They were just a bit too good. What he needed was a wife who could make him laugh at life's difficulties and then help him through them with a smile.

He walked slowly along the corridor, breathing in the scent of newly arranged flowers; they were roses, for no others remained in the garden and he was amazed that such a delicate bloom could withstand the cold of winter, as many of theirs did. Passing the foot of the stairs on his way to the morning room, he felt the smooth wood of the banister under his fingers and wondered how many of his ancestors had trodden this way before him. His eyes lifted to the beautiful, corniced ceiling high above him and he almost sobbed at the thought that his time for doing such mundane things was limited. Now, to tell mama, about the letter from his sister – for Marianne had ceased writing to her mother since she had become aware of her mental instability. He pushed open the door to the room, rehearsing his words as he had become used to doing recently.

"Good morning, Mother. I hope I find you well."

"I am well, Marshal. To what do I owe the pleasure at this time of day. I thought you usually inspected the estate in the mornings."

"I have been quick today, Mother and have some good news to impart – so that is why you find me interrupting your quiet time before luncheon."

"No worries, my boy. What is your news?"

"I have received a letter from Marianne and she is coming to stay for a short while, perhaps next week."

"Oh, why didn't you say so at once? My Marianne, my daughter, is coming home to see her mama. I must make sure all is ready for her stay. Have the housekeeper sent to me immediately and I will organise her room."

"Mother, we have not had a housekeeper for twenty years. Housemaids do all the work – you remember, the girls from the village – and Walford keeps them in order, along with Alexandra these days, I have to add."

"Alexandra? What has she got to do with my household? Send Walford to me then – tell him I have some very important orders for him."

"Would it not be easier for me to pass on the good news to Alexandra and she will ensure that Marianne's rooms are arranged to her satisfaction?"

"You will keep mentioning the name of that girl – that doorstep child – your penniless cousin. Tell me, why should she have anything to do with the arrangement of this house, when I am fit and well once more?"

She had completely chosen to ignore the fact that the person who made her fit and well was the girl she was abusing so readily. He should have told Alexandra about her cousin's visit and left his mother until last. The less she knew, the less trouble she could cause.

"I will see if I can find Walford. If not, I will ask Alexandra to come to you."

"I hope you find him quickly."

Marshal left the room, feeling frustrated at his mother's manner. As master of the house, he wanted to make his own decisions but he must listen politely to the views of his only parent and then decide. If he chose not to find Walford and asked Alexandra to wait on his mama, it would put her in the position of underling and yet to go over her head and send the butler in would be even more denigrating to his kind, helpful cousin. He knew where to find her – in the kitchen. Even though she no longer played around with a wooden spoon in the bowels of the house, she was happy talking about food and ingredients with Cook and this time of day was when she tended to do so. As he passed through the staff doorway, he tossed his present problem around and almost crashed into Walford on his way through. He mentioned nothing to the old man, so his decision had been made for him.

Cook sat in her rocking chair by the range and Alexandra was beside her on a high-backed pine kitchen chair, a book on the huge, well-scrubbed table beside her. He could hear their low tones and picked up a few words, such as Mrs Beeton, steak pie and remainders. So, she was still showing interest in the presentation of food. She would be a good wife for some man.

"Hello Cook number one and Cook number two," he said, smiling affectionately at two women he had known all his life.

"Oh, sir, you surprised me there! Whatever are you doing,

down 'ere in the kitchen?"

"I might ask the same of my cousin."

Alexandra marked the page in her Book of Household Management and smiled up at him sweetly. So, she had forgiven him for being the bearer of bad news. Perhaps the next news would improve matters – or perhaps it wouldn't.

"Alexandra, I came down to inform you that your sister… cousin… Marianne, is coming home next week for a visit…" Before he could finish, she swung round on her chair and looked up at him expectantly, saying,

"Is Ralph coming as well? Oh, that is good news. I must prepare Marianne's rooms for her this very minute." She looked too happy to be seeing the girl who had treated her like a minion for years – or was it the idea of young Lawrence that put her into such a tizzy? Surely not.

CHAPTER 18

When Marianne arrived, it seemed that all she wanted to do was show off her London gowns, even if they were all in mourning; if she changed during the day she changed completely, down to her frilled petticoats and bloomers and wanted Alexandra to examine every tiny piece of stitching. Inspections were done by the girl, more to see the happy smiles on her cousin's face than because of any true interest, but it did keep any churlishness at bay.

The third evening of the visit, Marshal thought it was time to tell his sad story. Both Ernestine and Marianne were in reasonably good spirits, discussing other girls' wedding gowns and the length of time required for ordering them to be made. Alexandra had separated herself from the rest, by taking out a novel and, with great difficulty, trying to read by an oil lamp. She could hardly bear the dreadful smell, sitting so close to it? It was too late for Marshal to consider installing gas lighting, which would have looked good as well as being more civilized, although none of the women knew this, yet. True, he had been told that it also was dirty and smelly and corroded picture wire, silver and some furniture but it would take some work away from the maids, who had to clean all the kerosene and oil lamps daily.

"Mother," Marshal said into the busy female conversation, knowing his mind had gone off at a tangent again, but desperate to tell them all the reason which had been upsetting him for days.

"Marshal, can't you see we're busy."

"I apologise for interrupting but I have something important to tell you and Marianne."

At this point, Alexandra put down her book and looked over at him. She knew what was coming.

In a fevered rush, he blurted out his dreadful tale of how the house must be sold and the reasons for it. She could see Marianne staring at him in wide-eyed disbelief, just waiting until he finished so she could interject with something she thought much more reasonable than he had been foolish enough to disclose – and she did.

"Don't be ridiculous, Marshal. Papa would never have allowed that to happen. I expect your solicitor has given you all the wrong information. You know what these legal people are like."

"No. I'm afraid there's been no mistake. The house and estate must go. I'm sorry, Mama," he said, turning for the first time to his mother on the sofa beside his sister. Her head was down and he could see her hands trembling. Her knees started to knock together and he recognised the signs of anxiety that had appeared on other occasions.

"Mama, I'm sorry I said that."

"Don't trouble yourself, Marshal," Alexandra said. "I see the signs. Your mother is unwell. Ring for the maids and we'll get her upstairs."

Oh no. This is what he had dreaded, yet expected. This is why he waited until Marianne was home - but she did nothing. Once again, the problem was left to their cousin to disentangle.

Together, Alexandra and two maids managed to manhandle his mother up to her bedroom and Marshal knew the woman would be shivering and shaking before they managed to get her undressed and into bed. Part of him felt guilty for bringing her illness back and the other part was ashamed of such a mother. How had he managed to remain so sane with a parent like her; no doubt because of the strong influence of his father. Anyway, the deed was done and he must continue the process of selling up, moving his mother out and, yes, moving out Alexandra also.

000

The following day, Ernestine remained in bed. Marianne did nothing but scoff at the feebleness of her own mother and more-or-less ordered Alexandra to get her out of her room and back downstairs.

"You did it once, I'm led to believe. Why can't you do it again? There's obviously nothing wrong with the old dear, in fact I truly think she puts on a big act to make everyone feel sorry for her. I'm so glad I'm going back to London within the next few days. At least I will be free of such childish tantrums.

You sort it out Alexandra. You're so good at such things, my dear."

There was no answer to such selfishness. And why did she call her 'my dear'. No doubt because that was the way the London set named their staff.

Marianne went off to London once more, without bothering to see her mother before she went and Alexandra was left as nursemaid, knowing she must bring her aunt to some understanding of the true way of things. Marshal had found her a dower house on the estate and intended to furnish it with items from the big house, to make the move easier for his poor mother.

ooo

The week passed and still Ernestine refused to be moved. She was suffering from an embarrassing loss of personal control and her bed linen had to be changed daily. The patient maids dealt with this new trial stoically and Alexandra was amazed that neither had refused to attend their mistress at such a time.

"Don't you worry, Miss, we'll cope. I've had worse than this from me old father and I'm sure Ethel's the same. We'll get her through this for your sake, Miss."

The maids thought this Yorkshire lass was a tough one, no doubt about that. Diarrhea and vomiting must have been caused by her aunt getting far too upset and when it passed she would ensure that those girls had some time off, with pay if she could manage to persuade her cousin, Marshal.

But it didn't pass. There was more and this time it was the absolute opposite of the week before. Alexandra had reports from the girls that her aunt had not passed any water for a day and a half and she looked a bit of a funny colour against the sheets. She went upstairs to see for herself and certainly what could be seen of her aunt was a strange, wrinkled purple colour.

She ran down to Marshal in his study and said,

"We must call Dr Beecham. Your mother is ill, really ill. I thought at first it was all the same as previous times, but this is different, Marshal. She needs the doctor."

"Oh, come along, my dear. You know what she's like by now. I'm sure it's just the same as before and she'll be right as rain in a day or two. We can't bother the busy doctor for a pretender."

"No, Marshal, it's different. I know what I'm saying. Please send a boy for Dr Beecham."

"No, I do not believe there's anything wrong with my mother. Please stop worrying."

"But this time there is a problem with her... water retention... and... the other department." It was so embarrassing to speak like this to a man, even if he was a blood relative.

Marshal understood and, instead of turning a bright shade of pink, as he would have done in his youth, he remained businesslike and merely said, "Alright, Alexandra, for your sake I will – but only for your sake."

A messenger was sent for the doctor and he arrived within the hour. When he appeared at the bedroom door, Ernestine peered around her bedsheets. He walked straight in.

"Now, my dear Mrs Turner, what's this I hear? I was told to come here post haste, because you were a strange shade of purple and all creased up. What do I find but a lady of a normal colour, peering at me from her pillow. Let me take your temperature and we'll soon find out that all is well."

He put a thermometer in her mouth, discreetly placed his stethoscope under the covers, then placed his fingers on Ernestine's wrist and stared at his pocket watch. His expression was not one of satisfaction and his brow creased as he turned to Alexandra and the maids.

"Give me the full story, ladies. I must know everything, be it ever so nasty."

One at a time, the maids related the sickness, the swollen abdomen, the cramping pains everywhere and Mary pointed out that she had been extremely thirsty for some hours, and drinking only led to more stomach pains. Then the other girl, Ethel, interrupted with her favourite symptoms, which had been the purple, wizened face and the lack of control that had sent Alexandra off to tell Marshal. When they had finished and Dr Beecham had questioned further, he spoke,

"Well, Mr Marshal, Miss Alexandra, I'm sorry to have to tell you this, but your mother is suffering from cholera and she must be isolated immediately. I will try to restore her body's fluids and you must also see that she drinks a vast amount of water. It must be boiled first because one of the main causes of this disease is a poor water supply, which is usually the way people catch it. However, in your case, I think it unlikely or the rest of you would have gone down with it and the staff as well."

"So how do you think she caught it, Doctor?" Marshal asked, nervously.

"I have known patients catch it from contaminated food as well as a poor water supply, Marshal, so I think you should have a talk with your Cook."

"It could not possibly have come from the kitchen," Alexandra said, loudly and angrily. "I have never seen anyone as clean as our cook in her dealings with food. She even makes me wash my hands, when they've just been washed."

"Yes, my dear, but cook can't keep her eye on all her kitchen staff and I'm sure some of them escape her eagle eye on occasion. The trouble is, there's a lot of cholera in the poorer houses at present, due to sewage problems around the Tees. We've been told in the medical profession of reflux by the incoming tides and there's not much that can be done about it at present."

"I know all about it, Dr Beecham," groaned Marshal. "I've read enough books to line the sewers of Middlesbrough single-handed."

"Then you'll know what I'm up against, my boy. Just make sure everything is spotlessly clean at Grangely Hall and you shouldn't come to any harm. I don't see much point in moving your mama at this stage because she's passed through the worst stages. She's in remission at present and all we've got to do is make sure she doesn't get pneumonia on top of everything else. I'll call daily until things improve – which I sincerely hope they do. You did the right thing in calling me out today. Now take care of yourselves, you two, and I suggest a bit of bathing for you both, and these girls."

After the doctor left, Marshal gave orders that every person at the Hall should bathe in hot water, if it meant heating it up the whole day long and that the only drink, apart from precious cups of tea, was to be boiled water and beer. This made some of the male staff extremely happy because they took this to mean they could sup ale throughout the working day.

Cook and Walford were not so happy when Alexandra told them what had taken place.

"Eeh, to think it could have been passed to the mistress in my good food. I've always been the cleanest cook I know, since I was a little lass. Don't you remember, George, how I made you run to the tap and wash your hands when you fell over as a little 'un?"

"Aye, I do that, Aileen. You were as clean as a new pin your whole life."

They had reverted to using first names in their panic and Alexandra felt she must put their minds at ease.

"Now Cook and Walford, I want you to know that not a hint of suspicion lies with you. Dr Beecham himself said that this terrible disease can be spread by anyone in contact with food or drink, so it could be a housemaid, a kitchen maid or anybody who has been less than scrupulous about washing their hands before they touch our meals."

"I'll teach 'em what for, you see if I don't..." cook started but both Alexandra and Walford jumped in and said together, "Now then, Cook." They all looked at each other and smiled before going their own separate ways.

Because of the dreadful, dramatic situation, no more mention was made of Marshal's bad news. It took second place to the illness of Ernestine, but there was another worry in the minds of both cousins – Marianne. Had she gone off to London laden with bags full of cholera bacteria? There was only one way to find out quickly and secretly and that was for someone to travel down south. Alexandra wanted to see Ralph again but, if she went, she would have to be accompanied by a chaperone of some sort and no-one could be spared at such a time. It was quite clear that no-one could go until the end of the incubation period anyway, which Dr Beecham said was five days at the most, and a week later Marshal decided to take the train to the big city.

Alexandra was left alone in charge of house, aunt and the whole staff.

"I intend to return as soon as possible, in fact as soon as I have ascertained my sister's health and explained to her what has occurred. I entrust everything to your capable ministrations, dear cos. and will see you within a few days."

They embraced goodbye and gave each other filial pecks on cheeks and he left in the trap which took him to Stockton Railway Station.

CHAPTER 19

On the train, Marshal perused his books on sewerage and by the time he reached Kings Cross station, he was convinced that the piping to Grangely Hall could not be improved for health reasons. Underground lines and cess-pits out in the country were completely separate from those in the iron districts. A Parliamentary Inquiry had gone ahead this very year and it had been suggested that local corporations should buy the now private water utility, to ensure there was always finance for constructing reservoirs and filtration plants. As there was constant contact between the chief Medical Officer for Health and the Local Government Board in London, it was felt that all was being done that could be done. Water throughout the area was said to have been contaminated by sewage washing up on the banks of the Tees, due to night-soil being dumped, thus the disease must have been brought into Grangely by a member of staff.

His arrival at Marianne's hosts' house was full of pleasurable greetings and he was forced into staying with them himself, after he had explained that his trip would be a short one. He was therefore able to talk with his sister the following morning, after suffering the most dreadful fears all through dinner that night, when he saw her unusual recalcitrance in company. He had to appear charming and cheerful to her friend, Hannah and inform Lord and Lady Brownlie of the potentially lucrative future of the steel industry in Yorkshire until bedtime. Never had his powers of diplomacy and tact been tested more fully.

When he finally had his sister to himself, in their spacious London morning room, which was full of female knick-knacks and paraphernalia which suggested that this is where Lady Brownlie usually did her household accounts and interviewed her staff, he was almost shaking with worry.

"Marianne, I have come all this way, on an errand of such importance that I could hardly wait until now to speak with you."

She sat, her skirts all around her, hands clenched in her lap, sitting bolt upright as if her bodice were far too tight, no doubt boned ridiculously tightly. He was glad Alexandra did not feel she needed to wear such fripperies – but he must keep to his subject.

"Marianne, when you left for London, our dear Mama was stricken down with an illness…"

"I know what Mama was stricken down with and it was an illness of her own making. She is a past-master of dramatic behaviour or perhaps I should say past-mistress of an imagined disease."

"No, sister, this time it was real. We called out Dr Beecham and he said she had contracted cholera."

"Don't be ridiculous, Marshal, cholera is what the filthy poor get in their hovels. Why do you think I had no interest in the iron towns of Yorkshire – they are all steeped in foul stenches and evil disease."

Marshal decided that now was the time to behave like the elder brother and cleared his throat loudly before saying, "Marianne, nothing I have said is from the realms of fantasy and can be borne out by our family doctor. Our mother has contracted cholera and the whole reason for my visit to you is to ascertain whether you are well. I must ask you if you have had an signs of illness since you came back here>"

"I have to say, I have been vomiting on occasion and feel a little faint," she grunted in a low voice totally unlike her own.

"No! When was this? Have you reported it to anyone else? Have any of the family seemed to be suffering from the same symptoms?"

"Hold hard, dear brother. One question at a time, if you please." When she saw the desperation and worry on his face, she seemed to cheer up somewhat and Marshal found this rather strange, although he knew how she loved to be the centre of attention.

"I must know, dear girl. Are you still feeling sick in the stomach?"

"At this moment, no, but only because I have spent some time hanging my head over an enamel pail in my bedroom. No doubt I will be free of my indisposition tomorrow."

"Marianne, please do not make light of this matter. It is life or death we talk about, not something you can recover from easily. Please allow me to call your physician for you, to find out what stage you have reached in this dreadful illness."

"As you will, Marshal, but please do not call the physician who attends Lady Brownlie. I would die of shame."

"Do you know of any other then?"

"No doubt Ralph has a doctor, who could attend me. He is calling this morning, so you can ask him yourself. Telling him I need a consultation is bad enough but I suppose I can accept informing my husband to be."

Sure enough, an hour later, Ralph Lawrence appeared, unaccompanied, and Marshal was able to arrange for his family doctor to visit Marianne – without informing him of any of his suspicions. It had to be said that Marianne behaved nothing like his diseased mother and, after his long and detailed conversation with the girl, he doubted she had been smitten with cholera. Perhaps she also had inherited the capacity for deluding herself that she was ill, probably to gain sympathy from all around her, as was usual. He very much doubted her tale of vomiting into a bucket, now he saw how cheerful she had become at the entrance of her betrothed but such symptoms must be checked. They could even be attributed to typhus, which would be just as bad as cholera and he alone seemed to be doing the worrying for both of them.

The doctor arrived that afternoon and luckily the rest of the family had gone to call on an old relative. He took Marianne into the library to interview her and left Marshal hanging around in the entrance hall, beside a roaring fire. His forehead sweated partly from the heat and partly from fear as to what the doctor would ascertain but within half an hour he reappeared.

"I see no symptoms of any disease in your sister, young man, but I would suggest that you take her home to her mother as soon as you are able." He said no more about his patient, except to state his fee, put the sum in his top pocket and walk out.

What on earth did he mean by that curt, dismissive tone of voice. Surely, a doctor should have more sympathy than that. Marshal went into the library to talk to his sister but found her in tears in a corner of the room, facing a wall full of bookshelves.

"What has he discovered, Marianne, my love. Is it something dreadful – and yet he said there is no sign of disease. Tell me what he said, dearest."

"Oh Marshal, Marshal. How can I ever hold up my head again?"

"I don't understand. You must tell me all Marianne."

"I can only say this because you are my brother and not another soul must know about it." She turned around, mopping her red eyes with a lace kerchief. "I am enceinte, my brother. I am expecting a child. Now what can I do?"

"You can tell me who's done this to you and I will fight him to the death, that's what you can do!"

"Marshal, you are not a soldier in the old days. This is the year of 1875 and I have just admitted my immorality to you, my brother. What am I going to do?"

"Who is the father of your child, Marianne?"

"I must be honest and confess that it is Ralph, for there has been no-one else."

"Then your problem is solved. You must marry early, as soon as possible and not a soul will be any the wiser. Leave this to me, sister. I will speak with the man in question and you will be married as soon as you come home."

"Oh no. I do not intend to come home. I have no home but London now. Ralph and I intend to set up here, as we had indeed intended to marry. We have decided that is what we will do after our wedding."

"Then come home with me and you shall have a fine wedding – a little earlier than anticipated."

"No! I will marry here, from the home of Lord and Lady Brownlie You can explain to Lord Brownlie that I have no father and ask him to do the honours for me, then I can have the wedding of the year, as I planned to do anyway. Yes, you are right, all my problems are solved. Now, off you go to see Ralph at his club. I have the address right here."

Once more, she was manipulating him and all he needed to do was spend money; money he hadn't got, but she would refuse to believe that. If he dug deep into the coffers, no doubt he could produce enough to marry her in style and then, hopefully, she would be off. Another man would have the great responsibility of taking care of his selfish sister and her child.

ooo

After he had found Ralph at his club in London and managed to drag him away from his many acquaintances, into a dark corner of the room where the only noise was of snoring old gentlemen, he explained the situation.

"Don't be ridiculous, my friend. As if I would let your sister get into that state. As for the actual fact of my being this child's father, I say no. Our relationship has been one of style and elegance, not a sordid dalliance, as you suggest."

"I am sorry, Ralph, but I must believe my own sister and she would hardly tell me about your close relationship unless she really needed to."

"She would hardly tell you about any other man in her life either!"

"You don't mean to say…"

Knowing he would have to marry the girl anyway, Ralph decided to change his tactics; a volte-face was the only way. There was no point in people thinking he was marrying a slut. He must take the 'whiter than white' line. "Sorry, old man, of course there's only me. Why would she want anyone else? And I have to confess we were a little bit careless on one occasion. You know what it's like, old boy. When a girl dresses up and flaunts herself… I mean when there's a beautiful creature and you find yourself all alone with her, what can you do? I confess, this baby will be mine. Now don't do the old pistols at dawn routine on me, will you? I was going to marry the sweet Marianne and we will just have to speed thing up a bit. I presume you have the wherewithal for a London wedding?"

"When I spoke to Marianne, she also said you both wanted to stay down here for the wedding. I suppose it's absolutely necessary?"

"Of course, my friend, I wouldn't think of anywhere else. You don't suppose we're going to trudge all the way back to the land of my fathers, to get married in the filth of Cleveland – in haste at that? We would be the talk of fine society when we got back here. No, it has to be in London, so get your pot from under the bed – your money pot I mean, not your chamber pot!" and he went off into riotous laughter, waking up old Colonels and Brigadiers all round the room. How could he joke at a time like this? The man had no shame.

Marshal left London in a miserable frame of mind. He knew he should have been glad to hear that Marianne was in good health and that she had not passed the cholera symptoms around the drawing rooms of London but his money worries overshadowed relief for his sister. He was not looking forward to explaining himself to Alexandra and he half-hoped she would be out when he arrived, deep in thought, from the station in the trap, after his long journey.

Walford opened the door for him and did his usual small bow, as he marched past and up the stairs, after handing over his coat and hat to the butler. His intention was to go straight to his room upstairs, where he could get his thoughts in order ready for his explanation to his cousin – and that is what he did, for there was not a murmur in the house from any quarter. The stairs were silent and not a soul passed him as he made his way along the first corridor. As he walked somewhat noisily across the carpet, he wondered if this is how it felt to be a bachelor, living in a large house alone, with only the butler to greet him as he came home – no matter how long he had been away. Not a pleasant thought. He must think about getting a wife; but this was not the way to consider it, like buying a new horse or another cow for the herd.

Opening his bedroom door, he was stopped in his tracks by a loud scream from further along the corridor; his mother. It had to be mother, judging from the direction of the noise and he dropped his small bag at his own door and ran along the short distance. He turned the handle and walked into the room, to find Alexandra struggling with mama in her white, lace-trimmed nightdress.

"What is happening?" he said and they both stopped to stare up at him. "Why do you ladies look like all-in wrestlers?"

"Because this person insists that I take yet another spoonful of her odious medicine, that is why. I refuse to be told what to do by a mere back-street girl!"

"Mama, whatever Alexandra is administering is not of her own making. She has instructions from the doctor to ensure you take your medicine, in order that you recover speedily."

"Well, it is not having any effect at all. If anything, I feel worse after it and I have been taking the dreadful stuff for weeks." Her idea of time was nothing to do with reality.

"That is not to say that it's having no effect. You must do as Dr Beecham directs." Marshal looked sympathetically at Alexandra, who had taken the bottle and spoon away from the bed and was straightening bedclothes around Ernestine. "Let me give it to you, Mama," he said.

He picked up the bottle and poured out a spoonful, holding it in front of his mother's mouth. She whisked out her hand from under the covers and flipped the spoonful of sticky liquid into her son's face, disappearing under the sheet like a naughty child. Marshal felt his hand go up as if to strike her but remembered in good time that this was his ill mother he was dealing with and let it fall, covered in a brown-coloured mess.

"Here, Marshal, allow me to wipe you," Alexandra said and came forward with a cloth. "Now you realise why I was employing some force as you walked in. Your mother's symptoms have returned and, as she refuses to take her medicine, I think we will have to call out the doctor yet again. I'm so sorry, Marshal."

"Alexandra, there is really no need for you to be sorry, about anything. You are not an employed nurse and yet you are doing all the things a nurse would do. I am very grateful to you for your patience."

She smiled, as she dabbed away at the back of his hand and he lifted his other and stroked her cheek. How he wished he did not have to relay the full story of Marianne and Ralph. That was something else to cause this girl to worry.

"Just leave the medicine, my dear," he said "I will get one of the maids to clear up this mess." And he beckoned her to come out of the room with him.

They walked along together, until he reached his own door, where he picked up his valise and made to go inside.

"Marshal, I have to tell you that your mother is not

recovering as we hoped she would. She coughs a great deal and appears to have trouble breathing, particularly when lying down. I really believe the doctor should call again. Will I send for him?"

"Tomorrow. Send for him tomorrow. I have some other news to pass on today. Meet me in the drawing room for afternoon tea. I will see you there."

Alexandra just nodded. This was something to do with Marianne as she knew he had been to visit her. She hoped against hope that she had not contracted cholera. Marshal's face was serious enough for him to be carrying such a burden and he had not had the time to mention anything about his trip down south due to his mother's tantrums.

ooo

When they saw each other again, they were both sitting comfortably in the large chintz-covered chairs, sipping tea from delicate china cups. The light outside had gone, although it was just after four o'clock and Mary had been asked to draw the curtains. If it were not for the disappointing news he was about to impart, Marshal would have called it a cosy, fireside scene.

"Alexandra," he said, pronouncing each syllable slowly and carefully.

"Yes Marshal," she replied quietly.

"Our sister is in trouble."

"Oh no, Marshal, she has not contracted cholera!"

"No! no! Don't think that, my dear. I'm sorry if I led you to believe that. It is something altogether different. The trouble she is in is of her own making, I'm afraid. When I asked her to see a physician to ensure that she had no symptoms of cholera, he found something else."

"Oh no, not typhoid. I know there is a great deal of typhoid, also due to the poor quality of the water along the Tees but surely not!"

"No! I can't seem to spit out what I want to say. Oh, help me Alexandra, by remaining silent until I have told you the real reason for my hesitation.

Marianne is expecting a baby. That's what the doctor found down in London and she has admitted to behaving immorally with Ralph, who has also admitted that he is the father of the child, so they are going to get married as soon as possible."

Alexandra said nothing. She just stared at her cousin with her mouth slightly open and said not one word.

"What do you think of that?" he said, hoping at last to be able to discuss this dreadful situation with an understanding person.

She hardly moved, just looking down at her hands.

He continued, thinking that Alexandra was too shocked to reply. "They had planned to hold the wedding at the house of Lord and Lady Brownlie and they intend to keep to their plans, with one big change, they will bring the wedding forward – to accommodate their secret." He smiled but there was no return smile forthcoming. "I will be expected to finance a big wedding in London, instead of a family celebration in Yorkshire, so there will be even less left in the coffers than we thought."

"It all comes down to money, doesn't it?" she said, gloomily.

"I suppose it does but what do you mean by that comment. Surely, it all comes down to love, doesn't it?"

"I didn't see much love between them. It was more a business arrangement, wasn't it?"

"I expect it started off like that but their emotions became too much for them."

"Emotions, you say."

"Yes, I suppose they were unable to wait"

"I suppose not," she said and, placing her cup and saucer on a side table, she left the room, leaving Marshal now in that open-mouthed position, his own cup and saucer still in his hand.

As she made her way up to her bedroom, Alexandra considered the

dreadful situation which had arisen. How could Ralph treat her so badly? It seemed that as soon as he found himself in the company of one woman, he forgot the promises made to the one before. She had offered him love and truly believed that he had reciprocal feelings but it seemed he did not. His loyalty lay with the person he attended at the time and he was unable to keep his masculine instincts in check. She would have to try to forget about him and hand him back to Marianne, who felt no more love for him than she did for the birds in the air. This marriage of convenience would go ahead, a child would be born and a new Lawrence family would be instigated due to a careless evening. She could have loved Ralph with all her heart had she been given the opportunity and now he would descend into the kind of life lived by rakes the world over, as he sought tenderness from other women to compensate for the lack of emotion in his marriage.

CHAPTER 20

Alexandra was very aware of a lack of money within the house and was determined to help Marshal in any way she could. She decided to start with food. Down in the kitchen, cook was also aware of their problems, due to hearing on the ever-present grapevine all conversations which had taken place between the cousins. She sat by the fire and talked to her brother.

"Oh, Walford my dear, whatever are we going to do. It would be easy to make food for a working class family, using cheaper and more plentiful ingredients – but our Grangely Hall family is slightly different, you have to admit."

"Yes, Cook, I admit it but surely you can economize by cutting down on portions, now it's only Little Miss and Mr Marshal. The amount the mistress consumes now could be balanced on a serving spoon."

"But what about the staff? We still have a plentiful number of people rushing around after the missus alone, and Mr Marshal, God bless him, has not even mentioned cutting back on the downstairs folk."

"Staff's easy. Give 'em a good bowl of soup for their midday meal and they're happy. As for dinner, what're leftovers for?"

At this point in the conversation, Alexandra walked in. She was glad she had heard them mention leftovers because that was one of the reasons she had decided to come down to the kitchens. Walford stood up and gave his little bow. Cook, having grown accustomed to her presence in the past, merely dipped her head and said,

"Hello, Alexandra, or should I say Miss Alexandra now? What brings you back to the Palace of Fun, as you used to call it?"

"Show a bit of respect, Cook," muttered Walford under his breath.

"Mmm," mumbled cook and gave him an icy glare.

"I hope you don't think I'm poking my nose in where it's not wanted," Alexandra said in kitchen jargon, "but I found my

Mrs Beeton book beside my bed and wondered if the part about leftovers would be useful, now we're heading for the breadline."

Walford's eyebrows tried to hit the ceiling, as she continued,

"Don't think I don't know what goes on downstairs, you two. I was around the maids long enough to find out quite a lot of your little secrets. Nothing passes the lips of the family, without one of you making mental notes – to be used in the best possible ways I must add."

"Oh, Miss, we would never think of doing anything that would harm our family, now would we?" Cook looked near to tears, as she looked at her from over her glasses.

"I know all about that, Cook. Don't ever think I'm criticising. Our downstairs family is precious to us – and no doubt always will be, as long as we have you. That is why I thought you could use the book."

"So kind, my dear Mi… Alexandra. Don't you think I don't appreciate your kindness, 'cos I do."

Alexandra wanted to rush across and hug the dear lady but she knew that would be carrying things just a bit too far. As for Walford, he was still standing to attention, looking as watery-eyed as his sister, so she said,

"Walford, do sit down. You look so untidy standing around like that," which made him smirk to himself, recalling how he would say these very words to them when they were little children.

Having succeeded in her mission, she went back to the morning room, where she had some correspondence to catch up on. The main letter she wanted to write was to Marianne, saying how pleased she was to hear her (unmentionable by name) news and how she looked forward to the forthcoming wedding. It was a pack of lies but it must be done, one cousin to another. Writing the letter would put her feelings once more into turmoil, as she thought of Ralph making love to Marianne. It was just as well she had not succumbed to his charms in the woods because, who knows, there could have been two women expecting babies and one of them would have been thrown out of her home, not given a spectacular wedding and a town house in London.

She settled down at the desk by the window, thinking once more of papa and how he would spend many hours doing just this in the library. He would have been so disappointed in his daughter and her wanton behaviour because the results of an unofficial liaison were always blamed on the female of the species, regardless of the pressure put on them by the male. She heard the wheels of a carriage outside on the gravel but chose not to look because she knew it would be Marshal going off to the bank or his club. The door to the room opened at precisely the same moment and it was Marshal.

"I thought... I was sure... Who has just arrived then, cos?"

"I have no idea. Let's have a look."

They both went to the window and, wiping their steamy breath away, saw Ralph Lawrence dismounting from a hired carriage. As he casually waved away the driver who had helped him out, they saw Walford come out to meet him. Marshal looked at Alexandra and she looked at him. This was unexpected, under the circumstances. Before long, there was a tap on the door and Ralph walked in front of Walford to greet them with outstretched hands.

"Good morning, my almost-relatives. It is so good to see you here together."

"Er, Good morning, Ralph," said Marshal, slightly nonplussed.

"And you, Alexandra, are you well?"

"Quite well, thank you," she said icily.

"Good, that's very good."

Then the room turned silent as each one wondered how to start a conversation with the man who had dealt so badly with their sister. There was no need to worry, however, as the confident Ralph stepped into the empty chasm, without preamble.

"I thought I should come and talk to my father, as he's down here on business. There was no need to get mother involved in wedding plans before I found out how pater felt about all this speed."

"Yes, I suppose that was a good idea," said Marshal, scratching his head and wondering how a man could be so blasé about such an important mistake – but to Ralph this would be a mere trifle.

"So, I've seen the parent and explained that the wedding will be six weeks from yesterday. You see, the invitations have gone out already and I believe you ladies insist on six weeks' notice for a wedding," he said, looking down at Alexandra affectionately.

He was treating her like a sister, after all that had transpired between them.

"Yes," she said and turned away, most impolitely, "I'm afraid I must leave you men to your plans. I propose to go for a walk before it becomes too cold. Goodbye."

"No, wait, Alexandra. May I come with you? I have spent so long travelling and staying at stuffy inns – I need a breath of truly fresh air. Would you excuse me, Marshal. We will continue our discussion over lunch."

So, he'd come for lunch. An invitation had not been offered but doubtless family did not require one. This was not what she expected, nor had she hoped this would happen – but how could she refuse without seeming churlish? They collected outdoor clothing and set off down the drive together. She could feel her body tensing up each time he came too close and refused to look at him; he did not exist, as far as her mind was concerned. After they had rounded the first bend, so there was no chance that anyone from the house could see them, Ralph put his hand on her shoulder.

"Please, take your hand away, Ralph."

"Why? Oh Alexandra, please forgive me. The only reason I'm here now is because I had to see you and talk with you."

"Now it is my turn to say, why. You are about to marry my cousin, Marianne, under the worst possible cloud and yet you want me to forgive you for your… for your… non-foresight, is all I can call it."

"I'm not even sure that is a word, dear Alexandra but if that's how you want to describe it, please go ahead. The fact that I have been seduced by your dear cousin, in fact I would even say trapped, has not been considered by any of the Turners in their judgment of me."

"You, seduced! You must think I am a child. You are the seducer, Mr Lawrence, not cousin Marianne."

"But it is true. She flaunted herself before me like a harlot and, being a red-blooded man, who had been turned down by the woman he loves, what could I do?"

"You could have broken your engagement to my cousin and asked the woman you love to marry you."

"Do you mean that, Alexandra? Do you really mean it? If so, I will cancel my engagement this minute. I will cancel the wedding. I will cancel anything you like and we will go away to a foreign land and you and I will get married."

This was not the way it was supposed to go. He was now saying he loved her; loved her enough to break off from Marianne and never see her again. Oh, why did their two fathers set up their business arrangement in the first place? But it was alright now! Papa had gone. There was no business arrangement to honour. Ralph could be free – but no, he could never be free because Marianne was expecting his baby. What could she say to him?

By this time they had walked past the animal cemetery and across to the wood Alexandra thought of as theirs and, after a period of silence, during which Ralph inspected her facial expressions, he decided to take her in his arms. At first she struggled, then, remembering how it used to be, relaxed into his embrace and allowed him to kiss her. His arms felt so strong around her body and she was made to realise how much she had missed him.

"Oh, darling Alexandra, how can you ever forgive me. I have committed a mortal sin and there is no way out for me – for us," he said, stroking her forehead, where her hair had come out from under her hat.

His voice was low and sensual, her defences were firmly down and being trampled underfoot. She loved this man and wanted to be with him. Anyone who would come all the way from London to speak with her, particularly if he thought she wanted nothing more to do with him, must care very deeply. They kissed again and when they returned to the real world, Ralph said,

"We must be together. The thought of never seeing you again fills me with dread. Leave it to me, dear girl. I will organise something for us."

"Oh, I don't know..." She was so ignorant of the ways of the world.

"Leave it to me, little one. I know what I'm doing."

They walked back through the wood and then released each other for the final hundred yards up the drive. Walford opened the door for them and she saw his pursed lips as they divested themselves of outdoor regalia. It was nothing to do with him, what she chose to do.

As they passed Marshal's study and saw him inside, Ralph gave her a surreptitious pat on the arm, then formally thanked her for her company. He knocked at the door and entered at Marshal's call, turning to close it behind him.

What would he say to her cousin? Would he say anything at all? How did he presume to reorganise his life with regard to Marianne? How could he leave a baby without a father? These were the questions she would mull over until he gave her some answers. He had said they could marry and go to a foreign land; but she knew that was impossible, due to the coming baby.

000

Unbeknown to Alexandra, Ralph went back to his father that very day, telling him he had changed his mind about marrying the Turner daughter because she had lied to him and pretended the child she was carrying was his. He said he had gone through his own calendar and reckoned that he could not possible be the father, as he had been here, in Cleveland, when she would have conceived. He also told him he was in love with the cousin, who was a chaste, beautiful and intelligent girl and he wanted to cancel, rather than organise, the proposed wedding. Walter Lawrence, being a bluff Yorkshireman, believed everything his son told him because he had never been found out in a lie before. The boy was too good for the Turner brat and he would see what he could do to sort things out. The other girl was a beauty; there had been times when he had not been able to keep his hands away from her himself.

Amazingly, Ralph went back to his fiancée to carry on the fantasy of preparing for a wedding, although in fact preparing to ditch the pregnant girl and marry her cousin – but nobody knew.

Walter called on Marshal at the club the following day. Ralph had decided that the best person to call off the impending marriage would be his father because Marshal trusted older people and respected them. If he had blurted out a few sentences about dates not tallying and his sister lying through her teeth to the girl's sibling, there would be no chance of escape. His father could state a fait accompli and Marshal would just accept that Ralph was not allowed to marry his sister.

He had no idea what all this was about but Marshal had consulted his books and papers on new steel industry proposals anyway, so he would be ready for any practical queries. As the stout Yorkshireman entered and was pointed in his direction, he stood up, realising just how different he was from his son. Ralph must take after his mother because he was tall and slim, good-looking in fact and this man was small and rotund, with a balding head. Like all overweight gentlemen, he kicked out his feet as he walked and his stomach seemed to precede him down the long, dim, carpeted expanse and into Marshal's favourite corner. He held out his hand, officiously and clasped Marshal's shoulder with his other.

"Hello, my boy. How are you this cold and frosty morning?"

"I am very well, thank you, Mr Lawrence. Now, come and sit down and tell me how I can be of assistance. Your message was brief and gave nothing away."

"I'm not prone to giving anything away, lad. I wanted to talk to you about your sister and my boy, Ralph. You see, I know what's been going on and I came here today to tell you that I won't stand for it."

"I'm sorry but I have no idea what you mean, sir."

"I don't suppose you 'ave but I'm here to tell you. Your sister has been having a gay old time down in London and she thinks she can blame it all on the lad. He's told me how he checked his appointment dates and it seems he was up here in Middlesbrough at the time he's supposed to have... fathered her little 'un"

"Ssh! Could you keep it down, Mr Lawrence? I'm not

exactly proud of the fact that Marianne's expecting."

"Oh, sorry, lad, but this had to be said. My Ralph had absolutely nothing to do with your lass, Marianne, getting in the family way. Do you understand?"

"I can't say I do. You see, the last time Ralph and I talked, he was full of his plans to get married and even said the invitations had gone out."

"That must have been before he put himself to thinking it all out. Oh, you know how persuasive women can be when it comes to arranging things, balls, soirees, weddings, you name it. Anyway, there's to be no wedding and them invitations'll just have to be got back again."

"But, my sister, how will she manage. She was so looking forward to it – and the… the… little problem?"

Walter bent down and whispered in Marshal's ear.

"I know what she can do, my boy. There are ways and means and she's in the right place to do it. You know what I'm getting at, don't you?"

"I'm not altogether naïve," whispered Marshal. "You mean an abortionist, I take it?"

"Aye lad, you've got it and to show you how serious I am, I'll pay for it. All you have to do is get her to the best aborchin… aborsun… oh, hell's teeth, the best bugger for the job, and I'll foot the bill. That's it then. That's all I have to say. Now, I'll accept your offer of a large Scotch whisky and then I'll be on my way."

Marshal could not believe he felt so calm about all this, knowing he had to explain to Marianne that there was to be no wedding, nor was there to be a baby but it was probably because he realised how little she felt for Ralph and how upset she had been when she knew she was expecting. In a warped way, Walter Lawrence had solved many of their problems, not least that of his gallivanting son, who could now get back to beguiling the female population of the south of England.

CHAPTER 21

After Marianne's speedy and rather seedy abortion, in one of the backstreets of London – the same backstreets where Ralph had had so much masculine fun - she came home. It had all taken place so quickly that Alexandra and Marshal were not ready to accept an unmarried sister into the house; getting used to a potential wedding had been bad enough but to harbour an escapee from matrimony was even worse and she was now a second invalid needing care.

"I expect you know everything, Alexandra," she said, when her cousin came to her room to visit for the first time.

"Yes, I do," she said, feeling as a royal traitor must have felt in Elizabethan times.

"Then you will understand when I say I do not want to hear another word about weddings, babies or Ralph Lawrence. They all reside in a closed book. When I return to London, as an independent woman, I intend to take up a social career suitable to my position."

Alexandra wondered what her position was: seductive female, jilted woman, old maid in disguise, thwarted concubine. By her comments, she did not seem to be at all worried about the man she had previously called her beloved or the foetus which could have become a copy of them both.

"I am totally suited by that," she replied.

"Good. Then you may leave me to recuperate. If anyone calls, say I am indisposed – then run up and tell me who called. It might be someone of worth."

This comment was far too ridiculous to answer, so Alexandra simply nodded and left the room.

She left one selfish woman, to visit another but the second was indeed poorly. None of her medication was helping her to surface from the terrible disease and she felt so sorry for the aunt who had prided herself on her looks and her dress, who had gone into a decline and was slowly wasting away. There was no point in trying to talk to her because she either did not hear or chose not to. When a maid appeared, even before any medicine was offered, she made a faint fanning movement with her hand and often covered her shrunken mouth with the other. The odd purple colour had returned and, apart from this, her complexion was a monotone, wrinkled to her hairline which was dishevelled because she refused to allow anyone near her face.

Both she and Marshal knew it was just a matter of time and, although Dr Beecham continued to call, his cluck-clucking as he left the room had come to be a habit, saying, without words, 'no hope'.

It was therefore an expected and accepted disaster when Mary knocked on Alexandra's door, one dark night and said,

"She's gone, Miss. She just heaved a big sigh and left this world for the next. I said a little prayer for her soul, Miss but I expect you want the vicar to do the honours properly for our mistress."

Mary was always correct, to the letter. She must have seen this kind of thing many times, down in the village, to be able to handle such an illness and eventual release with the minimum of fuss and she could only be in her thirties herself.

"Thank you Mary. I will put on some clothes and come and see to things."

"If you need me, I will be around, Miss. You only have to call."

As she pulled on a robe and some stockings and shoes, in order to keep warm in the cold, night-time house, she wondered how this latest tragedy could be explained to the hysterical Marianne but why was she thinking of such a thing? That was Marshal's job, not hers. She should have told Mary to go along the corridor and wake him. When she left her room, Marshal appeared, fully clothed, so Mary had done just that.

"So, it's all over, little cos. Our suffering mama is dead."

To hear him say it so calmly, so quietly, came as a greater shock than if he had burst into tears. To voice the word, dead, was a miserable thing for a son to do about his own mother. Dead was such a definite word.

"You will have to tell Marianne and I don't know if she's strong enough to accept it just now,"Alexandra said quietly.

"She accepted the death of her unborn child, without

comment. Why should she care about her old mother?" he said, through tight lips.

Oh, this was not the Marshal she knew. He had become hard and crusty, like an over-baked pie in the oven of discontent that was his life. Too many things had gone wrong for Marshal. He deserved better and yet the worse the situation became, the stronger the man appeared. What a twist of fate.

Without stopping to think what she was saying, she uttered the foolish words, "Would you like me to break the bad news to her?"

Of course, being a man in conflict, he said yes and Alexandra found herself in the corridor, making her way to Marianne's room in the middle of the night, while Marshal made his fond, or otherwise, goodbyes to a mother who had seemed to have disliked him throughout his life.

Marshal had been right. Marianne did not erupt. She hardly bubbled into life when her cousin appeared at her bedside, waking her, and said,

"My dear cousin, I have sad news for you. Your mama passed away in her sleep and Mary has just been to tell me."

"Why couldn't it wait until morning, you silly girl? You know I am not well and I should not be disturbed by something so traumatic," she said, as she wiped the sleep from her eyes.

"What kind of daughter are you?!" she said, as she fumbled for a match to light a candle at the bedside, before lighting and bringing over an oil lamp.

"Please don't shout at me, cousin. I am unwell and know not what I say."

"Then wake up and listen to me. Your mother, not mine as she constantly told me, is dead." There, she had used the word now. It was so much more powerful than saying she had passed on or quitted this mortal coil or some other euphemism that would be used at the funeral service.

"I heard you the first time. I feel awful. Send Mary to me immediately. I must have something hot to drink, before I faint away."

"Selfish to the end, Marianne. You cannot have Mary. I will send Ethel to you as soon as she arrives. Until then you should commune with your inner self and try to find something fond to say of your mother. Goodnight – or is it good morning – I have no idea."

She went back to her room, not trusting herself to speak to Marshal. He would suppose she was too upset to reappear, as most women would be. The light was beginning to creep up from behind the trees and she sat by the window to watch the sunrise. Little by little a pink, then salmon, then deeper red appeared in the sky, until there was a pure brightness lighting up the tops of the trees, waking up the friendly wood of her past life. She could hear birds beginning to call, as they woke from their freezing cold slumber and started to search for food to warm them through another winter day. The rest of the sky was streaked with long, flat stratus clouds, a beautiful cerulean blue in between, and higher up the dark grey cumulus clouds shrouded the rest of the picture. It looked as though it was going to be a fine day.

Fine it was not. First Dr Beecham arrived, to declare the very dead woman deceased. Then the funeral director was called and details were explained to Marshal alone. Needless to say, Marianne did not make an appearance, although she was quite capable of leaving her bed – indeed had been from the moment she entered her room. It looked to Alexandra as if she were intent on copying her mama's lifestyle even now.

000

The funeral passed, unheeded by the local people who had attended that of William Turner - but they had loved him and despised his pretentious wife. Not a soul lined the road on the way to the village, although the cortege for Ernestine was equally as large and important as that for her husband. Marshal was suitably pious and attentive but as soon as the church service was over he went back to his own worries about the estate. Marianne did not attend because she was ill, reminding Alexandra of the number of engagements Ernestine had missed for the same reason. Having her upstairs was just like having her mother there; the maids were treated similarly and she had tried to debase her cousin on more than one occasion. When they were alone, she said to Marshal,

"I want you to know something, cos. I will not become a

slave for your sister, the way I was forced to become for your mother. Nor will I treat her as the mistress of this house – for as long as we still have a house. Incidentally, have you discussed our situation any further with her?"

"No and I don't intend to. As far as I'm concerned, Marianne left us when she went to London. The best thing that could happen is for her to recover quickly and go back where she feels she belongs, although where I will find the money to allow her to continue such an exhorbitant lifestyle I do not know. She has already asked me for an increase in her allowance and refuses to hear me when I tell her how little we now have."

She never thought she would hear this from compassionate Marshal but she had never expected him to change so much after the death of his dear father either. Then, it had been as if he had inherited the character and kindness of papa, just like taking over his greatcoat. Or perhaps she should say, like taking over his riding whip, because he had become a force to be reckoned with, now he was master of Grangely.

000

Days passed and weeks passed. She heard nothing from Ralph, and Marianne stayed. It seemed he had been talking nonsense when he had mentioned their togetherness; obviously the bright lights and even brighter people had taken over when he left Yorkshire.

Alexandra decided to apply herself to something new as, despite her comment to Marshal, Marianne had decided to manage the house and nobody stopped her, probably because this was far better than the alternative – her return to London with a propensity for spending every penny they owned. During the long period when she had dined and conversed with papa's friends around the dinner table and afterwards, she had ingested much information about investments and the way to go about making them. Obviously the discussions were not meant for the ears of a woman but she had the habit of remaining silent when seated at the end of the table, thus enabling her to listen-in to more interesting conversations than those going on between the women. It was a matter of casting back her mind to those times and straining her memory on names of companies, types of businesses and heads of corporations and with her wonderful capacity for recall she found it stimulating, rather than tiring. She invested in several notebooks, for use as journals, and jotted down everything that came into her head. It was not long before she was ready to approach Marshal with her ideas for investments which she was certain would help in their time of need, which was now.

She found him in his study one morning at the end of March, where he sat gazing out of the window at a robin, tapping on the newly softened earth to fool a worm into thinking it was raining. Nature had ways of feeding its birdlife. She had spent long minutes watching pigeons beneath a dried seed-head where sparrows had been feeding and felt they were behaving as employers, setting the small birds the task of shaking the plant so the ground feeders could reap the rewards as seeds dropped down. Her cousin rose as she entered.

"Marshal," she began, without recourse to the weather or the state of his health, both of which she knew and therefore found the exercise useless. "My dear, I have been studying the possibility of investing in the new steel industry, as discussed in the past by papa and his friends…"

Before she could continue, he butted in to say,

"Alexandra, how many times do I have to tell you, the subject of investments, business and the like are nothing to do with the female of the species. Kindly get on with your own affairs and leave me to mine."

She had never known him so rude, so dismissive and certainly never so unkind. This obviously was not the time to broach the subject of finances, so she changed her tack and said,

"This is not why I came down to see you; just an afterthought in fact." It was sad how easily lying came to her, when it was due to an important problem – but papa would have called these 'little white lies'. "How is Marianne coping, now that she is back on her feet again. Walford tells me she wishes to involve herself more in the running of the house and I wanted to ask you if you have impressed upon her that we must economize as much as possible."

"I have tried to mention such vulgar things as frugality,

restraint and indeed thrift to avoid poverty but she insists we have enough money now she is not getting married or returning to London. It seems to be her one aim in life to spend the amount I would have expended on her wedding on trinkets and trivialities for the house – even though I tell her repeatedly that we will not be here for long. Her ridiculous laugh rings in my ears when I go to bed at night. Now do you realise why I cannot listen to another woman telling me what to do!"

"Poor Marshal. I had no idea."

"Of course not, you never seem to pass the time of day with your cousin. Why is this so?"

"I have better things to think about than the fashions of the day and the colour of curtains, Marshal. That is why."

"Oh dear, what a family we have become since papa and mama died. Do you ever think we will come to terms with life and do something worth remembering. It doesn't look as if any of us are going to have children to take on our non-existent fortunes anyway."

"I can see you're depressed but please, please try to think more objectively. There has to be some way of retaining Grangely – if nothing else."

"Oh, here you go again. We will be back where we started soon, with your idiotic ideas about investments. Please go, Alexandra, before I say something I don't wish to say."

She felt a mixture of regret and anger, when she remembered how she had tried to help this family, one way or another. Now, both her cousins seemed to have turned on her. It would serve them right if she left them to their own devices. If only Ralph would contact her, then she would know if she were leaving this family forever or remaining as the poor relative for the rest of her miserable days.

CHAPTER 22

"What I would like to know, Alexandra dear, is which colour of velvet do you think we should hang in this room. Now that Mama is no more, I can please myself about the organisation of rooms and Marshal has agreed that we may replace the curtains in here at least."

The room under scrutiny was the large drawing room and it would take yards and yards of expensive fabric to re-curtain, not to mention the services of a needlewoman for weeks. If Marianne had been told she could not return to London, why was she trying to spend as much money as possible, here at Grangely?

"Please don't ask me, Marianne, because you know I am happy with the ones your mother chose. Curtains in a house like this should last for years and, as we will soon have to leave, why purchase new ones for a future occupant?"

"What a silly idea, cousin. You know Marshal tends to err on the cautious side. I don't suppose we have anything to worry about, in actual fact."

"But you must listen to him. There is only a limited amount of money in the bank and that is insufficient to run the estate indefinitely. What we need to do is invest in the new steel industry, then maybe we will be able to ride out the storm."

"Oh, you are so clever when it comes to bright ideas, Alexandra. Why have you not mentioned such things to the man of the house, so he can mull over the practicalities of such a proposal."

"I have but he put it down to female interference; didn't want to know."

"But this is ridiculous. You are equally as astute as he is. I must do a little interfering myself. Leave it to me."

Why was Marianne trying to curry favour at such a late stage. She had been the total opposite for so many years and Alexandra began to think there was some plot in her mind. However, another opinion on her own, hopefully sensible, views would not go amiss, so she let it go.

Marianne disliked being out of friends with her brother. For one thing, he was now the only person who could finance her and it was late spring now, which meant a whole new wardrobe if she were to make a mark for herself even in Yorkshire society.

When Alexandra was out on one of her many rambles, Marianne went to see him in his study.

"Brother dear, I wish to speak with you about some senseless comments I've been hearing from Alexandra. She has some harebrained scheme for investing our money in an industrial project. I have come to ask you if you agree with her half-witted opinions."

"Of course not, Marianne, and I've told her so myself. Why she has to come running to you with the same idiotic ideas, I do not know."

"So, you are not planning to take papa's inheritance and squander it on the filthy iron industry?"

"Definitely not. Whatever made you think it?"

"Alexandra, of course. She said you were in total agreement and were discussing the project with the bank manager. It would only be a matter of weeks before we invested."

"That is so wrong! I told her I had no interest in her words about business ventures and to go back to her loom, or somesuch."

"Not only that, Marshal dear, but I have detected signs of insanity – or maybe that is too strong a term at present. She is ... eccentric I believe the word is."

"What on earth do you mean?"

"Oh, nothing I can really pinpoint but just certain conversations we have had seem to me to be ... unusual, unreal to say the least."

"I never thought…"

"You never think about women at all, dear Marshal. What I have in mind might just solve our little problem. What do you think about moving Alexandra out into the Dower House which you planned for mama? In that way, we will be able to keep a close eye on our cousin and she will be absolutely unable to interfere with our own plans."

"I don't know about that. She and I have been together for so long."

"And *we* will still be together, brother. Think about it – in fact wait a little while and then ask the girl herself what she thinks."

The seed had been sown. If she were to remain mistress of this house, she must ensure that Alexandra, with her bright ideas, was elsewhere. It was bad enough having to miss the London season and all the excitement a true coming-out would entail but to be dictated to by her own door-step cousin was preposterous. She would make sure that girl never interfered with her plans again and that Marshal and she led the lives they surely should lead, being the children of the squire.

000

From that moment on, Marianne behaved like an angel to her cousin, yet turned her every thought into something foolish. She hid Alexandra's possessions and brought them back again after long searches around the house; she passed on messages giving the wrong time or the wrong date, then swore she had said otherwise when Alexandra appeared confused; she told the servants to do some senseless task and informed Marshal that the order came from the other girl. Her enjoyment was greater than she had known for some time and she even walked around the house smiling, much to the surprise of the housemaids. The downstairs staff were given a long break from the temper tantrums of Miss Marianne but they also wondered about the strange behaviour of Miss Alexandra.

It was weeks afterwards that Marshal decided to have words with his cousin and felt it should be in her room where she would be surrounded by everything familiar; for he really believed she was losing her mind. Situations reported by Marianne, combined with Alexandra's miserable features led him to think their cousin had succumbed to a form of madness and, after his mother's deterioration due to something similar, he could not handle it. He knocked at her door one evening before dinner.

"Come in Marianne!" she called and Marshal wondered why she imagined this was his sister.

"It's not Marianne, it's Marshal."

"Oh, wrong again," she said, most unlike her previously bright self.

"I wish to have a few words with you, Alexandra."

"Yes," she said, as she moved her book to one side. He noticed it contained a long laundry list as a bookmark.

"What a strange bookmark," he said by way of conversation.

"I don't know why it's there. I didn't put it there," she grimaced. He looked down at the floor to allow her to compose herself and noticed several small bows of ribbon on the carpet; there was one in the centre of each medallion of pattern. This was so strange.

There was a knock at the door and he watched as his cousin opened it to admit Mary.

"Here are the empty bowls you asked for, Miss. They've been scoured with salt as you asked."

"But I didn't…" Alexandra stopped speaking, looked at Mary and said, "Thank you, Mary. That will be all."

Marshal made up his mind in that one moment. "I came to ask you if you would like to move into the Dower House, cos? It seems to me that you need a little more independence than you have here. Alexandra looked at him in way he could only describe as sympathetically and said,

"I think that would be a very good idea. When do you want me to go?"

This was bad. She thought he wanted to be rid of her presence, which indeed he did if she proved to be insane but they had been so close in the past and it felt wrong, totally wrong.

Alexandra had thoughts of her own. She had no idea what was happening to her. Staff members said she had been giving orders for what she thought of as ridiculous items to be brought to her room and had found things placed foolishly all around the house, yet she could not remember doing these things. Marianne had assured her that she had and had explained that sometimes people were unaware of their actions when their mind was deranged. A move to the Dower House would be right at such a time and would allow her to relax into her insanity without others seeing what was happening to her. The strangest part of this was that she was able to study and write intelligently, while her idiocy continued through the small facets of life. If Marshal wanted her to go, then go she must and it would be something of a relief.

Her personal possessions were taken by cart to the house which was halfway down the back drive, along with pieces of furniture she had come to know as her own. Marshal added some fine pieces of downstairs furniture for her rooms and, before long, she was established as the spinster sister in the Dower House.

000

Ralph Lawrence had made his plans, which had taken longer than he expected, and was now in a position to collect Alexandra and take her away. When he had told his father about it, he was so pleased that he said he intended to settle a fair amount on his only son after his marriage. Ralph told him he wanted no fuss for this wedding and they would sooner go off to Europe and marry quietly, rather than upset everyone who had been involved in planning the first celebrations with Marianne. Walter agreed. The less fuss the better and, as long as he got this nice little daughter-in-law to produce future generations of Lawrences, everything was fine.

Ralph turned up at Grangely Hall one bright spring day and glanced around at the new pale green leaves appearing here and there. It would be nice to live in the country with his new wife. He could hide her away in the Yorkshire Dales, where there were no distractions, apart from a few cows and sheep and country yokels to jump to her bidding, then he could go off to London on business and enjoy the high life, knowing he had the handsomest woman he had ever met, waiting on the doorstep for his return. He would have to get her a staff of, preferably ugly, servants to look after her until he came back and no doubt she would start to breed as soon as they were wed, which would ensure she stayed in one place. This was the best idea he had had for years.

Walford opened the door and he asked to see Miss Shankland.

"Sorry sir, Miss Shankland's gone."

"What do mean, gone, Walford. Where's she gone?"

"I am not at liberty to say, sir. Miss Turner's in the drawing room, if you would care to follow me."

"I don't really care to..." This was stupid. One did not show one's feelings to the hired help. "Yes, Walford, that would be fine," he said, removing his coat and hat and handing them over.

Marianne sat in a newly decorated drawing room. It was light and airy in the Arts & Crafts style and, Ralph thought, unsuitable in such an old building.

"Good afternoon, Ralph. What a lovely surprise. We haven't seen you for a long time."

"There's no need to be polite to me, my dear. We both know what happened to cancel our friendship – if we ever had one – and now all I wish to know is where is your cousin?"

"Not available is my answer to that. You will never see her again, Ralph. Don't think I didn't know about your sneaky plans to get together with Miss Goodie-goodie. Forget all about her, as we in the family have."

"What are you talking about, Marianne. You say you have forgotten about her. What have you done with her?"

"We have done nothing. She decided to go insane, so we sent her off."

"Not to a mad-house, an asylum or whatever they call them?"

"No, just to a lovely little house in the country, where you will never find her. Goodbye Ralph, that's all I have to say."

At that moment, Marshal came in and Ralph stood to shake hands.

"I hear your cousin has gone to recuperate in the country, Marshal. Please could I have her address, so I can visit her?"

This was the last thing she needed. Why was this nincompoop still hanging around, after all the trouble he had caused?

"I'm afraid not. She is not to be disturbed. Nobody must know her whereabouts, then perhaps she will recover from her temporary... er... trouble."

"Your sister tells me she has gone insane. Surely this is not true. I have never known a more sensible and sane person in my whole life."

"I'm afraid it is true. She started to show signs of mental illness, almost as soon as mama died. She may make a complete recovery but, if not, she is in safe hands."

"Then I will leave you. I have to admit I only came to visit Miss Shankland. We had a little unfinished business to discuss but now..."

They all said their farewells and Ralph left Grangely House for the final time. As he travelled along the road to Darlington, to catch a train back to London, he thought what a lucky escape he had had. Just imagine if he had married the girl and placed her in a house in the country, he might have been tied to her for life. There were novels about such women – Jane Eyre wasn't it, where the hero, Rochester, had a mad wife in the attic – and he was not the kind of man who wanted to be saddled with such a responsibility. He would find a little piece back in London. Perhaps he would not marry at all – just go from attractive mistress to the next one, until his time ran out. Girls did not worry about a man's age; it was his performance and his money that mattered to that class of woman.

CHAPTER 23

In the Dower House, things started to come right immediately. Because there were no servants, nothing odd was ordered by Alexandra; there were no strange items in wrong places and she loved living in a small house near the woods. In fact, Marshal could not have given her a finer present, had he tried – apart from the fact that she missed Grangely, as if it were a person. All her days had been spent in the big house and each piece of furniture told its own story, mostly of papa and his loving kindness.

So, who was it who had tried to drive her mad? Could it have been any of the downstairs staff – someone with a grudge, due to her friendship with Walford and Cook? Surely not. She had always felt close to the maids, after her spell as a kitchen helper. What if word had spread that they were all to lose their jobs and she had been the target for their persecution – but if that were the case they would have chosen the master or even the superior Marianne. No, everyone thought Marianne was only there temporarily, even if she had turned the house upside down during her stay. Oh, the worry of trying to pick out an assailant from the people around her. She really *would* go mad if she continued.

Her room was small compared with those at Grangely but the familiar pieces of furniture gave her a comfortable feeling of belonging. She sat in the window seat and looked out at birds flying back and forth to the woods with bits of straw and old leaves in their beaks; the nesting season was really underway and she also had been nest-building. If only she could depend on spending the rest of her days here. She looked out at farm workers going up and down the back drive and felt sad on their behalf, even though they knew nothing of the shocking alteration their lives would take. Perhaps a new owner would keep the old staff on.

When looking for inspiration, sitting quietly alone was the best thing to do and when it came it came with a loud bang inside her head. The perpetrator of all the trickery at the Hall was Marianne. It had to be. She was the person who gave out orders and had access to her rooms; she had an axe to grind regarding Ralph; she wanted more from Marshal in the way of financial help for her own scatter-brained schemes. It was Marianne and she had been clever enough to persuade Marshal to believe her. If only she had known for sure but at the time she had been so depressed and so gullible she would have believed anything about herself. Once she had started to think her mind was going, she had no option but to trust the girl who had seen her through childhood. What a childhood it had been though. Every time she stepped out of line, Marianne had run to her mama with tales to tell and she had tried to turn Marshal against her on more than one occasion. It was Marianne – and left to her own devices she could well have made her lies come true because Alexandra had felt sanity slipping away like sand from the shore of sensibility. She easily could have become that insane spinster sister in the Dower House that Marianne desired. Once again she had been gullible and trusted someone she had known all her life, even though that person had given her no grounds in the past to believe that she had an ounce of affection for her. Now she had come to a conclusion, her mind raced on to remember all the stupid deceptions she had suffered and believed. If she had read them in a novel she would have put down the book as being far too unbelievable to enjoy – but tricks had been played upon her and she had fallen for the wicked girl's ploy.

She wanted to dash off to Grangely Hall that minute and tear out Marianne's hair but she stopped herself from flying to the hallstand to grab her bonnet by telling herself she had no proof. The only person who knew – and yes, she knew without a doubt – that Marianne was the prankster – was herself and chances were she could not even persuade Marshal to believe what had happened. How could he trust his cousin over his sister? There would come a time though, when she felt more confident in herself, when she would enjoy dressing up and would go to the hall and explain all. The only thing to do now was to sit tight, enjoy her solitude and prove herself to be sane. Ralph would come to collect her soon and she must be as well as she could be, in order to prance away with Marianne's erstwhile man-of-her-dreams, waving her bonnet-ribbons at the foolish Turners.

Once again Alexandra needed an outlet for her newly revived intellect and this time she decided to research her own family. She had never been told the real truth about her birth and, indeed, either of her parents and this quiet time would be perfect for accumulating some real facts. She must know that she was the child of her parents after they had married because the thought of being illegitimate had nagged her for too long. That could have been the reason her aunt had been so cruel and so disparaging to her all those years.

000

Grangely Hall was a noiseless place without Alexandra. Marshal walked about the hallways and up and down stairs, listening to his own footsteps and remembered how there had always been voices around the rooms, particularly during the day, when maids were working. They had laughed with each other and with Alexandra, for she refused to succumb to the mistress-servant regime operated by his mother. Whenever she entered a room to find a maid raking a fire or dusting ornaments she would stop and chat to her about something pleasant like the fine day or a certain bird in one of the trees outside. Work then must have been worthwhile for his staff. Now, Marianne insisted on silence at all times; she believed that servants, like children, should be seen (as little as possible) and not heard (ever). His sister was a carbon-copy of her mother. He also missed the efficient housekeeping done at Alexandra's behest because it all seemed so effortless. She would issue orders in the morning and by evening-time the whole house would radiate cleanliness and the warmth of friendly people. Unfortunately, there was now a chill about the place, with servants skulking around corners and work left undone because they all feared a meeting with the self-styled mistress – and even himself. He had been placed in the same container as his sister, purely because they were siblings and yet he had always enjoyed the odd word with a maid or with Walford.

The butler had become extremely subservient recently but Marshal knew in his heart this was mere subterfuge; the old man had been with the family for so long that there was no need for him to behave in such a humble fashion. Even when he tried to engage him in conversation, the replies were stilted and far too polite. The whole house suffered from the loss of his cousin. Why had she become so disturbed? He had done everything within his powers to make her feel at home – as indeed she was – so what had rocked her into mental illness?

He went to his study, which was the only place he could pursue his still vigorous interest in iron. There was no-one to listen to his contentious comments, as he shouted back at the authors of books and newspaper articles, nor argue with his assertive comments about the industry, now that papa and Alexandra were no longer in the house and misery sought to overtake him, as he perused his books. As an intellectual student, it was necessary to have an adversary, otherwise life itself became like a re-read volume; there was always the knowledge of what came next. As soon as he sold up he would try to find work in or around the new steel industry but for this he would need to take a course at university, to prove himself for the first time in his life, in his thirties.

The door opened, without a knock.

"Oh, there you are brother dear. I expected to find you here, with your nose inside a book. What you find in such a dry subject is beyond me. I came to tell you that we must start holding dinner parties and social evenings, if we are not to sink into a mire of obscurity out here in the country."

"It sounds as if you have already decided, so why mention it to me, sister?"

"Because you must appear as host and will need some new garments, if you do not wish to be outmoded by petite moi."

He hated it when she added phrases in French to the perfectly adequate English language. Presumably, that is how they all spoke in London. "I don't really care who outmodes me, be it lord or tinker. I don't see why I should attend your ridiculous charades, while you are here, in down-to-earth Yorkshire."

"But that is why I must entertain – to show that we are not down-to-earth but high on a pinnacle, compared with the puddings of Yorkshire. Ha-ha, I made a pun about the Yorkshire Pudding! Please be good enough to laugh at your witty sister, Marshal."

"If that is wit then I must be uproariously funny. Kindly leave me to my own, boring devices and continue with yours. I think cook is a more appropriate person for you to discuss your social gatherings with."

"Oh, that dimwitted old thing downstairs. I doubt she would know the difference between entree and entrance when it comes to entertaining the gentry."

"And where do you expect to find this gentry you speak about?"

"I have my contacts – but I must have your agreement that you'll host parties with me. I must find suitable gentlemen to escort me while I'm here, at the family seat. Not that I haven't got plenty of male admirers down in London – just not up here, you understand."

"Oh, count me into your numbers, if it will keep you quiet. Now leave me. I wish to do some reading, in peace."

"Thank you. I anticipated your answer and have sent out half a dozen invitations already."

This was unbearable. She really was behaving like the mistress of his house; not even waiting for his affirmation before going ahead with her plans. It was a pity he could not afford to send her back to the capital city, where she could organise her friends as much as she, or they, wished.

ooo

Marianne's first dinner was planned for three weeks hence. Everyone in London knew that less than three weeks' notice was vulgar and more was seen to be full of fear that people might not come. She had planned the menu herself and made sure that cook was given instructions to use the best butcher and to try to excel herself, with the sweet course in particular. The guests were from the best houses in the district and many older couples had sons who were also invited. She saw to the dressmaker personally, driving to York to find the best person in the county and she insisted that Marshal also chose a tailor in the lovely old city for his own outfit. The way she organised the world was hard on the limited finances of her brother and, subsequently, their pot of gold went down and down with every new venture.

The evening before the party, Marianne and Marshal sat together at the dinner table. She talked about nothing except the feast to come, the hired staff, how inefficient their cook was compared to those in London and all the rules to which Marshal must adhere if he were to become the best host in Cleveland. Just before the dishes were removed after their main course, Walford came into the room and bent down to murmur in Marshal's ear,

"Someone wishes to speak with you, sir."

"Now, Walford. Surely you have explained we are at dinner."

"Yes sir but I thought you would wish to see this particular person."

"Why? Who is it?"

"It is someone you know very well, in fact a member of the family, sir."

"A member ... we have no family, apart from Alex... Oh, is it my cousin, Walford?" He felt a finger of fear run down his back. Surely, his insane cousin had not appeared, at this time in the evening. Perhaps she had come for dinner. What could he say to Marianne, to stop her from marching out and haranguing the girl? What could he do? "I think I had better accompany you, this very minute. Hold on a minute, Walford."

"It's quite alright, sir. She has taken a seat beside the hall fire and seems quite comfortable to me, sir."

Marshal found the whole situation extremely hard to handle. Walford was behaving as if Alexandra were a visiting guest and not the worrying, unstable girl who lived in the Dower House for her own good. He must put Marianne off the trail.

"Marianne, it seems that I am needed regarding some estate business. Walford says it cannot wait, so I have agreed to go with him to find out what is up." To mention estate business was the right thing to do because Marianne thought everything to do with the estate involved pigs and dirt and ploughs.

"Oh, as you wish brother. I presume I am allowed to continue with my meal whilst you converse with the outdoor help?"

"Of course, of course," he said with a feeling of relief. "In fact I do not wish to eat any more. Have your dessert and I will meet you in the drawing room later."

He followed the smiling butler into the hall and turned into the front alcove where a small fire was burning. The sight that greeted him was totally different from what he had expected because there, on the settle, sat a beautiful woman. Her hair was done up and she wore a fine, green silk and satin gown, worthy of any drawing room in the county.

"My dear Alexandra, what brings you here, in the evening." He must tread softly here, because she may be under some illusion, not knowing what she was doing.

"I am sorry, Marshal. I was under the impression that you ate dinner earlier, as we did in papa's day."

Of course, Marianne's new refinements had involved changing from the sensible hour of dining in the early afternoon, to a much later time dictated by the smart sets in London.

"Ye...e...s, it is Marianne's idea. She thought we were behind the times."

"I'm sure."

"I thought you were... I thought you had to keep to the house. I never... I never expected to see you here, particularly in the evening." He cleared his throat, looking around to see if his sister had appeared from the dining room. She must not see this new, elegant Alexandra. He must get her away from the house.

"I'm afraid I must leave you, cos. May I say how lovely you look and apologise profusely for not being able to receive you in the way I would wish to. I would rather you didn't confront Marianne until I have had a chance to talk to her. Please, Alexandra, try to understand my reasons for sending you away. I promise I will come to see you tomorrow."

"I had a feeling I had outlived my use to the Turner family," she said quietly. This was not something she had expected. Marshal wanted to keep her away from his sister. He had said it was until he had had a chance to talk to her but how could she be sure; he probably just wanted to rid himself of an embarrassment. Her bravery vanished in the knowledge that Marshal had refused to listen to her but her new self-confidence came to her rescue. "I just came to say something to you and to Marianne but far be it for me to spoil your evening, despite your sister's attempting to spoil my whole life. As you recommend, I will return in the trap to the Dower House and leave you.. Believe me when I say I had no idea you would not wish to see me." She rose, elegantly and walked slowly to the big double doors, where Walford waited with her cloak. She turned to him, smiling and said,

"Thank you so much Walford. You are so kind" and made her way to the trap which was waiting at the front of the house.

"Oh no," Marshal said, his hands over his face, "What have I done? Walford, what have we all done to that girl."

"I think it must wait until tomorrow, sir. Your sister will be coming out to go upstairs, as we speak."

Sensible to the letter, Walford was right. He had obviously heard everything from Marianne and from Alexandra. Marshal dragged his feet back to the dining room, where Marianne had indeed just risen to leave the room.

CHAPTER 24

The next day was one which Marshal dreaded all through the night. Because he did not sleep well, he was awake early and decided to walk along the back drive at eight o'clock in the morning, in the hopes that Alexandra would be up and about. He should have remembered her penchant for early rising for, as he neared the Dower House, he could see someone in the little garden tying up rambling roses near the back door. What a pity she had been sent away from the big house and made to live the life of a servant, alone.

He approached cautiously, so as not to frighten her, as she stood on a kitchen chair, string and scissors in hand. The sun was shining somewhat weakly over the trees and there was no wind and no rain, so it could be seen to be a fine day. As his boots made a crunching sound on the path, she heard him and jumped down lithely from her perch. Gone were the fine hoops and petticoats of last night and in their place were the more practical skirt and blouse of a working woman. His cousin was capable of being anything she wished and he was not sure which character he preferred – the fine, satin-clad lady of last night or the pleasant gardener of today.

"Hello, Alexandra, I have come to call as I promised yesterday evening."

She smoothed down her skirt and straightened her lacy white cap, before answering him in the same well-modulated tones of their previous encounter. She sounded more mature, older and, yes, more sensible – as if she understood more about herself and about him. This was a wise woman, who replaced the laughing, fun-loving cousin of the past. It was such a pity that it had taken something so vile to change her character from lively girl to mature woman.

"Please, come inside and join me in a cup of tea. Whatever enticed you to venture into the great outdoors so early in the day.?"

"I was unable to sleep. I wanted to speak to you. I feel so bad about what happened to you, Alexandra."

"Come along inside, cousin and we will talk about it."

He followed her into the small, comfortable room and was glad he had had the place renovated for his mother – because previously it had been two estate workers' cottages. He recognised the small pieces of furniture he had chosen for Alexandra himself when he thought she had lost her reason and he chose a chair which had been a particular favourite when it resided at Grangely.

After she had made a pot of tea and served it, surprisingly, in fine china, they sat for a while, staring at each other. They were like strangers. He must make the first move.

"Alexandra, I was not aware of how this dreadful thing happened... I want you to know that I was under the impression that you were unable to understand what was going on. Do you believe me, cousin?"

"Of course I do. If you imagine I think you had anything to do with my removal from the Hall, you must also believe I was insane. It was Marianne who masterminded the whole scheme and you were taken in as much as I was. I know I speak of your sister, your own flesh and blood, but she can be a wicked person, Marshal, and I advise you to take care in your dealings with her." Oh, she had not meant to say all this at first. Her general idea had been to lead up to an explanation of what occurred – not to jump in with both feet, like a duck into water.

"I had no idea... Alexandra, tell me what happened, why it happened and how we were all misled into believing you were out of your mind. I always think of myself as an intelligent human being and, when it comes to practicality, there is no-one more so than Walford, and indeed his sister – so how could we all be taken in by lies and stories?"

"Marianne has been blessed with a very definite and compelling personality. When she speaks, we immediately believe her views – was she not always that way, even in childhood?"

"Yes, she was but..."

"Nothing has changed. She has the manner of the mistress of the estate; the manner of her own mother. I don't think we need say more."

"But we must. I want to know everything. Start from the

beginning and explain it all." His own manner had become more definite and he now sounded like the master, so she had to comply.

When she had finished the whole sorry tale, Marshal ran his fingers through his hair, then looked deep into her eyes.

"Will you come back home, cos? Come back to Grangely Hall, where you belong."

Her only answer was, "No." It was hard to say this to him but she had made up her mind to stay where she was. There was no point in explaining all about her and Ralph at this time but she would tell him later, when things had calmed a little.

"Well, if I can't persuade you, let me send over some more furniture. I hate to think of your living like an estate worker, with nothing but the necessities of life."

"Surely, that is all anybody requires – the necessities. All luxuries are the icing on the cake and I personally prefer my cake plain." She laughed, as they had laughed in the past, without feeling a great knot of a problem between them.

"Then come to the house more often. Come every day if you like and we will walk in the grounds as we used to."

She was convinced her heart missed a beat, as that of a Bronte or Austen heroine would in a romantic tale, because she remembered her walks – not with Marshal but with Ralph. She desperately wanted to tell someone about her love for him and fought with herself about whether she should break this comfortable mood by mentioning a man her cousin could not abide. It would have to be said sometime and perhaps better sooner than later. Leaving the telling until she had to say she was leaving Grangely estate forever would be a cruel blow to her cousin, just when he imagined he had regained his true friend. She straightened her body in her chair and put both hands on the arms, as if to steady herself – for steadying she would require when she issued her ultimatum.

"Marshal," she said in her new calm, low voice. "I have one other thing to say. It is about my future plans and I want you to be the first to know because we have always been such friends. The last time Ralph Lawrence was here, he did not come to see Marianne or yourself; he came to see me. We walked and talked for some time and the result of all our deliberations was that he and I are going away together and plan to marry in time. Because of the many plans made for his wedding to Marianne, we intend to do it quietly, probably abroad and no-one needs to know."

"Oh, my dear Alexandra, what a shock."

She had anticipated his being surprised but definitely not shocked. Surely, he had chosen the wrong word in his confusion. What was there to be shocked about? His cousin had fallen in love with his sister's fiancé – it must happen all the time. "I had not intended to tell you yet but it occurred to me that Ralph may turn up sometime soon and whisk me away before I had a chance to explain my feelings to you, my dear cousin."

Marshal had no alternative but to tell her what had transpired, due to her move to the Dower House. This was going to hurt her and she might blame him for the change to her expectations. "Alexandra, I have something to tell you and you won't enjoy hearing it at all. The last time you saw Ralph was not the last time he called at Grangely. When we all thought you had become deranged, Ralph came to the house, presumably to whisk you away as you have just mentioned. Marianne had to tell him what had transpired and I am so sorry to say that he left, without wishing to see you. I don't know what thoughts went through his mind but I have a dreadful feeling that you will never see him again."

She sat, bolt upright, facing him and looking straight ahead beyond him. All her most private thoughts came rushing out. "This cannot be true. The thought of going away with Ralph was the only thing that kept me calm throughout my terrible period of isolation. His was the face I saw in my mind every morning when I woke and when I retired at night. If I felt anguished or depressed, I reminded myself of my wonderful future with the man I love and it was enough to bring me back to an optimistic frame of mind. What will I do without Ralph?" She held her head in her hands and appeared to be weeping. Then her sensible side took over and she smiled into Marshal's anxious face, saying, "Of course, when he has time to think this over, he will realise that someone as level-headed as myself could not possibly have gone insane. He will know it was yet another ploy by Marianne to keep us apart, due to her jealous nature; if she couldn't marry him then she would hate to think that I did. Yes, I'm sure I'm right. He will return when he thinks everything over."

She seemed so sure of herself – but then she always was. Could he ruin her dream or was it better to let her go on thinking that Lawrence would return. As the days and months passed, she would finally realise that nothing was going to come of their relationship. The only trouble was, he was relegating her to the life they all thought she would have. Perhaps another day would be better. Let her think her preposterous thoughts for a little while at least. So he said goodbye.

It seemed as good a time as any to leave the house and make his way back to the hall. Everyone would be up and about now; fires would be lit, curtains drawn back and Marianne would be about her dubious business, planning the evening's party. He held Alexandra close and kissed her cheek, before saying farewell and telling her how welcome she would be up at the big house, at any time of day. Then he left, turning at the gate to wave to his cousin once more. It was good to have his best friend back.

000

In the evening, as guests arrived, Walford appeared on top form. His formal manner was entirely in keeping with that displayed at bigger houses in Yorkshire and, had he been asked, he would have said how much he enjoyed playing the role for which he had been employed all those years ago. In fact the whole house came to life when it was once more full of people, as it had been in the old days and even Marshal admitted grudgingly that Grangely Hall was meant to be a place of entertainment. The fact that it took his sister to make it so was the bitter pill.

The guests were seated at the long mahogany table, after initial conversations in the drawing room And dinner was laid out a la Francais, with dishes for Marianne and Marshal to serve at either end of the table and many corner dishes to which people could help themselves afterwards. Marshal had no idea that their cook could produce such a feast and made a mental note to go down and thank her personally, as he knew his sister would not.

The first courses were removed and various sweet delicacies appeared, to the obvious admiration of all around the table. They were the only topic of conversation for the ladies, as they withdrew after the meal and went upstairs to the drawing room for further dissection of the evening. Marianne was not happy and let the fact be known by refusing to gossip, as all good hostesses should, despite the efforts made by all and sundry to amuse her and draw her out. The men invited for her inspection were not the suitable beaux she had expected and she could hardly wait to wave them off in their respective carriages. None of them was ever seen again.

CHAPTER 25

Although she had been confident with Marshal about Ralph, once left alone Alexandra feared the worst, as he was not the kind of man who would relish taking care of an invalid of any kind, let alone somebody without intelligence. He had always told her how her intellect had drawn him to her initially and to find out what he imagined had happened must have been a dreadful blow.

However, she must not dwell on a pessimistic outcome to their romance; it was better to hope for the best. The worst thing in the world about being a woman was that they were at the mercy of a man's notions and, if Ralph did not want to see her, there was nothing she could do to encourage him. Her fate was in the lap of the gods.

She must occupy herself fully, in order not to disappear into her own misery. Her earlier idea of researching her family tree had not been brought to the fore; now was the time to investigate it. All her life she had been aware of Somerset House, where modern records of births, marriages and deaths were kept. If she contacted them, she would not have to suffer the time-consuming and exhausting travelling to parish churches in the back of beyond to find out about her mother and father but her first call must be on Walford and maybe cook because they had been around for so long they must have more than a passing idea of who her father could be.

As she dressed suitably for making calls, she remembered how she had planned that intrepid evening drive to the Hall. It had been so exciting, getting dressed in her finest gown and applying subtle face paint which she knew would rival Marianne's. Her hair had been tamed under a silk-satin bonnet and each piece of broderie anglaise, both at neck and face had been washed and starched to equal that of any woman in Bond Street. That gown would most probably spend the rest of its days in a trunk because she did not visualise wearing it again in Yorkshire. No, she would not think such dismal thoughts.

The back entrance to Grangely would have been an easy

option and she could have spent all her time explaining her enforced absence to cook and any serving maid who happened to be around. However, she decided to enter the house by the front doors and to behave as a person of her rank should behave. What a sensible mind had emerged from the milieu of fears and torments which accompanied her to the Dower House. Hopefully, with her own family as paradigm, nobody would ever treat her so badly again.

000

Arriving, this time on foot, no-one was alerted to her presence, so Walford took some time to hobble to the door after her ring. She knew the brass bell down in the kitchen hallway would have been clanging loudly and she could see in her mind's eye the old butler, picking up his black coat and making his way to the hall door to answer it. Even though he was unsteady on his legs, no-one else was allowed to answer the front door, even if a maid should be polishing its large brass knobs at the time. He was jealous of his position of guard to the great doors. Eventually, he came and pulled back the middle door. When he saw who it was, it was as if somebody had given him a sovereign.

"Oh, Little Miss. How we've longed to see you again." All formality left him and he grasped her hand in his, patting it with his other. "You left this house without sunshine when you went off down the back drive – and we were all told to leave you alone, on pain of unemployment, what's more."

"Who would say such a thing?"

"Your cousin, Monstrous Marianne, as she is called downstairs. Oh, begging your pardon, Miss but you know how it is down there. I forgot meself for a minute."

"Don't worry, dear Walford. I'm so pleased to see you again. Now, if you'll let me in…."

"Sorry, sorry, Miss. You see what you've done to me, just appearing on the doorstep like this. Please, enter."

"I must have a word with Marshal and then I'll come down and see cook and the girls. I have a favour to ask of you and all I want to say about it just now is – make sure your memory is in full working order."

After leaving the old man with a puzzled expression, she went straight to Marshal's study, where she knew he would be incarcerated at this time of day. It was wonderful to see the old place again and she was glad there was no-one about, so she could peer up the stairs and round corners as she walked down the corridor. There was obvious redecoration everywhere, which looked far too modern for a house so old. To come back would be lovely but not with Marianne as mistress. She had been told by papa that if you speak of the Devil then he will appear and certainly her particular devil did just that.

"Good morning Alexandra. To what do we owe this debatable pleasure?"

So, Marshal had spoken to her about Alexandra's situation. Well, she was prepared.

"You need take no pleasure from my presence, Marianne. I come to speak with Marshal and the downstairs family."

"Why do you always refer to servants in such a childish way? They are the staff, no family of mine."

Rather than continue with such a snobbish and trivial conversation, she lifted her skirts and walked around her cousin, heading towards Marshal's study.

"And you will not find him in there. I saw him leave the house earlier."

This girl could not help herself; she still lied about what she had seen and not seen. Obviously, Walford would have told her if Marshal was out, when she had mentioned going to see him; it was a butler's job to know such things. It was hard not to reply but Alexandra kept her own counsel and continued walking in the same direction. Because she had said nothing, Marianne had no adversary and she in turn kept walking in the opposite direction.

Marshal looked up from his ledger as she entered, after a light tap on the door.

"Ah, Alexandra, I'm so glad you've come," he said. They had returned to their easy relationship. Without polite preliminaries, he went on, "I have been thinking over some of the comments you made before... before... before you were ill. The main opinion you had at the time was that we should invest in the new steel industry. I have been in contact with some of the managerial staff in the iron works and they all agree with you, that it could be the new way to go. I would like to discuss it in more detail, when you have the time that is."

This was quite amazing. After being ignored and seen to be insane, he now expected her to join him in discussing plans which had been hers initially. No doubt he would tell everybody that he had discovered this gem of information and present it to his friends at the club as his own project.

"I'm sorry, Marshal, I have no time at present to go over suggestions I made to you some time ago. I'm sure you can work out the best investments with financially lucrative companies, without my help." She was furious but all Marshal saw was a cold, dispassionate exterior to the woman he had known as sentimental to a fault. His friendly cousin was going to be more difficult to handle these days. He decided to treat her more as an equal, less as a foolish, unknowledgeable girl.

"Alright, cos. I'm sorry to interrupt your day but it is still good to see you again. I hope you will continue to visit, anytime."

"Unfortunately, I met my cousin in the hall and she told me you were not in your study. Luckily, I do not believe a word she says now, so all was well. I'm going down to see cook and will leave by the back exit, so I will have to see you some other time. Goodbye, dear Marshal."

She saw no need to protect Marianne from her own deceitful character. She had only come in to let him know where she would be in his house and hoped she had not been too harsh with him. Had he been more conversational, she would have tarried but all he wanted to do was pick her brain, now he knew she had a healthy one. It seemed as if he had decided to try to do something about Grangely at last and he would be more proud of his actions if he carried them out personally.

As she pushed open the door into the hall, she almost knocked over Marianne, who fussed and primped as she made her sophisticated way back to the morning room. Had she been listening at the door? It mattered not, for she had only heard the truth. Just before she pushed the door to go downstairs, her voice rang out,

"I hope you're not going downstairs to upset my staff again!

They each have their jobs to do and must not be interrupted by an upstairs person who thinks she can cook like a servant."

Oh, how she wanted to fly back at her with words of similar hatred but she must not sink to her level. Marshal had mentioned her imminent return to London, so why was she still here at the Hall at all? There was only one way to handle this person – with silence. When they were children, it was the only thing that could truly infuriate her – because there was no answer to nothing. She behaved as if alone, pushed open the solid door and almost skipped downstairs in childish enjoyment. On the stairs she saw Mary and noticed how she reacted, partly pleased to see her but with an element of suspicion as well.

"Hello Mary. It's very good to see you," she said, calmly and Mary just nodded but with a smile.

There must be a way to assure everyone at the Hall that she was not deranged and was not going to revert to her old, maliciously invented, ways. Perhaps cook was the woman to approach.

There, in amongst steam and the appetising smells of the kitchen, stood her friend and erstwhile mentor, stirring a pot as usual. She looked up, myopically, at the intrusion from upstairs and said, joyfully,

"Little Miss! I wondered when you would find your way down into the bowels – begging your pardon, Miss – the bottom of the house. I take it you're completely recovered from your nasty ailment?"

"No, Cook, I'm not. The thing is, I find it difficult to understand how anybody could recover from something they never had. I'm very well, if that's what you mean but I never had an illness, I never went mad, I was no more deranged than you are and I did not lose my reason – not for a minute. I'll leave it to you to decide how I was given such a reputation but I'm sure you know from conversations with your brother. What I would like from you, Cook dear, is a promise that you will spread the right kind of rumour about me, from one end of this house to the other, including the gardens and stables. I want no more strange looks from anybody, do you understand?"

Cook stood with her mouth wide open while this speech went on and then she put her hand over it and laughed long and loud. When she had finished, her eyes were dripping tears and she had to lift her apron to wipe them away. "Well, Miss Alexandra, I've never heard such a long 'un. You must have been saving that up for months, to judge by the speed of your prattle. I'll certainly tell 'em all to mind how they treat you in future – and don't give the other thing a minute's thought. You know you can depend on Cook to spread the word for you. Now, come into my little room and we'll have a cup of that special tea I save for important folk."

The room looked no different from the last time she had seen it and for this Alexandra was grateful. So many changes had taken place upstairs that she even dreaded going to her own old room to see what she found. There, up against the wall was the comfortable chair she had relaxed in on many an occasion and there was the old brass poker leaning on the fender for Cook to snatch up as soon as she came in. As soon as the noise of feverish raking ceased and the kettle was put on a black swinging trivet to boil, she said,

"Cook, I told Walford I would be down to talk to both of you about something I've had in mind for quite a while. Do you want him here now, or shall we two talk privately and I'll catch him some other time."

"It's all the same wi' me love but I think he'd have been down if he was free. No doubt that cousin of yours has found something more for him to be doing – at his age an' all. I wish she would realise he's an old man now and let him relax a bit."

"Oh, she's not having a go at Walford as well, is she? I thought she'd have had enough with the maids."

"Not 'er, she's full of her own importance, that one."

"Well, I think we'd better start without your brother and you can tell him what I asked you later. I have decided I would like to know more about my birth and background and I believe, from your comments in the past, that you know who my father was and what happened to the marriage of my parents."

"Ooh deary me, that's a tough'un me dear. As you know, my own mammy had a lot to do with your adoption to Grangely but I swore on her death-bed that I would keep my mouth shut."

"But Cook, this is the story of my life and I must know how I came into the world at least."

"I know love but put yourself in my position. I've kept certain secrets all my life. To tell now goes right against the grain."

"Would you rather talk to Walford about it first, then let me know some other time?"

To cook this was a let-out clause and she grasped it with both hands. Her clever brother would know what to do – he would advise her.

"Yes Miss, that's a good idea. Walford and me'll talk about it and you come back again after we have and we'll tell you what we've decided."

This was not going to be quick and Alexandra knew she could not drag the information she desired out of the stubborn old woman. But when she said something, she meant it, so she finished her cup of tea and left the cosy little room, and before she went she said,

"By the way Cook, I heard all the ladies saying wonderful things about your dinner party last week. They compared it with a feast at Castle Howard and wanted to steal Marianne's cook away."

"No chance of that, there is. I've been here for forty years and I expect they'll carry me out in a box when I go."

"You're a superb cook and the family is grateful," she said, as she left the smiling woman in her hideaway. She knew the dear cook loved a spot of flattery.

Cook was worried about her brother though. If he knew Little Miss was coming down to talk to them he would definitely have been here. Apart from anything else, this was the time he came down for his cup of tea with her. Where could he have gone?

Half an hour later, she found out, when he was brought down to her, half carried by one of the boys. Seemingly, Marianne had decided to move some pictures around in an upstairs corridor and, because she said they were valuable, she wanted no garden boys or boot boys fooling around with the large canvases and had called for Walford to appear with his white gloves, to help her take down some paintings from the high picture rails.

"Now, Walford. You just get up on this chair and unhook those pictures from the rail one by one and hand them down to Ethel, who will steady them to the ground. Do you understand what you must do, Ethel?"

"Yes'm, I understand but are you sure Mr Walford should be up on a chair like that at his age – sorry Mr Walford, sir."

"Stop panicking girl and do as you're told. The butler has been doing such things all his days, since before you were born I expect," she smiled.

"That's what I'm worried about," she mumbled, as she looked dejectedly down at the floor.

All this time, Walford had said nothing. He had to obey orders, that was why he was here and if he took it slowly he would manage. After all, his leg only gave way occasionally, not all the time, and he could hardly expect the mistress to get up on a chair to hand down big pictures like that.

The first one was easy and it felt so light in his hands, he could hardly believe it was so big, so he handed it down very carefully to the girl standing next to his chair. Feeling full of confidence now, he flipped the next painting's chain off the hook on the long maghogany rail above him with one hand and steadied it with his other but it started to fall sideways and he knew, if he let it go, the frame would be damaged when the corner hit the ground. So, he leaned to one side to stop its fall and, by doing this, he fell himself – off the chair and onto the floor beneath, with a mighty crash. By this time, Ethel had sprung to his aid but she was too late to stop him and he landed right on top of the old landscape. Owing to the ancient canvas being so brittle, it parted company with its stretcher all along the top edge and Walford just sat there, surrounded by Scottish mountains and highland cattle, feeling extremely dazed.

"Just look what you've done, you silly old man!" Marianne shrieked. "That painting has been there for hundreds of years and now you've split it right along the top!"

"I'm terribly sorry, Miss, I really am," the old butler murmured, rubbing his jaw where he had bumped against the wall on his way down.

"Don't you yell at Mr Walford like that, you awful woman," shouted Ethel. "He's worth ten of you and don't you forget that."

"How dare you?" Marianne spat out.

"I'll tell you how I dare, you besom. You should never have sent an old man up a chair like that in the first place and I don't know why you have to keep on wrecking this lovely old house. That's how I dare."

The noise had been heard by all and sundry in the house and Marshal appeared in the midst of this female tirade, not noticing his butler sitting down on the floor in the middle of the debacle.

"I'll thank you to go to Mr Walford this minute," said Marshal in his authoritarian voice.

"I can't sir."

"Why ever not, my girl?"

"Cos he's down here on the floor, sir."

"He's what?"

"He fell off a chair and he's hurt his leg. He's down 'ere under us."

Marshal ran up the stairs, to view the havoc caused by the falling painting and he took in the scene in seconds, noticing the first picture on the floor, leaning against the wall and his butler prone on top of the other large oil painting.

"It's alright Walford. Just sit tight and I'll get one of the strong lads from the garden to give you a hand downstairs. Don't even move an inch until he gets here."

"No, don't you dare to move an inch while you're lying in the middle of that valuable painting. Have you seen what he's done, Marshal?"

"I see everything that's happened here, Marianne. Would you mind going downstairs to my study where we can have a little talk."

She thought he meant to commiserate with her for the inefficiency of the staff, so she pursed her mouth and sailed off downstairs without another word. Marshal turned to Ethel and asked her if she was alright, to which she nodded and he told her to take herself off downstairs. Then he went down on his knees and took a look at the poor old man, looking so sorry for himself lying in the middle of the canvas, with the frame over him.

"As for you, Walford, I know you're as tough as they come

but I'm counting on you to tell me the truth. Does anything hurt badly. I'm not talking about the odd bruise here and there but – oh, you know what I mean."

The old butler was more embarrassed than hurt and he tried to look in control as usual, as he said, "No, sir, nothing hurts much. Me jaw aches a bit, where I knocked it on the wall going down but, apart from that all's well – and you know I'd never tell you a lie in all me born days."

"Alright man, as long as you're not hurt badly. Anyway, what on earth were you doing up on a chair, at your ..." He was going to say, at your age, then stopped himself. The old fellow did not need to be reminded of his increasing years at this time, not when he was feeling so stupid. "...in your position. I thought you gave orders to other people to do daft things like that."

"That's right, sir, I do but when the mistress says jump, I jump, if you see what I mean." He was grinning at his foolish metaphor and Marshal laughed along with him.

"Well, in future don't," he said and turned as he saw one of the biggest garden lads coming upstairs in his stockinged feet.

"Thanks for coming. What's your name?"

"It's Alan, sir, you know, it's Beckett's son, Alan," Walford chipped in.

"Now Alan, you see the problem we have here. Do you think you can get Mr Walford down to his quarters, without hurting his leg any more than it's hurt now."

"O' course I can, sir. You leave it to me. Come on Mr W. We'll soon have you down in the kitchen and you can have a nice cup o' tea with cook" and he heaved the old man off the picture and onto his feet in no time at all. When he had stood for a minute and looked capable of being moved, the strong, young boy half-carried him all the way down the stairs, without even looking breathless. Marshal caught up with them at the bottom and took a coin out of his pocket and put it into the boy's.

"That's for your trouble, Alan. I won't forget this," he said and thought he sounded just like papa in the old days.

So, when cook heard the commotion on the stairs, having been briefed by Ellen, she came out of her room to see the sorry sight of her brother being hauled along by a garden lad in his socks.

"Where do you think you're going, Walford," she said, as they turned off towards his room. "Get him in here, whatsyername, so I can have a good look at him. He looks as though he could do with a cup of tea. As for you, lad, get yourself over there to Mary and she'll see what she's got for a Good Samaritan. Did you hear that Mary!"

CHAPTER 26

Once again, Marianne was spending. It seemed as if Marshal had no control over his wayward sister, not even if it meant becoming bankrupt before the year was through and this time she had decided that electricity would be installed in the house.

"If we are to remain at the zenith of society in this godforsaken place, Marshal, we simply must be in the vanguard. Absolutely everyone I speak to is installing this new wonder because life is changed by the flick of a switch, from a collection of dark and dingy rooms to a fairyland of light. I have asked an engineer to call to measure up or whatever they do."

"I hope you realise, Marianne, that our honeypot is almost empty. Once father's money has run out, we will have to depart from our home – this home which you continually insist upon modernising."

"Oh pooh to that Marshal, you are far too cautious. I expect you've been listening to our interfering cousin again. Just make yourself available for the electrician this afternoon, if you please."

Marshal had always been one to hide away when his sister began to organise him and this time he went off to Alexandra's house. Unfortunately, their paths had crossed, for she was at the Hall talking to cook and Walford, so he was forced to turn around and make his way back home. Before he went, however, he took a closer look at the Dower House and liked what he saw. Alterations had been made sympathetically to the estate cottages, so it was almost impossible to see what they must have looked like as two small dwellings. A little further on, down the lane and around a bend, there were two other similar houses and he stood for a while contemplating their use as a domicile for himself. Why not? When the big house was sold, he would need somewhere to live and why not remain close to his favourite sister. Surely, he could make a deal with the new owners. He always thought of Alexandra as his sister and had more affection for her than he had for Marianne, mainly because she would listen to him and never made him feel inferior. They had plenty in common as well, with their longing for knowledge and the intuition to carry through self-devised projects. They were a partnership and always had been, even though Alexandra had become a little too domineering since her removal from the house. At least she never tried to hoodwink him, nor did she lie to facilitate her own ends.

As he walked slowly back to Grangely, the idea grew in his mind and by the time he reached the back of the house his mind was made up. He would call a builder to do the same alterations to his cottages as had been done to Alexandra's. They must change the name of her place also; a Dower House was meant to be for an aged mother, not for a young, attractive woman.

Going in by the back entrance, as he had done since he was a child, he could see cook with Walford in her sitting room, talking to someone whose face he was unable to see. It would have been rude to move closer in order to crane his neck and find out, so he turned onto the back stairs and went up to the main house. Unfortunately, he bumped into Marianne with her electrical man and she haughtily said,

"Oh good, here comes my brother, Mr Harforth. Now you can tell him your plans also. Marshal, this is the electrician I mentioned and he feels we will have no problems connecting ourselves to the main cables on the road at the end of the drive."

"No problems at all, sir. All we have to do is dig a trench the length of your drive and plug you in."

"I see, that is all you have to do is it. I hope you know how long that drive is. It will take several men several weeks to dig a trench as long as that."

"But Mr Harforth can summon the labour immediately, Marshal. Seemingly, there are many Irishmen who have been laid off their work in the iron industry, just itching to dig our trench. Is that not correct, Mr Harforth?"

"It certainly is madam. I can 'ave the men as soon as you say the word go."

Marshal replied to him in his father's indomitable way. "I fear I will have to think over this subject, after I have your estimate of cost, Mr Harforth. Would you like to come with me to my study and you can give me details? There is no need for you to involve yourself in this, sister. I will keep you informed."

"But, surely, you need a woman's point of view, when it comes to deciding how many lamps and the design of fittings etcetera."

"We won't get round to that for quite some time, madam. I think Mr Turner's right when he says we men should 'ave a talk about the boring, monetary side of things."

"Oh, alright – but I wish to be informed as soon as your talk has finished. I will be in the drawing room, Marshal dear."

The two men went off and so did Marianne.

In the study, Marshal decided to come directly to the point of their conversation and asked him outright how much the project was going to cost. After some humming and haaring, Harforth gave him the bad news. The price he gave was only guesswork but he based it on a job he had done for Ormesby Hall, along the road and, as the house was of a similar size and period, there should not be too many differences. Rather than explaining that they were too poor to pay the price – a tasty piece of gossip which would circulate the area like a whirlwind – Marshal told Harforth that they would be in touch when they had made a definite decision.

As the door closed on the electricity expert, Marshal felt a door close in his mind. There would be no more luxuries in this house and he would press Marianne to cease her spending. The ignominy of discussing such vulgar subjects as price and cost hurt like a physical wound and he was not prepared to put himself through such an interview ever again, so he went up to the drawing room with a tightness in his chest and even tighter lips.

000

Some days later, downstairs, Alexandra, cook and Walford were deep in a conversation cook thought she would never hold with anyone. After Alexandra had been taken from her dead mother's side and cared for by her own mother at the Neville's home, it was assumed by them that the baby would be taken to an orphanage. The main reason for this was that Vincent

Neville had gone to France with a companion. Vincent's mother had taken pity on the girl and allowed her to lie-in with them, unusually using the family's doctor for the birth and hoping the baby's father would return if he received her letters telling of the birth.

That happy conclusion was not to be; not only did Sarah Neville, nee Shankland, give birth to a girl but Vincent never returned, not even when he was told by letter that his wife had died in childbed. After that letter, they moved across Europe and were never seen again.

Cook, knowing the truth, could not bear the thought of a daughter of the gentry going to an orphanage and secretly contacted her own daughter to tell her of her opinions on the matter – adding that her younger daughter Annie was quite prepared to look after the bairn during the day, until she arrived home after her work at the Neville house. Cook was a young woman at the time and knew many maids in service at the Neville's, so she found out all the gossip her mother refused to tell her, about how the baby's father had sped off on his travels.

Aileen (cook later) went straight to William Turner, after encouraging her brother to get her a private interview with the master – a thing unheard-of between kitchen maid and employer. She told him, without embarrassment or fear, what was about to happen to his son's baby, and wheels were put in motion for him to adopt the tiny child as soon as possible. That is why Alexandra, named by Vincent's own mother, knew no other parents but the Turners – although she was told in no uncertain terms by Ernestine, when she was able to understand, that she was *not* a Turner.

"So I still have relatives in the area, Cook? Where do they live? Is it close by?

Cook kept up the fairy tale and said, "I wouldn't say close but not too far either. It's up in the hills beyond Redcar on the coast and they live in a big house something like Grangely Hall."

"Do I still have relatives living there though?"

"Yes, m'dear but I wouldn't recommend you trying to see them. For one thing they're very old now and, for another, they wanted nothing to do with you and never clapped eyes on you from the day you were born. They blamed your ma for making their son go abroad."

"I understand and I won't ever give away the secret you've told me. Thank you for that. Just one more thing, did my father ever come back to this country? Perhaps I could surreptitiously find out where he is."

"No, he didn't come home alive – not even for a visit – and me mam told me he died of influenza, when she was still working at the Nevilles. I think his body was brought home to be buried though but it was only a bit of gossip and that's not much good to you is it?"

"I don't think so but thank you again, Cook. Now I feel I know who I am, even if I never knew any of my relatives."

All this time Walford had remained silent. He was confined to a chair most of the time since his fall and spent a lot of it in cook's warm little sitting room. He felt his sister had given Little Miss all the information she needed at present but, as he looked at the pretty girl's eager, curious face, he wondered if he should offer anything further. The secrets of a family were indeed sacrosanct but this girl was one of the family, wasn't she? If she ever needed to know any more, as long as he was alive he could feed her curiosity. He had written it all down and Aileen knew where to find his personal notebooks if anything happened to him. She was sure to outlive him, being ten years his junior.

Alexandra went back to her house, with a feeling akin to contentment. After all these years not knowing, she now understood what had happened to her poor mother. What a dreadful life she had led. After running off with a handsome young man (as cook described him) she had been left to her own devices when expecting a baby, then was taken in on sufferance by his family, only to be discarded in death. Her own life was luxury compared to that of her mother.

She still had a niggling desire to search for the Neville family, particularly as cook had said that her own Shankland family lived close by. She supposed they had been in service also. However, she had promised cook not to reveal the source of her knowledge and this would surely come out if she found anybody. Maybe sometime in the future.

CHAPTER 27

The need to know more niggled at Alexandra in every waking moment. She had a picture in her mind of her parents as young people, much in love and rejected by their families. It was a romantic story and she was pleased to be part of it. Surely, her father had not been as bad as people – at least two people – had supposed and, if she knew more of the miserable tale, she might find out for certain but there was only one sure way to discover the truth and that was to go to the Neville house.

Her trips in the trap had been few and far between because she enjoyed walking to local points of interest or down to the village, so it surprised the grooms when she asked for a horse to be harnessed. It was a sunny day and the eight or so miles to Redcar were lined with trees all the way, some of them hanging down onto the road, so horse-drawn traffic had to veer around them to ensure the driver remained in his seat. There was plenty of traffic on the dirt road out of the village and the horse enjoyed his jaunt because it was downhill most of the way, so the driver found himself holding the keen animal back as he tipped his hat to other drivers, most of them farmers. Smoke and steam made by iron workings on the shoreline could be seen but Alexandra chose to look the other way, up into the hills, over newly grown pasture. There were cattle in some fields and sheep with their grown lambs in others; even a few goats roamed around cottages at Lazenby. This farmland was similar to their own and she felt that the same builder must have erected farm cottages at each village along the way because they all looked the same; a little shop and a line of red brick houses with tiny gardens at the front. Some people had grown roses over their doors and filled their little plots with flowers, creating a splash of mixed colour every few yards along the road and the trip itself was a source of pleasure, so it really mattered not if her search were fruitless.

Soon the road passed the old gates of Kirkleatham Hall and went downhill once more, much to the delight of the horse, as it entered the seaside town of Redcar. The smell of the sea was strong and Alexandra found herself taking deep breaths through her nose, to savour the ozone she had not experienced since childhood, when papa had brought them here. They trotted sedately now towards the esplanade at Coatham, a little village just before Redcar, which ran seamlessly into the old fishing town. There, on their right was the huge, grey-stone building of the Coatham Hotel, with its several slated turrets and little iron railings at each window along the front. It was a self-styled advertisement for the present iron industry and yet looked very much like a large, misplaced French chateau. How many families could this vast emporium accommodate during the holiday mania which had swept the country? Alexandra had never stayed in a hotel in her life of almost twenty-one years.

Farther along the seafront, she shuffled over on her seat to peer down onto the beach, where many fishing boats sat on their wheeled trailers, up on the soft sand beyond high tide line. Some laughing children played with little spades and doting mamas watched over them as they dug in their long, cumbersome skirts. No doubt these little ones were feeling the heat of the sun in their many layers of petticoats, stockings, dresses and aprons, topped by large hats. Some of the boys, who had been working energetically, looked like over-ripe plums in their jackets and knickerbockers, with perhaps an inch of flesh showing between clothing and footwear but no doubt they cared less about their smothered dressing than the fun they were having.

At the junction of Newcomen Road and the Esplanade stood Coatham Pier, with its flags already flapping to signal the holiday season. Two brick kiosks at either side of the metal sign saying, very obviously, Pier, seemed rather incongruous beside the iron legs of the pier itself and the ochre of the sand below – but it was newly built and would probably weather into a more mature colour eventually. Further on, looking up the street at the famous Redcar clock tower, like a solitary castle turret which had torn adrift from its building, Alexandra noticed it was well into the afternoon. Neither she nor the driver had lunched but she was not even slightly hungry. When they arrived at her destination she would tell Coverdale to go off and find something to eat.

They moved quickly along the straight road which followed the line of sea and sands, from one pier to another. The Redcar version was more oriental in design, due to complicated toll-collectors' offices jutting out onto the pavement. She had heard that this pier had been financed by the sale of shares and a generous donation by the Earl of Zetland, who owned rights to the foreshore, so it was more exotic, to show off its superior pedigree. Soon after they passed it, they turned right and soon found another country road leading uphill to a small village.

"Would you mind leaving me here for a while, Coverdale. I wish to inspect this area at my own pace."

The driver knew Miss Alexandra had a mind of her own so he didn't argue with her. Even though she was unaccompanied, there was little danger here and he could come back and find her easily enough in such a small place. Anyway, it would have been plain daft to dispute her decision as his family came from Redcar and he knew his way around the town, so he could find himself a tankard of ale and a bite to eat – and maybe a bit of gossip from the local worthies. Once he reached the gates of a large house he was able to turn the horse and Miss got down. He was a bit worried she hadn't bothered with anything to eat herself but there was a shop and a little inn, if she felt brave enough to venture in and, before he thought it, he knew being brave was no problem to this one; she was the toughest person in the whole family.

Alexandra watched the disappearing back of the trap, then turned to look closely at the gate in front of her. It was tall and once more made from iron but was unlocked, although there was a lodge keeper in his small house keeping an eye on her. She decided to have a word with him but he was quicker than she was and the little man darted out like a ferret from his hole..

"Hello, madam. How can I help you, this fine day?"

"I was wondering if this is the home of the Neville family?"

"Yes'm that's correct."

"Is the family at home today and does Mrs Neville accept calls?"

"I'm afraid you must be new here. Both the master and mistress have passed away since winter an' there's only a skeleton staff up at the big house, until Mr Humphrey comes down from Scotland that is."

"Oh dear, I'm so sorry. You're right, I am a stranger to Redcar and have travelled from near Middlesbrough today."

"Then you've had a wasted journey, madam, I'm sorry to say."

"Perhaps not. You may be able to help me. Would you know of a family of servants called Shankland. And do they live on the estate."

"That I do. Or should I say, that I did. You see, Miss, all the Shanklands have gone to meet their maker. The young footman went off with his master to foreign parts and came back in a box some years ago."

"Oh dear. I know this is a strange request, but could you tell me where your master and mistress were buried?"

"In the local churchyard, not a hundred yards from here. You just walk on up the road you're on and you'll see it. The Nevilles have a large crypt in there, where all family members are buried. It's a fine day to be taking a walk to the churchyard but, begging your pardon ma'am, a bit of a miserable reason for going."

"Yes, I know but it's something that has to be done. I presume some of the servants are buried in the same graveyard, as is the custom. Thank you for all your help."

He went back into his tiny house, thinking this fine lady must be a family member wanting to visit the graves of relatives.

She followed the road up past the long brick wall of the estate and soon it narrowed down to little more than a dirt track. People visiting this church on Sundays must arrive covered in dust or mud. The gate was small compared to that of the Neville house and it squeaked loudly on its hinges as she pushed it open to enter the graveyard through a little tiled, arched entrance. The church was small and built from grey stone and stood a little way back from the many tidy graves surrounding it. She looked around to find something resembling a mausoleum or crypt and saw a large walled area to the left, its top half circled in iron fencing. There in front of her was a large stone sarcophagus with a figure atop it and a metal plaque at the end, stating the names of those underneath it. She read quickly down the names until she came to one, Vincent Alfred Evison Neville – the one she was searching for. The man who had taken her father abroad.

Now she cast around to find the more humble graves of the servants of the Neville household and, before long, she saw a very plain mound bearing a gravestone, with the words, ???? Shankland lies here. That was all the life of her father was worth to the family who caused his death?

Having found the final resting place of the man who gave her life, it was tempting to kneel down on the short grass and offer up a prayer to God for leading her to this place but her faith had never been very strong and she thought how dirty she would make her clothing, so stayed on her feet. She continued to stare at the place where her father had been buried; brought home from Europe in a coffin and interred with the rest of his family in this common grave for all the local people to see.

Then, another thought came into her head. If he had been buried here, perhaps he had been baptized here and what was more important, married here. If so, there would be ledgers noting details of his marriage to her mother and she could close another chapter, the final chapter, of her search.

When she had embarked on this journey into her past, she had kept the reason for doing it a secret from cook, from Walford, even from herself in the logical hours of daylight. It was in the depths of night that she had admitted to herself that she wanted only to know whether she had been fathered by another man maybe a lover taken by her mother – and that was why she had been foisted onto her uncle. The thought of her own illegitimacy had lurked in her subconscious mind for so long – every time Ernestine had said doorstep baby and refused to call her daughter. Her mother must have lived here with the Nevilles for some time before her birth and there was a slim chance that her little daughter had been baptized here also when she was born.

She walked firmly but slowly towards the church, her mind set on one goal. She was not worried about what she would find; fate was a thing you could not change; she was who she was and if that was a person without a legal father, then so be it. At least she would know.

The church door also creaked as she opened it and there, inside the plain, old building stood the vicar, his hands clasped before him as if they had been set there for ever to prove who he was.

"Good afternoon, my dear," he said in a cheerful, kindly voice. "I don't think I know you, do I?"

"No, Vicar, I don't live in Redcar."

"Then come and enjoy the peace of the best little church in town. I will leave you to your devotions."

"No, no, don't go away. I came to find out something about... about a distant relative. I saw the Neville crypt outside and the name of the person I was searching for but I wonder if you have any more information about him."

"I'm sure I can help you there, my dear. You just take a seat in one of the pews and I will go and seek my ledgers. Now you tell me for whom I'm looking."

Alexandra gave him as much information as she had and he unclasped his hands and threw them up in front of him, as he said,

"Oh yes, that's an easy one. I christen all members of society, marry them and, sadly, I bury them but you probably know all that. A distant relative you say. May I enquire as to which particular family?"

She felt flustered for the first time, wondering how to explain and then realised she would not have to, for the kindly vicar said,

"It's alright, I have no right to delve into your private thoughts. Forget what I said and I'll go off and find those ledgers."

He had obviously been sensitive enough to catch her expression and knew how she felt, although he was certain, on account of his meetings with so many troubled souls and his own sensitivity, that this girl was searching for her own roots - nothing as trivial as a distant relative or even a sweetheart.

When he returned he was empty-handed and Alexandra was sure he had been unable to find what she had been searching for.

"I'm sorry Vicar," she said. "I didn't think you would be able to help me" and she turned, as if to leave. What a misery.

She had been certain that her story was about to terminate, here in this lovely little church.

"But that's where you're wrong, my dear. It's just that the books are far too large to carry around. I've found all the relevant pages but you will have to accompany me to the vestry and sit down in front of them, if you want to read comfortably."

She felt almost excited, although that was definitely not the word to use about the sad details of her long dead parents. Then they went together, into the small room on the right and Alexandra was able to read beautifully scripted notes about her father's baptism, then the marriage between him and Sarah Beatrice Turner and finally the entry of her own baptism. It had been done when she was two days old, no doubt in case she died early and spent her afterlife in limbo - instead of which it was her mother who had died.. The name of her father was quite clear and she felt the presence of the vicar, as he looked over her shoulder while she read every detail about the baby, who he now knew was the woman in front of him. She looked around at him and he brought his finger up to his mouth, then said very quietly,

"I think you need some time to yourself. Let me lock away these great big books and you can take that seat I offered you some time ago in the church. No-one will trouble you further, so you can stay there as long as you like. I hope you feel happier now you have found what you came to look for. Goodbye, my dear. It was good to meet you."

CHAPTER 28

In the kitchen, Walford was still fretting about his secret. Should he ask his sister what she would do? Women were good at such things but the fact that only he had heard the conversation between the young Ernestine and her friend made him hesitate about letting on to another soul. He had locked the information in the depths of his mind for all those years. No, he would not tell anybody. There was no reason to divulge what he knew.

When Alexandra returned from her trip to the coast, the first place she thought of going was the kitchen. Marshal was her best friend but she chose to tell the two people who had set her on the road to investigating her origins, rather than the one she called brother. She would tell him her wonderful news later, perhaps at dinner as she had been invited to stay that evening.

"I have had such good luck in my search today, Cook," she said, smiling brightly as she strode into the kitchen. "I found the church where the Neville family have been buried for centuries, along with their servants, and the lovely old vicar was so helpful to me. I am now certain about my parentage and have seen the final resting place of my mother and father, at last."

"Well, if that isn't amazing and here we were not knowing whether your da had been left in foreign parts all those years." She had heard rumours but no solid facts.

"No, he was brought home and buried with my own dear mother, so she found peace at the end with her husband."

It was enough to make cook start to weep, just thinking of their lovely young girl thinking she had found both her dead parents like that, in an obscure little church near the sea. At the time, the Turners – or rather the master, not that heartless woman he married – thought young Sarah should have been buried here but the thought of her lying beside a crowd of servants was so wrong.. She pulled up her apron and wiped her eyes with it then turned when she heard Walford enter the cavernous room, still limping slightly.

"Do you hear that, Walford? Little Miss has found the graves of her mam and dad in Redcar. Did you know where they were buried?"

"Aye, I knew where they were," he said somberly and shortly.

"Then why didn't you tell the girl before she went off?"

"I suppose the answer to that is I didn't know she was going. It would have been a bit pointless to tell her – and might have upset the lass – just out of the blue, wouldn't it?"

"I would have liked to have known, Walford. Even when I was quite young, I always wanted to know about myself. You must have known how my aunt belittled me for being what she called a waif and stray."

"You seemed to handle it so well, that I didn't want to cause any more problems for you." What was the point of bringing out old stories?

"Oh well, I found out for myself and it didn't take long to do it. Let's forget about it now, shall we?"

"You can only forget if you know the honest truth, m'dear. Those Nevilles were quite an important family in the area and you're a direct descendant to 'em. It was nothing to do with one of their servants. It was the young master himself, you see. It's a pity they disowned you when you were a baby or you might have inherited that big place in Redcar now the old 'uns have gone."

Why was it that the butler knew everything and always had? "What are you saying Walford. It was there, in pen and ink, who my father was. He was Vincent Neville's footman, Shankland, not his master."

"Aye, that's what them Nevilles wanted you to think. But you're born with their name, little lass. What do you think of that, now/"

"I can't say it means anything to me, Walford. All I know is that I went on a wild goose chase and I could have stayed here and heard the true story from you. Money and status don't matter to me. I'm very happy with my little house up the back drive."

"Aye, you've always been easy to please, lass." He sounded so miserable today. Perhaps his leg was hurting.

However, the conversation ended on a happy note when cook got out a cake and made what she always called 'a nice cup of tea', a panacea for all ailments mental and physical, then Alexandra went back to the Dower House to change for dinner.

What a turn of events. And presumably Ernestine knew nothing about all this. If she had, perhaps it would have meant an easier life for her.

000

At dinner, Alexandra told Marshal all about her solitary trip to the Neville house and informed him with a big smile on her face. Then she surprised him by telling him that she now knew for certain that she was Neville descendant. She omitted to mention that she had heard the truth from Walford.

"I'm not even slightly surprised, cos. You have always had the air of the aristocracy, even when Marianne and mother constantly put you down. But I am surprised that you wanted to find out all this from a solitary visit to another town. It was rather reckless, even for you."

"Oh, I suppose it was just female curiosity and the way I was always pushed to the back when your mother was alive. I thought I had been the daughter of a fine lady and a footman but I did sometimes wonder if there had been another man in my mother's life, which would make me illegitimate. Now I know for certain that I am a bastard. But my father was a gentleman, not a servant." She knew she should not be talking in this free way to a man but this was Marshal, her brother since childhood; she could tell him anything.

"Well, cos, I am very pleased for you but I hope it will never change anything between us. We must remain close, no matter what the circumstances."

This was unusual for Marshal, to speak out in such an emotional way. Surely he knew they would always remain close no matter what happened. Knowing she was a true Neville could never change that. Her thoughts were in turmoil and she had no idea why. Perhaps it was because Marshal had voiced his inner feelings when they were alone.

After their meal, Marshal approached Alexandra with his idea about turning two cottages into one for himself, thinking it was a splendid solution to his problem of housing, so he was not prepared for her onslaught.

"How could you even consider it, Marshal,.a Turner living in farm cottages on his own estate. You would be a laughing stock. Imagine how the estate workers would talk amongst themselves. No! I cannot allow you to demean yourself like that!"

How could she allow or disallow it? Who did she think she was? If he wanted to live under a hedge, it was nothing to do with his cousin.

"Don't speak to me like that, Alexandra. You remind me of Marianne. I thought I had managed to retain my independence by informing her of her rightful place in this house. Now you are starting to undermine my decisions as well." His voice had taken on a hard, serious note she had hoped never to hear from him.

"Alright, Marshal. You have made it quite clear how you feel about me. I will not stay a moment longer. Please call for the trap to take me home."

They had never had such an argument, not one which resulted in their parting under a cloud and Alexandra was sorry she had thought of confiding in him about her trip to Redcar. She would hide herself away and never return to Grangely Hall for dinner again. She felt totally at ease in accepting a roof over her head, and a small stipend, as payment for all the favours she had done the Turner family during her life with them. Marianne had been confronted by her brother but she would not be browbeaten in this way. Perhaps she should consider taking employment as a governess or a nanny, rather than being dependent on Marshal for her survival, now he had changed beyond recognition since the death of papa, becoming totally self-confident to the extent of hurting the feelings of others.

Back at the Dower House, she gave way to her feelings of distress. It was right what Ernestine had always said: she was not a Turner, but now she knew for certain she was a Neville. She would revert to her mainly solitary ways, only this time she would have no fears for her sanity.

000

Marshal also was furious at the way things had turned out. Alexandra was becoming far too overbearing and he was not prepared to take this treatment from anyone, let alone a woman of his own family. She could remain in her house but he would be damned if he would give in to her foolish behaviour. Knowing the details of her birth had gone to her head and she was trying to behave like a Neville, like the upper crust.

His plans to convert the cottages had been shattered in one evening. Part of what she had said was true; no-one should live in an inferior way to his own workers but no-one should be told that in such plain terms.

To avoid confronting his inner thoughts, Marshal threw himself into his paperwork. His investments were doing much better than he had ever imagined they would. The steel industry was now well underway and anyone who had backed major businesses such as those of Henry Bolckow and John Vaughan or Arthur Dorman and De Lande Long at the outset were reaping fine dividends. He had hardly dared to expect this from his investments but interest at such a level was gratifying. Recalling that Alexandra was the person who had actively encouraged his speculation at the outset only made him irritated again; he would much rather think the ideas were his own – and so they had been, later. In fact, initially, he had read so much about the blast furnace being built at Redcar and the basic oxygen steelmaking plant at Grangetown that he should have known it was worthy of a monetary outlay, right at the start. Unfortunately, he lacked the drive and ambition of his assertive cousin and he had to admit he was a little worried about disposing of all his inherited capital in an untested industry. The only contribution he had made to the consideration of investment was to visit the Royal Exchange in Middlesbrough to check on prices and contact some of his father's friends on the subject. Alexandra should have been born male, particularly in these days of ineffectual women.

So sending Marianne away was the next thing he did, after finding her a suitable property, with the help of a friend of the family. She had gone fairly impassively, only saying how cruel he was to throw out his only sister when she had done so much for him – but that was her way. No doubt she would live in comparative luxury in her own establishment, as papa had intended, and she would cultivate many friends of the local gentry on whom she could sponge when the fancy took her. She was so good at that. He had not troubled himself to contact her at all, even though she was a mere ten miles away. He could hardly bear to be in the same room as her these days, probably because she had matured to be so like his mother.

His mother; that was another subject he preferred to keep in the locked box of memories within. Why she had treated him so callously as a child he could not fathom and he could never remember close contact with her, ever. Everyone knew that children were brought downstairs to see their mama and papa at certain times but his father had been such a modern man, preferring to make his own domestic rules rather than copy those of a previous age – and surely some of this should have rubbed off onto his mother. Her embraces were like being held in a brown paper parcel and she tended to ignore his comments whenever he so much as opened his mouth. If it hadn't been for papa, he would have run away to sea as soon as he was old enough. No wonder he had remained silent when in her company. No wonder he had been wary of any move made by any woman, apart from his little sister Alexandra – but he must stop thinking of her as his sister if she wanted to treat him similarly to his other female relatives. Oh surely not, she had always been the one he could turn to - and now there was no-one. He could not be seen to be bowing down to her wishes on this occasion or any other. So he was alone with his thoughts and that is the way he would stay. All women were fickle and uncaring.

The thought did cross his mind that he was behaving just like his mother also but his pride had been so badly dented that it was only a fleeting thought and made no impression. It had taken some time but he now felt totally independent of everyone and would run his life to suit himself.

So, unwittingly, both Alexandra and Marshal had come to the same conclusions about their lives and their plans excluded each other.

000

Walford took in the letters which had arrived that morning,

put them down on the desk where Mr Marshal had been working and let his eyes linger over them. The first two were business communications but the last one, at the bottom of the pile, was from Miss Marianne. He knew the writing, even before seeing the postmark from Darlington and he wondered why it had been so long since she had visited. It was very unusual for a sister to write to a brother, when she could easily have come to see him.

The door opened and he rearranged the envelopes on the blotter, so they would be right in front of his young master.

"Thank you Walford. I see your leg has improved considerably recently. I hope you have taken my advice and rested more recently."

"Yes indeed sir but I have to add that part of my recovery is due to cook's comfrey cream, which she insists on plastering all over me before I retire at night. It's just as well it's at night, sir, or you wouldn't want me in the room with you."

They had a good laugh at cook's expertise in the medical department, then Walford left him to read his mail.

Why had Marianne sent him a letter after so long. It would be interesting to hear what she was up to. He picked up his paper-knife and ripped along the envelope, opening out the two sheets of paper and pulling his chair closer to the window to get more light.

Dear Marshal,

I suppose you are wondering why I have remained silent since I left you. The main reason was because I felt we parted on poor terms. I also looked up some old friends and have been flitting from pillar to post, as well as having a wonderful social life.

I write to you now to tell you my exciting news. Ralph and I are reinstated and intend to marry. Our wedding will be a small affair and all I require from you is the wherewithal to finance it. Please write by return and tell me how much money I can expect from you.

Your happy sister, Marianne

He could not believe it. After making his life a total misery by spending every penny of papa's money that she could lay her hands on, she now expected him to finance yet another wedding to that reprobate, Ralph Lawrence. He would indeed write by return, telling her she could expect the grand sum of nothing from him.

He moved back to the desk, picked up his pen and dipped it in ink. This would be one of the shortest letters he had ever written. He would tell his money-grasping sister to stay out of his life forever. At last she would have a husband to pander to her wishes, the same husband she had anticipated some time ago. So, he had come back to her, after leaving her to pursue a dalliance with Alexandra and, when that came to a humiliating end, he was prepared to take second-best, no doubt anticipating an inheritance.. Oh how those two unscrupulous people deserved each other.

His letter went off that very day and he imagined that would be the end of it but the end of the week brought another missive from the same source. This time it was more a pleading note, intended to stir his sympathy.

Dear Marshal

I must have some money now. I understand that you are furious about the

turn of events but I need the cash to facilitate my wedding immediately. I must be honest with you and tell you that Ralph will not marry me without a sizeable dowry and I cannot live without him. Please listen to your distraught sister.

With my fondest wishes and earnest hope for your speedy reply,

Marianne

He would have to send enough money to keep Ralph quiet, otherwise he would desert her and she would be back here, living with him and making his life hell. No doubt the rake had some gambling debts and Marianne had told him about papa's inheritance to her. Most of her allotted amount had gone into her house and she had managed to spend most of his on Grangely while she resided with him. The thought of such a man marrying his sister should have filled him with horror but all he felt at the moment was potential relief at the expectation of her having a husband, any husband would do.

If only he had someone to talk to. Why had he fallen out with Alexandra? There was so much need for a sympathetic ear and sensible comments.

CHAPTER 29

Ralph Lawrence gloated at his good luck. Admittedly, he had been rather careless once more at the cards and he knew Marianne had a small inheritance. Of course his whole life would change if he married her, but change for the better if he played his hand correctly. His first ideas regarding marriage with the Turner woman could come into play again and her foolish brother would be sure to pay to keep her happy. He had considered asking his father to bail him out but that would be rather stupid on his part, for he must have his own inheritance intact when the time came around and, if he confessed to gambling debts, he could easily find himself cut off without a penny.

So, he was about to become a comparatively rich man due to his own attraction with the opposite sex. The cousin was now out of the question due to her insanity but there were plenty of others longing to become his paramour. How he loved women and the novelty of that first attraction. Once he was a married man, he would be able to offer himself to many debutantes without having to worry that they would catch him in their lacy nets. He had the ultimate excuse for escape – my wife must come first. He started to rehearse his speeches, which always came at the end of an affair, laying on the paste of loyalty with a trowel: I love you desperately but I am the sort of man who could never leave his wife; how would you feel if you were she and I ran off, leaving you with a baby to care for alone – for of course there would have to be a child, almost immediately. There are two kinds of men – those who care nothing for their women and those who remain faithful for the sake of the children. Yes, he could have a wonderful time making up complicated stories in order to leave one beautiful girl after another before they became too serious.

His first action, on receiving money from Marshal, must be to pay off his debts. If he wanted to continue at the gaming tables, he had to ensure his credit was good. Nobody would play with a rake who did not pay his commitments when he had the bad luck to accrue them. Of course this was just a bad time and Lady Luck would smile upon him once more, as soon as the worry of bankruptcy left him. Marianne would be his Angel of Mercy.

000

The Angel of Mercy was miserable. Her second letter had gone unanswered for some time and she was so despondent that people were not inviting her to their events due to her dejected appearance. Who wanted a dreary companion at a soiree or a dismal neighbour at the dinner table? Oh how she needed her friends at a time like this.

Since she had explained to Ralph that she had written to Marshal and would get him enough money to continue their boisterous social life, which had indeed improved for him when he was in London due to invitations from her gentrified friends down there. Without a promise from her brother, she was unlikely to hold him and that would be the end of her world. The longer her letter went unanswered, the sadder she became.

000

Marshal could not come to terms with his apprehension about his sister and, after spending many sleepless nights, decided to try to make up his quarrel with Alexandra. After all, who else did he have in the world who would advise him on such an urgent, personal problem.

With this thought, he walked off down the back drive to the Dower House. He started by marching firmly along the stone path, then slowed to an amble and eventually found himself strolling across the track from side to side, kicking stones onto the grass verge. He was afraid, not of the girl herself but of the way she would (or would not) receive him and he realised for the first time in his life that he cared what she thought of him. Not only that but he loved her as a person, not as a sister but as a strong, intelligent woman and her approbation was important to him. This was all wrong. She was his sister. No she was not, she was his cousin and that was totally different. People often used to marry cousins in order to keep the blood line pure. Wasn't that in the previous century though? His thoughts went off at a tangent regarding the legality of marrying blood relatives and saved him from delving too deeply into his own affections. Before he could continue his first line of thought, he stood at the front door of the large cottage. He rapped the knocker. The door opened. She stood there, staring at him, not looking very pleased to see him.

"Alexandra… I had to come to see you… I… I'm sorry about the way we parted the last time… Please, let me come in and speak to you… I need a friend…"

"Don't stand there, stuttering and stammering your apologies. I forgave you a long time ago. Come along in and sit down." If only he knew how she had longed for this day. She was like that. As soon as the fire of an argument died down, she was able to forget the reason for it. The only thing she had decided was that she would not be the one to apologise; that was a man's job.

"Alexandra, thank you," he said, before choosing a chair and flopping down in his usual relaxed way.

"Did you really believe that we would remain enemies forever? We have been brother and sister all our lives and friends all our lives also, so there is no need to stop caring for one another. Now, tell me the real reason why you came to see me."

She knew him too well. He supposed it was the family blood that did it. Nobody else would have known so quickly that he had a problem.

"Apart from wanting to become friends again, I have had two letters from our sister in Darlington and things are not good."

"I thought she had returned to her high society acquaintances and would never darken our industrial doorstep again."

"That's probably how it would have been, had she not become embroiled with one Ralph Lawrence once more." He did not stop to check how she felt about this but continued, "She is yet again going to marry him and this time she wants money from me. From the way she explained it, it appears he will not marry her unless I give him money to do so."

"Oh what a lucky escape I had! That man is unbelievable. Not only does he keep on proposing to her but he wants to be paid for doing so."

"The trouble is, I feel I would rather pay Marianne to stay away than have her back here at Grangely, managing (or should I say mismanaging) all the staff and changing the decorations. Tell me, cos, how should I handle this?"

Alexandra sat perfectly still in her chair, looking serenely out of the window at the trees and breathing quietly. Marshal could not interrupt this calm moment and merely waited until she looked back at him and said,

"How much can you afford?"

"Since my investments are doing so well – thank you my dear – I find myself reasonably well-off."

"Then give her a sum which guarantees she will marry and stay away. That is what you want and that is what you must insist upon. My advice, such as it is, would be to have a document drawn up by a solicitor, to be signed by Ralph, which ensures he will not approach you again for money. It must be the last time."

"I knew I could depend on you for sensible advice. I will arrange it immediately. I feel rather strange, paying my own sister to stay away from me but it is the only way I can have a problem-free life. If she is married, surely she will behave a little better than she has in the past."

Remembering the conversation the two girls had had regarding marriage for the sake of the family and the way she intended to cuckold her husband, she very much doubted this statement. "You must say it is no longer your worry. Accept she is a grown woman and should not need to be looked after, financially or otherwise, by her brother. She has treated you like a father for too long. You also have a life to live."

"You are so right and I intend to live it. What about you? What kind of life do you intend to live?"

"The same kind I have lived so far. I am happy in my surroundings, happy in my pursuits, happy knowing that we are no longer enemies. What more could I want?"

"What about a husband and children? Do you never think in that way, cos?"

"I can't say that I do. I have no desire to join the socially elite and attend parties and the like. I have a few friends and acquaintances and they are enough for me. What do you suggest – that I marry the pig man?"

They laughed together but Marshal did not find it in the least bit funny. He had a very attractive young cousin and she was more or less condemning herself to a lifetime of loneliness. He alone could do something about it but did he want to? Deep down, he wished he could keep her for himself so there would always be someone to run to, should life treat him badly, but that was not all. She always appeared so strong but should she ever need a shoulder to cry on, he wanted to be the one, not some stranger picked out for his wealth and not his character. She would make such a good wife for somebody.

No, this line of thought was one he should not pursue; she was his cousin and he had no right to entertain such ideas. He would consider holding some social evenings, inviting some acceptable young men – as soon as he had enough money to do so. For the time being, every spare penny would have to go to Marianne.

Their time together reinforced a friendship which had never really died but had just gone into an ice house for a while. He should have known better than to think such strong ties could be snapped in one ridiculous argument, for, apart from anything else, their fight had been about a situation which might even right itself due to the good advice he had had from this sensible person. He would go back to his figures and project the costs of keeping Grangely. If only it were possible.

CHAPTER 30

Marshal's payment to Marianne sufficed. She wrote and thanked him for his generous donation, as she put it, which was delivered by a solicitor on behalf of her brother's legal representative. The man had waited for Marianne and Ralph to sign the affidavit and it was now in the hands of the Turner agents.

It would take some time to accept his own cold-blooded actions but he agreed with Alexandra that this was the only way to keep himself and his estate out of Lawrence's clutches. The man had proved himself to be deceptive and would swindle anybody who came between him and the high life. Goodness only knew what kind of husband he would be to Marianne – but he really believed she loved him and had done so for some time. Even a hard woman must have some loving feelings. They would have to wait and see.

000

When his steel shares started to climb in value, Marshal felt confident once more that he could continue to live at Grangely Hall. He had kept Alexandra informed of the way his financial state was progressing and she had joined him in his exuberance and excitement whenever a substantial dividend appeared. She had been the prime instigator of the plan which led to this new wealth and he desperately wanted her to share in the proceeds. Many times he had asked her to return to the hall to live but she always refused, saying,

"I enjoy my independence far too much and, anyway, you will marry one day soon and what wife would want the man's cousin living in the same house." She hesitated to say, unless she wanted a live-in housekeeper.

He hastened to assure her that there was no woman on his personal horizon and that the true test of love would be for his intended to accept the presence of his best friend and cousin in the house where she had been brought up.

After trying for six months to persuade her to relent, Marshal decided to carry out his second plan, which was to hold a party in her honour to introduce her to the men of his acquaintance, those who were still single. Admittedly, her age was something of a drawback to some men, as even the older ones wanted a slip of a thing in her late teens, not a mature woman in her twenties but there were some who had served in the armed forces and foregone marriage because they needed to prove their own worth before giving in to a life running an estate, who might be interested in an intelligent and interesting wife.

So he went down to see Walford in his quarters – a thing he never did – because this seemed the right place to discuss such a complicated event and he did not want the old man standing around with his hands behind his back for however long it took. The room was spotless and free of ornamentation, apart from some photographs of him and his sisters in the garden, which had been taken at papa's behest. He remembered the day well, when they had been made to stand in front of the house while the photographer hid his head under a black cover and shouted at them to 'say cheese'. Their smiles had frozen on their faces and it was quite obvious from the pictures what had been done – but it was kind of the butler to keep them in his room.

"Walford, I wish to introduce my cousin to the local gentry and thought you might have some ideas of how we could best arrange the first party. When I say party, I don't mean a big formal gathering, more a small collection of acquaintances who will come for dinner and stay for music and chat afterwards. What do you recommend?"

"If I could have some time to think it over, I'm sure we could organise the right occasion, sir. I will get together with cook and come back to you."

"Good. You see I worry a great deal that my cousin is not meeting people, with whom she can make friendships and enjoy herself."

"You mean you want to do what your father would have done for her and introduce her to eligible suitors."

"Yes, I suppose you're right in your assumption, Walford, though what I shall do without her I really don't know."

The old man heard the sadness in his voice and decided there and then that he would speak out.

"Sir, would you sit down with me in my humble abode, while I tell you something."

"Of course, Walford. You have no need to ask."

"This will come as a big surprise to you and, believe me, I have tossed it over in my mind for so long – ever since the death of the master, in fact."

"What on earth are you talking about. Come on old friend, spit it out."

That did it. Hearing the boy call him 'old friend' made him more confident and he went straight ahead with his secret, something he never thought he would do.

"Mr Marshal, I was in a position to overhear something many years ago, which I planned never to divulge to a living soul but, hearing you planning to marry Miss Alexandra off to one of your friends and hearing the sadness in your voice, has prompted me to tell you."

"Come on man, get on with it. I'm dying of curiosity. What have you got to tell me? Is she really my sister? Did mama have a torrid affaire with someone other than papa?"

"Just the opposite, my young friend. You are not even her cousin."

"What! I must be!"

"That is what I heard your mother say to her friend. She had no idea I had heard her, when she told Lady Simpson that she had given in to sins of the flesh and that you were the result."

Marshal went as white as his collar and rubbed his chin forcefully. His heart was thudding in his chest and his legs felt weak, even though he was sitting in Walford's comfortable armchair by the fire. All he could think was, poor papa. He thought I was his son and brought me up as his own and all along I was not his, a by-blow foisted onto him by my vicious mother. How could Walford have know this all the years of his life and never told a soul.

"I'm sorry sir, perhaps I should've kept it to meself. I've deliberated it 'til I was blue in the face but I'm an old man and I couldn't think of going to me grave and not telling you – just in case it made a difference to your life and who you marry, you see."

He was starting to recover and suddenly realised what it was that Walford was saying. He thought he should approach Alexandra, now that he knew he was not related to her. How would she take this? She had lived her life thinking of him as a brother, or at least a cousin and she was the one who had been castigated by mama for her parentage. He wished with all his heart he had known sooner – soon enough to tell papa what a dreadful woman he had married – but no, that would have been wrong and he understood why Walford had remained silent. His father died in the knowledge that he had a son who would take over where he had left off and carry on the blood line for him. It was right that he never knew - but how could his mother live with her secret for so long? Why had she been so dismissive of him? This must have been her way of handling her guilt; ignore him and the boy would be invisible, not remind her of her foolish mistake with another man. Who could it be?

"Walford, do you know who my father was, is?"

"No, sir. That is one thing I didn't overhear and don't you think it's better not to know?"

"Perhaps you're right there. I was given a life by the best man in England and I am proud to say that I have many of his characteristics. Had I been brought up by some cad, I might well have turned out differently."

"I always say it takes a minute to father a child and a lifetime to be a father. Your father gave you many gifts in his lifetime. Hold onto them and use them well, as he did. Now, I must stop preaching to you, the master, and get on with some work. What was it you asked me to organise now?"

"I don't think it matters any more, Walford. I need some time to digest all this and I don't think a party's on my agenda just now. Do me a favour, would you, and don't tell anybody else about this – not cook, not anybody. You've lived with it for long enough; just keep it to yourself, my old friend."

"Of course I will. But would you put my mind at rest before you go, sir. Did I do the right thing?"

"Yes, Walford, you did the right thing and I'll let you know how it has affected me at a later time."

He left the kitchen area and wandered back upstairs like a ghost of himself. This new information made all sorts of things possible but would it improve his life. The main question was, would Alexandra feel the same way? The only way to find out was to ask her and he felt so nervous about approaching her.

What if she had married Ralph Lawrence? Would Walford have told his secret then or would he have kept it to himself, so as not to hurt him? He had asked him not to tell cook but did she already know. Had her brother sworn her to secrecy as well? He must trust the old retainer not to have spoken a word to anyone. Also, would he gain anything by admitting to Alexandra that he was not who she thought he was. Instead of a fine father to be proud of, he had an unknown parent who had seen fit to compromise his mother and compromise was what she had done to her husband. The good, understanding man she lived with had been a cuckold and had reared another man's child, never knowing what had gone on under his very nose. He had hated his mother for the way she had treated him but, in actual fact, she was his only true relative. Only her blood and that of her lover ran in his veins. This was a sorry story and one which he wanted to keep hidden from the rest of the world.

He did what he always did when confused, he went to his study and got down his books. In the Journal of the Iron & Steel Institute, there were articles by renowned scientists lauding the invention of new processes. Steel-making companies could clear his head, whereas constant thinking about his own, now delicate, situation could not. Bolckow Vaughan were considering a steel-making process which converted low grade pig iron into steel, not wrought iron. This was an amazing new process which could raise the reputation of Yorkshire to that of a world class industrial area. How dear papa would have loved to have heard that.

Thinking about the man who he thought was his father caused a sadness in Marshal's heart which had to find an exodus; he cried, all over his papers, they soaked his handkerchief and his shirt front, until he ceased caring and lay his head down on his arms and wept some more. When he eventually came back to reality, the sky was dark and the room even darker. Because he had cut down on staff during the lean period, there was no-one to build up the fire for him and he was feeling cold but it was a good thing nobody had come into the room and seen him. Men did not give in to such emotions and weep; he had been told since he was a toddler to get up and carry on; only girls cried. Getting up and walking over to the fire, he found some red embers still alight and teased them into flame by careful application of small coals from the scuttle and use of the bellows. Before long, the room was full of an orange light and dark grey shadows moving about in the flickering light so he took up the matches and lit his desktop candle. Perhaps now he should install electricity.

ooo

Walford felt better, having divulged his tale of woe to Marshal but he was still the keeper of a final piece of information, which he could not bring himself to speak. The master had always known of his wife's adultery and had, himself, kept that secret until he died. It was only when he lay on his deathbed that he had written a painstaking note to his faithful old butler, telling him the secret that he also had kept. He knew all along about Ernestine's slip and had never mentioned it, probably because Marshal had been the son he always craved and had shown himself to desire a father he could emulate. This was why he had remained quiet over many personal matters and had buried himself in his library on so many occasions. His reluctance to leave an annuity for the upkeep of Grangely was in part his own knowledge that Marshal was not a Turner and the subconscious fear that his progeny might be throw-backs and ruin their inheritance in a tawdry fashion.

ooo

Alexandra could not cease thinking about her new relative, the Neville cousin who was coming down from Scotland to take control of the lovely old house near Redcar. How old was he? Why had he gone up north? Would he welcome the appearance of another relative when he arrived to take over his ancestral home? She would love to meet him and find out whether the older Nevilles had poisoned him against her. There was only one way.

The old gatekeeper had seemed to think his arrival was imminent, so she waited some weeks before putting her plan into action. Then, on the appointed day she once more set out for the coast and sent Coverdale away again. The old man appeared and she asked her question.

"Is your new master at home now?"

"Yes'm. He arrived just after I spoke to you last time. Did'y find the old chapel up the road, like I told you?"

"Yes, I did, thank you and I know much more about my relatives than I did earlier."

The old boy longed to ask many more questions but he had been in service too long to disobey rules which were now part of life to him. She looked like the old mistress but that meant nothing; it could be the tilt of her hat or the coat she wore. She might be a closer relative than he thought.

"Is there staff in the house, now that your master has arrived? If so, would I be able to speak to his butler about calling?"

"Yes ma'am, you could do that today. I believe the master's at home and he's a very approachable man, I might add." Oh dear, he'd gone a bit too far – but she was a nice young thing and wouldn't think him too impertinent.

"Then I think I'll walk up the drive."

Off she went, striding out like a farmer and not like the gentrified lady she appeared.

CHAPTER 31

She gave the knocker two good thumps and stood back. She knew she was behaving more like a man than a woman and here she was without a chaperone, knocking on the door of a man she knew nothing about, in the hopes he would invite her in. What would people think? The door opened and the butler stood there, staring down at her in surprise and looking around for a carriage which might have disgorged this nice little package.

"Is your master at home," she said in clear, pleasant tones, looking so confident he could not refuse to answer.

"Yes ma'am. Who shall I say is calling?"

"Miss Alexandra Neville, if you please. I am his cousin."

"Yes ma'am, of course ma'am. Please come in whilst I enquire. You can take a seat here in the hall. I trust you will be comfortable."

She walked slowly in to the quiet, old house and noted plenty of wood panelling, just like Grangely. In fact the whole house was another version of her childhood home and she felt quite at home here. There were one or two tapestry-covered seats by a small fire and she took one not too close to the heat, as her walk had warmed her through. It must have been a mere five minutes before the butler came downstairs, accompanied by an attractive dark-haired young man with a military style moustache, dressed in the height of fashion with a high fastening waistcoat of a bias-cut checked fabric, under a shorter jacket than usual and plain buff trousers. She had plenty of time to assimilate all these details as he passed from the first landing down to where she sat. He held out his hand in warm welcome.

"Good afternoon, Miss Neville. Oldwood tells me you are one of my cousins and I can't tell you how glad I am to see you. There are so few of us left that I feared I was the only one in Britain. How far have you come?"

"I live in the country, near Ormesby and this is my second visit to your beautiful house. The last time I came, I found no-one at home, so took a walk up to the chapel and deliberated the graves of our antecedents." He was so easy to talk to, paying so much attention to every word, that she found herself going on at length.

"Well, I am at home now and I must ring a bell and call for some afternoon tea." He moved to the fireplace and pulled on a cord. "Now, come along and we will sit in comfort in the drawing room" and he issued her in front of him to the staircase.

What was she doing? There were rules about such things and to keep company with a young man in his own house, without female company was simply not done. He did not seem to think anything was amiss and just kept talking as they mounted the staircase and turned into a pleasant room at the top. There were pictures everywhere on the walls and ornamentation covered each surface. The tall mirror above the fireplace was too far up for her to see her own face but she saw his reflection at the side of a glass dome which held a brass clock and he was smiling happily.

"Come and sit here, cousin. Auntie was very keen on comfortable seats for ladies in their wide apparel and installed several Prince of Wales chairs throughout the house. I will sit here close beside your chair, to make it easier for you to hand the cakes when they arrive. It is so long since I had a woman around that seeing you pour the tea will be a true treat for someone fresh from the Scottish Highlands."

This man could not stop talking. It was all very light-hearted and friendly but Alexandra could not help but wonder if he ever stopped for breath.

"You must tell me something about yourself and our relationship. You see, I had no idea that I was related to any other person in our age bracket, let alone someone…someone so…" He seemed to hover over the word, as if he would say more, then changed his sentence to something more fitting. "Someone from so close by." He knew she would have been the Neville heiress, had he not been around, but the subject was not worth pursuing as he was definitely alive and kicking.

"I have to say that my existence was denied by your aunt and uncle because I originated from an alliance between their son, Vincent, and my mother. Oh, don't think anything dreadful. They were married but my mother died when I was born and my father went away to Europe and died there."

"Don't say more. I knew my cousin Vincent when we were children and he was unable to take responsibility for even his old dog. It does not surprise me that he left you and went off to the Continent."

"You knew him! I thought I would find someone who knew my father if I persisted."

"You mean you never knew him yourself. I thought he must have gone off to France when you were grown, not when you were a babe in arms."

"I was about to be sent to an orphanage, when one of the maids contacted her daughter who worked for my uncle and he adopted me."

"You poor girl. You never knew your mother nor your father. What can I say, except that I feel sadness for you, as if it were my own story."

This man was strange. He seemed to want to suffer on Alexandra's behalf – for something that was nothing to do with him at all. She must go, as soon as she could but there was all the ritual of taking tea before she could do that. The maid came in with a tray and it was set down before her, as if she were the mistress of the house. This was the stuff that nightmares were made of. She did all she could to remain casual and poured the tea, handed the cake stand and passed the sugar with all the aplomb she could muster. Throughout, the cousin whose name was Humphrey, kept up his light chatter and, by the time she had to say farewell, her head was spinning.

As she left, insisting on walking down the drive because Coverdale would be waiting for her at the end of it, she was made to promise to return soon, which she did because she had no kind way of refusing.

All the way home, she mulled over what had taken place and she arrived back at Grangely, safe in the knowledge that she had a cousin who desperately needed her company due to his lonely existence. The fact that he had rambled on incessantly was only because he had seen no-one he knew since coming down from Scotland and he would, no doubt, calm himself before their next meeting.

She saw Marshal the following day as he was leaving the house and thought she would tell him her exciting news. However, as soon as he saw her, he behaved as if he had been heading off to an important engagement and could not even spare time for conversation. Her news would have to wait until he had more time. She went back to the Dower House and decided to trim her roses. Flowers had the effect of calming the mind and the soul and she spent more time than she had intended tidying up her well-stocked plot.

By the end of the day, she had decided not to bother Marshal with her gossip but to leave him to his more pressing business. Everything seemed to be improving for him and she would not wish to spoil any plans, by acting like the garrulous Humphrey.

000

One cousin took the place of the other and Alexandra found herself looking forward to Humphrey's regular letters, as she kept herself to her little home and Marshal conducted his affairs without referring to her. She would never know that he was nervous of approaching her because he dreaded her rejection of him when she found out he was a bastard. The fact that she had spent the whole of her own life not knowing about her own origins meant nothing; her parents had been married and his were not. The only way he could handle this affair was to avoid her – to avoid the person who had been friend, confidante and adviser to him all his life. When he was able to accept this state of things himself, then he would feel confident enough to tell someone else: but she was not just someone else was she? She was Alexandra.

The tolerant girl received a letter from Humphrey which made her heart race but not in the way that men usually affected girls. It was not the first one, for he had started to send her long epistles every week. This time, he wanted her to go with him to Scotland, to meet his friends up there, before he closed his residence but he was telling her very early because he was about to go to France on business first. She realised that she had no idea of his business; they had not discussed it. Why did everybody in the Neville family have to go to France on one pretext or another?

Replying to his letter was one of those difficult decisions. She liked Humphrey, now she had become used to his method of communication, at least by letter, but she was unsure of any further friendship with the man who called her cousin. Her relationships with cousins were doomed to failure – one was too amiable and the other seemed to have deserted her.

After a sleepless night, during which she tossed the invitation around in her mind almost as much as she tossed her blankets around on her bed, she came to the conclusion that she could not travel as far afield as Scotland with anybody, not Humphrey, not a single person she knew. So that was the answer she gave when she wrote her very sweet letter the following morning, couched in more polite terms than she had thought to herself. The last thing she wanted to do was to upset the person who had so recently come into her life, given her more facts to think about than she had considered for years and been a thoroughly pleasant person throughout. She wrote it, blotted it and walked down to the post office with it that very day. Hopefully, Humphrey would understand.

On her way home, the Grangely carriage stopped and Marshal offered her a ride back to the house. Seeing his extremely worried face, she had not the heart to refuse him although she still felt slightly piqued.

"Where have you been this fine day, cos? You come from the direction of the village," he said.

"Yes, I had an urgent letter to post, so thought I would take a walk."

"You know you can always add your letters to those of the Hall. Why did you not bring it over?"

"Because it was urgent." Why did she keep saying this? She knew he would enquire further. Did she want to tell him about her new-found cousin?

"May I ask why?"

"Yes, you may and I will tell you what I had planned to tell you some time ago. I went to the Neville house beyond Redcar and met my cousin, Humphrey. He is a man of your own age, perhaps a little younger. We got on very well together and he asked me if I would like to go to Scotland with him next month.

I know he is going to France shortly and I wanted him to get my reply before he goes."

"I take it you will go with this... this... cousin." What a situation. She had met another man, before he had had a chance to talk to her about his own problems.

"No. I have turned him down, if that is what you call it. I felt it was too far to go with a man I have barely come to know. We may find out our temperaments are not suited for a long acquaintance and then what would we do?"

She talked as if she wanted them to suit each other. "You find this man interesting?"

"Yes, he is very interesting and friendly as well. He is everything one could desire from a relative."

"A cousin, you say."

"Yes, a Neville cousin. We are related through my father."

"First cousin?"

"He is the son of my father's brother. That makes him first cousin, I believe."

She was being facetious. This was dreadful. He had always been her only first cousin and now she had conjured up another one, of his age – or younger. More suited to her own age, no doubt. "I am glad for you Alexandra. Ah, here we are at Grangely. I will send Lawson round to the back drive with you."

"No thank you, Marshal. I would like to walk. I will see you soon" and she left, waving her hand at him blithely, as she wandered off.

CHAPTER 32

The weather was warm and there were mature flowers in all corners of the gardens around the Hall now it was almost autumn. Marshal went out walking most days now, as he found this the best way to reflect on his problems. He still had not approached Alexandra. His main reason for not doing so was that he imagined she had formed a more than comfortable relationship with her cousin Humphrey and he dared not confide in her now. What if she told him his secrets during one of their 'interesting talks'? She had not been that kind of person in the past but who was to say how she had changed, now she knew her true family.

Birds were singing in the trees surrounding Grangely and the sky was light blue, with fluffy, cumulous clouds over the hills. It had not rained for weeks. This, in itself, was unusual but there was also a distinct lack of humidity, making everything feel airless and dusty, even on the edge of the woods. As he continued to walk, even though his mouth was dry, he could feel his sour mood lifting and wondered why he did not find himself a dog. A dog would be a companion indoors and out and would never say anything to upset him, as humans had the habit of doing. He picked up a stick and threw it deep into the shadows, imagining his dog rushing off to find it and bringing it back to his hand. They were loyal animals, dogs. They lived for the whims and fancies of their masters and all they required was a bed to sleep on and one meal a day. What pleasure it would be to bend down and stroke the soft head of his dog, as it lifted brown eyes to his face and it would never leave him.

There was a stone wall in front of him and he realised he had walked right round the house in the shade of oaks and elms and was now on his way up the back drive. There had been no conscious decision to walk this way; his feet had just taken him.

At the gate of the Dower House, he looked up and saw Alexandra collecting colourful blooms from her garden, right in front of him. It would be churlish to continue walking.

"Good afternoon, Alexandra. I see you are picking flowers

for the house."

"Yes, I always need to have my vases full, you know that."

He had always loved the way she had strewn her rooms and indeed the upstairs hallway with flowers from the garden at the big house and she was continuing this habit, even though she lived alone. He looked at her bouquet closely, as if inspecting each flower and she said,

"Please don't just stand there, in the heat. I'm sure you could take some tea with me to counter the dryness in the air, particularly as you have been walking. Come along in." It was so good to see him, after all this time and she was prepared to use every hook she could bait to bring him inside the house.

What could he say or do? He pressed the catch on the gate and walked in, hearing it click shut behind him. Her little stone path was strewn with wandering plants, some of them highly perfumed so he could almost taste the smell as he crushed them underfoot. She suited this environment, much better than that of an empty old house. Little wonder she had refused to move back to the Hall. He walked into the pleasant little sitting room and took a seat when it was offered.

"I will be back quickly with our tea. Please make yourself at home" and she laughed when she remembered that he was at home – everywhere on the estate he was at home. Why had she not returned to Grangely when he had asked her? Just to be in the same house as Marshal would be comforting. He was such a sympathetic listener. The sight of him walking the corridors would bring a smile to her face to take the place of the frown which threatened to take up residence permanently.

The ten minutes it took for her to deposit her flowers and brew some tea seemed like a year to Marshal because he used the time to dig deeply into the recesses of his mind, attempting to come up with a way of explaining himself. Even when she returned, tray in hands, he was unsure how to start. She helped by starting to talk about Walford and cook.

"Do you know, Marshal, I would not have known about my Neville relatives, had it not been for Walford and cook putting me on the correct track. How lucky we are to have two such caring employees."

"Yes, we are very lucky." Thank goodness she had reverted

to the 'we' they always used as children. "Walford told me something else recently and I have been longing to share it with someone – with you Alexandra, as we always shared everything, once."

"Then tell me, cos. I feel we have been too separate for some time."

"But you have a new cousin with whom to share now."

"That does not mean I must ignore you. You are both my family and I expect you will get on well together when you meet." She was not altogether sure about this but said it anyway. Marshal would not enjoy Humphrey's constant comments about everything and everybody, which flowed from her new cousins lips like a river in flood, even though she loved to hear a man talking to her. It had been so long. Even now, Marshal was sitting with compressed lips as she spoke.

But he was also thinking his own thoughts. Oh dear, this sounded ominous. How could he meet the man who was stealing his cousin and confidante away? Perhaps he had made a mistake, thinking they could have the same close relationship they had ever had.

"What did Walford tell you, Marshal?"

He started out of his reverie. He had to go on now. "He told me something so momentous, so frightening that I needed to mull it over for weeks before even admitting to myself that it was true.

Now she was worried. Would he explain himself?

"He said he heard mama talking to her friend when I had been born and she told her that I was not my father's son."

"Not a Turner after all?" Her eyes were wide and she definitely felt shocked at his news. He had taken away their relationship in one sentence.

"Not a Turner *at* all. Unfortunately Walford did not know who my father was and I shall never know from whence I came – not like you, who have discovered your true family."

"That is so sad, Marshal. I would never have suspected ma… Ernestine to have dealt papa such a blow. She did not seem the kind of woman who would stray and, particularly, as he was always so kind and caring to her?"

"Our dear Walford kept it a secret and it is only now that

both my so-called parents are dead that he felt he could confide in me – and only me, so you are the only other person to know."

"Well, dear cos, having suffered the same ignominy for years, you can rest assured that I will keep this in my memory box, as you called it when we were children."

"Thank you, Alexandra, you are too kind. Of course you realise what this means, don't you? You and I are totally unrelated and should not call each other cousin at all. Should we find another pet name for each other?"

"I ... I don't know, Marshal. You have been my cos for my whole life. I can hardly change, just like that. What would you suggest anyway?" It was true. He was saying they were not related at all. If they were not related...

"I would be happy to call you my dear, unless you object to being on such close terms with a total stranger."

"What a ridiculous thing to say. You have been my friend and confidant all the days of my life and when I had no family to call my own, you became my brother, as your father became my papa. I will not hear the word stranger issue from your lips one more time, do you hear?"

"Alright, my dear."

"Yes, I like to be your dear." It was comforting and even loving to be called my dear.

"Do you really, I mean do you have any affection for me that does not stem from our supposed relationship?"

"What are you saying to me, Marshal. Nothing has changed. I am still your cousin in thought and deed and you know you will be able to depend on me until the day we die." She must never give away the thoughts which had recently come into her head. They were wrong, in view of the way they had been for so many years. It was enough to turn him against her forever.

Marshal was unsure of himself. She looked so serious and had not even smiled at him once, while he had opened his heart to her. It was no good going on further with this personal line of enquiry. One surprise was enough for one day. Maybe he would bring up this subject of great importance at a later stage. He was happy enough knowing she still cared for him and should not push his suit until she got her thoughts around this new situation. So, he kissed her lightly on the cheek and left the cottage before she could realise that they had never been kissing cousins before.

The skin of her cheek had felt warm under his lips and she had longed for more. His hair had touched her lightly as he drew away and her desire had been to take his face in both her hands, drawing him in to her as she did so. Their lips would have met in a soft, perfumed kiss and she would then have known how much he cared for her – if indeed he did.

But he left. Just walked out of the cottage without a word and left her feeling as if she had been offered a cool drink on a hot day and seen it dashed to the ground instead.

000

Marshal's walk back was much quicker than his outward stroll and he entered the house, once more thinking about cousin Humphrey. Perhaps he should meet him – just to find out what the competition looked like. She had said he was going to France and had probably set off by now, so it would have to wait.

He was no nearer to voicing his inner thoughts to Alexandra. Perhaps he never would. He was frightened of the consequences. Surely, having the girl he loved on the estate where he could visit her any time he wished was better than scaring her off to that Neville man, miles away.

In the meantime, he had been voted onto a committee of steel investors and had meetings to attend in Middlesbrough. Over a period, he had been elected onto the Town Council and became even more knowledgeable regarding the results of a very poor water supply system, not only in the town but at Stockton, Hartlepool and Darlington as well. It seemed obvious to Marshal that this was the main factor causing epidemics of typhoid and cholera but this was because of his in-depth study of these diseases and the overworked water supply throughout the Tees valley.

Now he was in a position to let his opinions be known, he felt he could push and probe until water supplies were made safer for the many thousands of people living in back-to-back dwellings in the town he now represented. Middlesbrough's population had now reached a figure near 50,000 and it was imperative that so many water-borne and inhaled diseases were conquered. As well as typhoid and cholera, there was typhus, spread by lice infestations and smallpox had taken hold in some places also. It was amazing to Marshal that he, a studious son of the big house, had become involved in such specific medical subjects to such a degree that other council members would ask him for reports on numbers of people suffering pneumonia within the town boundaries or pertinent areas suffering water pollution by sewage. He had never been more pleased about his youthful interest in subjects not deemed suitable, at the time, for mixed company.

Of course there were real experts in public health and investigators were constantly being sent to different towns to report on outbreaks of infectious diseases. Vaccination against smallpox had been suggested but not carried out before over a thousand had been carried off. Once it had become commonplace the death rate diminished considerably.

It became Marshal's life's work to establish a pure water supply for the iron and steel workers and their families who, through no fault of their own, found themselves in pitiable conditions consisting of ash pits, open sewers, over-crowding and hence disease, just so they could earn a pittance in the heat and discomfort of Yorkshire industries. Sadly, he and his fellow councillors knew it would be many years before a substantial change was made.

CHAPTER 33

Whilst Marshal was working for the common good he had no time to debate the presence of Humphrey Neville nor was he able to see Alexandra, which he felt was all to the good, due to his unbrotherly feelings.

She understood his embarrassment about coming to tell her of his illegitimacy and put his absence down to needing some time to recuperate his mind after exposing his life to her scrutiny. The facts he had disclosed changed nothing in her eyes. He had always been her friend when a boy and she would always respect him as a man. He had become more erudite in maturity and exceedingly attractive. Surely, no woman would care whether he was the son of Grangely Hall or a hard-working councillor representing the poor families of Middlesbrough. And Grangely Hall would no doubt soon have a new mistress.

Being a woman who enjoyed the company of a man, Alexandra felt she must put Marshal out of her mind, as he had done to her, so she looked forward to the return of Humphrey instead. Marshal had obviously crossed her off his list now he had confessed his illegitimacy to her. It must have been something that was truly worrying him because they had been so close as children. All her unnatural longings for him were surely caused by a woman of her age being alone too much and she must put them behind her. Turning her mind to her Neville cousin, she ticked off the days on her calendar until Humphrey crossed the English Channel. Two remained and then, no doubt, she would receive a letter or even an invitation to dine.

She inspected her wardrobe and brought out two gowns which would be suitable for calling, either in the evening or during the day, and attended to some alterations and small mends. It was good to be thinking in terms of visiting once again, after so long without friends. She even wished that Marshal paid her more calls – but she knew how involved he became in new projects.

The day of Humphrey's return came and went. Then a week later she had still not heard from him. This was miserable. Perhaps he had decided she was not a suitable companion after all and had taken this opportunity to put an end to their friendship. She would miss him, if that were the case, but she still hoped he would contact her. He was not a truly handsome man but he was amusing and affectionate by nature and she had come to like him a great deal. Of course there was always something in the blood that encouraged a person to like their cousin. If that were the case, why had she felt so close to Marshal as they grew up together? Perhaps a family thought was enough.

The next day, Marshal arrived at her door looking quite miserable. Did he only visit her when something was worrying him. Surely nothing worse had happened to him since she saw him last. He came in and only looked at her fleetingly, before beckoning her towards him and holding out a copy of The Times newspaper.

"I really think you should read this, my dear," he said in the voice he had always kept for illness or tragedy.

Without speaking, she took the paper and read where his finger lay. It was the Obituary column. She read it so quickly, she had to rescan it, to make sure she had been right the first time. Oh yes, she was correct. It said, 'Drowned at sea, when his ship went down off Dover'. She had no sooner found her family than she had lost it again. Humphrey was dead.

Could she cry, for a man she had known just fleetingly? She did not feel like crying, not in the least, but she felt it was expected of her by Marshal. She had never been one to give way to her emotions and this was more disappointment than grief. She looked up into his concerned eyes.

"I am sad I knew him for such a short time. We never really became true friends. We were only correspondents."

Marshal's body seemed to relax as she said these words, or was she imagining things. Then he held out his arms and pulled her to his chest, as papa used to do when she pulled the head off her doll or lost a picture book. That is what it felt like now – her new family had been dismembered and one of the pieces thrown away. She could hear his heart beating loudly inside his warm body and she pressed herself closer, as if to join in a duet. This was so comforting, she felt so protected, so – loved. Was she being ridiculous to think of love at a time like this? One cousin had died and the other was protecting her from her own sad feelings – except that he was no longer a cousin and she had no sad feelings to speak of. Then, he bent his head and kissed the top of hers. She looked up and he kissed her mouth. It was a precious moment and neither of them wanted it to end. When it did, Marshal seemed different, so much in control and Alexandra felt like a new person.

"Are you annoyed with me?" he said, quietly.

"No. I'm surprised but not annoyed," she said just as quietly and then, because she did not want him to change back into the man who treated her as a sister, she lifted her face to his and allowed it to happen all over again.

"I love you Alexandra and I am sorry it took so much hurt and tragedy to reveal it. There is only one question I must ask. Do you feel the same way?"

"I have always loved you because I believed you were my cousin. We never indulged in physical closeness for the same reason but our minds have always been close and I needed that proximity. Now, I can allow my other emotions to surface, to eclipse the family ties which are no more. Is that how I should feel? There is no point in thinking I can suddenly change from being a companion to being a sweetheart. I could not change my feelings like changing a bonnet, but one day soon…"

"I understand absolutely and I am being crass to think otherwise. I have had longer than you to come to terms with my new self and during all my private thoughts you have been the one constant. I desperately wanted to tell you about my discovery but dreaded your saying we were friends no more. As if you could have changed so much. I suppose, secretly, I was happy that we could become more than friends, once the barriers were down. Is it a sin to love someone who once was your sister?"

"I don't think so, because an old love consisting of family affection and protection has metamorphosed into a new relationship involving deeper emotions. We must live with the altered state of affairs and find out if our feelings are real."

"Mine are."

"And I think mine are, dear Marshal."

They held each other close, cultivating the new experience of kissing, as if they were ten year old children practising on dolls. Each time one of them peppered the other's face, they felt a quickened heartbeat and a sensitivity of the flesh, which enhanced the knowledge that they were made for each other.

"This alters everything, my dear," Marshal said, when they came back to the real world. "I had been going to ask you to return to the Hall to live, before I had my revelation. Now that is impossible. I will, however, ask you an important question."

"Please do, my dear."

"When we are married and live together in the house we have always known, would you be prepared to share it with a dog."

They took each other by the hands and started to laugh. It was something neither had done for some time and the sound reverberated through the old walls, as their laughter had done in their childhood. When they were married, they would share their house with dogs, cats, children and laughter. 83,851

THE END